# Demons Are Forever

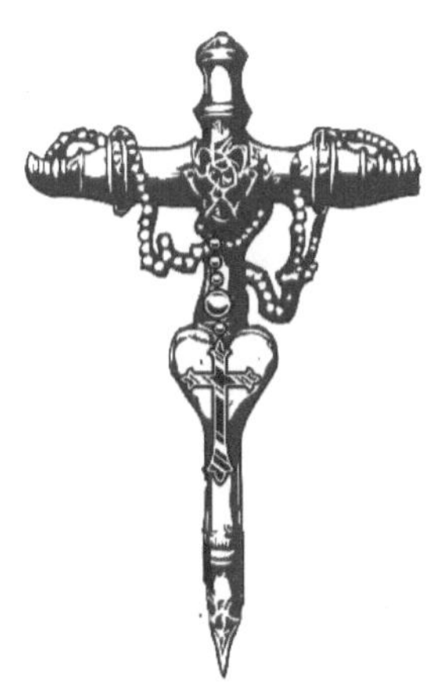

## Love At First Bite

## Book Two

By Declan Finn

Three Ravens Publishing
Chickamauga, GA USA

Demons Are Forever: Love At First Bite Book Two By Declan Finn
Published by Three Ravens Publishing
threeravenspublishing@gmail.com
P O Box 851, Chickamauga, Ga 30707
https://www.threeravenspublishing.com
Copyright © 2023 by Declan Finn



Publishers Note: This is a work of fiction. Names, characters, places, and incidents are a product of the author's imagination. Locales and public names are sometimes used for atmospheric purposes. Any resemblance to actual people, living or dead, or to businesses, companies, events, institutions, or locales is completely coincidental.

Credits:
Demons Are Forever: Love At First Bite Book Two was written by Declan Finn
Cover art by: Steve Beaulieu

Demons Are Forever: Love At First Bite Book Two by: Declan Finn /Three Ravens Publishing – 3rd edition, 2023

Demons Are Forever: Love At First Bite Book Two by: Declan Finn /Silver Empire – 2nd edition, 2018

Demons Are Forever: Love At First Bite Book Two by: Declan Finn /Declan Finn – 1st edition, 2018

Ebook ISBN: 978-1-951768-72-0
Trade Paperback ISBN: 978-1-951768-73-7
Hardback ISBN: 978-1-951768-74-4

*Dedicated in loving
memory to my good friend
Msgr. William J Rodgers
1949-2018*

# Table of Contents

# Prologue

April 16th, 2:15AM. Greenpoint, Brooklyn, NY

Amanda Colt was dead, and Marco Catalano looked like he had been through a war.

Both were technically true. The battle for Mount Olivet and for Greenpoint had been surprisingly quick affairs but had left hundreds if not thousands dead on the streets of New York City. It helped with the cleanup that most of those who died had already been dead – namely, vampires.

Amanda Colt was a vampire, and thus already dead – but she had looked more dead than usual when she came flying back through the air, impacting on the Brooklyn Street with a sick sound that was a cross between a splat and a crunch.

Marco, despite having had his left leg and his right arm broken by Mikhail the Bear in single combat, was at least still alive. Though he hurt to look at.

Despite all of that, Amanda still felt like jumping his bones. Even while she had sunk her fangs into his body to help him heal with a small sample of the vampire virus in her saliva. It wasn't enough to turn him, but enough to heal him. Like other viruses, her virus helped keep the host alive and well by keeping her "food stock" healthy and kicking. As long as he didn't try hurling more man hole covers, he should heal quickly.

"And yes," he said, "I'm serious. I don't care if Special Agent Mister Wizard offers to pay my entire way in San Francisco. I don't see a reason to leave here. Do you?"

Amanda winced. *That is such a poor question to ask me.*

Then her phone rang.

Amanda and Marco started. She pulled out her phone, looked at the number, and said, "Huh."

"Unknown?" he asked.

"*Nyet.* It is the VA."

"The Veteran's Association?"

She shook her head. "Vampires Association. Shh."

She put the phone on speaker, said her name, and the voice at the other end answered. "Miss Amanda Colt, this is Jagi Witzke, administrative assistant for President Bosley of the NYC-VA. Your presence is requested at our next meeting. There have been a few complaints launched against you that must be addressed."

The two of them exchanged a look. "Such as?" she asked.

"The destruction of several pieces of vampire property, as well as assaulting other vampires. And using your minion as a weapon."

Marco cocked his head, looking at her with amusement. He mouthed "Minion? You have a minion? Or am I it? Should I be honored or offended?"

"I'll be there," Amanda answered.

"Thank you. You know the time and location?"

"I do. I get the newsletter in the email."

"Thank you. We still have members who don't know what email is. See you there."

Amanda hung up. Marco's eyes narrowed. "So will the ninjas."

She shook her head. "No reason for that."

"We've blown up how many bars?"

"Only about three."

"And how many vampires have we killed? In the last six hours alone?"

Amanda winced. "We'll talk with Hendershot."

"Can we talk with Bram? I like him better."

# Chapter 1

# Physical Therapy

April 26th, 9 PM, Greenpoint, Brooklyn

Marco didn't think about Amanda. He had to make certain he didn't think about Amanda. Because if he did, he would probably fall into his thoughts and never fall out. After all, he wasn't easy to love, and didn't do much loving himself. He even surprised himself how deeply he fell into love once he was there.

And there was so much to focus on. She fought like a professional but was as intimidating as a chipmunk. And as sexy as the one that got away only better looking. Her 5'6" height made her a perfect fit when he hugged her, and her long red-gold hair went to the small of her back in a golden fall – he just wanted to run his fingers through it.

*Though with my luck,* he thought, *I'd find the only knots in her hair and pull them out.*

And her eyes – a warm, liquid Frangelico brown with her Siberia-pale skin. Her dress was casual, covering everything, but it didn't matter, she looked good in everything. It all seemed to be form-fitting, no matter the size. Jeans and a sweater *should* have covered her thoroughly, but somehow managed to be quite snug. Granted, it was a very nice form with curves that a Volvo would hug.

It gave him a warm feeling just thinking about her.

*Yes, I have to stop it. Dammit.*

After all, he was fully-healed, his bones knitted together, he had something else to focus on.

Staying alive in front of a half-dozen vampires.

Step one was easy. After the first three bodies were discovered around one construction site, Marco had no problem doing that math. He had contacted one of his people on the construction crew and had them lay the groundwork for his attack.

*But, hey, there are only six of them.*

Marco was crouched on an I-beam twenty feet up from where he had set his trap.

*This is going to be so easy.*

There had been *some* concern about staying hidden against vampires, but apparently, vampires were just as stupid as everybody else – nobody looked up.

*This is going to be so easy. No one ever looks up.*

On the top floor of the unfinished building stood a short, dark man, swathed in Armani and Prada. He was slender and unthreatening… until you looked at his eyes. The eyes were the tell – they were empty. Look at them too hard and too long, one could almost swear that they were lidless eyes of fire, straight out of *Lord of the Rings*, but most people never held his eyes that long.

The creature that looked like a human being gave a very tiny smile as he eyed his prey, Marco Catalano. It was strange to imagine that this child, this 19-year-old, had been such a threat. He wasn't even that big – a 5'9" blond dancer. That was it.

The creature that commonly called itself "Mister Day" chuckled to himself. *Dance of death, maybe.*

But now, it was time for him to die. And Marco would never see him coming.

Marco opened with a salvo of glass phials filled with holy water. As the holy water burned them like acid, Marco dropped down onto another vampire he missed, taking his head off with a knife.

Marco moved before that vampire turned to dust. He threw his entire weight into the next vampire, and slammed a stake into the vampire's chest, like a hammer blow. The vampire disintegrated into a pile of dust and clothing.

Marco spun, took the recently emptied jacket out of the air and hurled it at the third vampire, covering his face like a net.

Marco threw the stake in his hand, and it landed, point first, in the eye of the fourth vampire. Since the stake had been soaked in holy water, it not only penetrated the back of the eye socket, it lodged in the brain and started eating away at the gray cells. Undead or not, it was hard to focus when something was eating one's brains.

*Three down in a matter of seconds,* Mister Day thought. *Nicely done.* The creature lowered itself into a crouch, studying his prey with admiration. Marco was mostly human; the only improvement that Day could perceive was some residual after effects of a vampire's bite, but even that seemed to be mostly for healing fractures.

*Fascinating. But, sadly, time to end it.*

Day dropped from the I-beam of the top floor, and landed with a hard thud right behind Marco.

Marco heard the heavy body land behind him and, despite himself, didn't laugh. He merely gave a quick look over his shoulder, dropped his body in a bow, and shot his right foot backwards, cracking the newcomer in the sternum.

The newcomer only took a half-step back, and that was more than enough. The half-step took him onto a tarp.

This tarp, however, had nothing under it.

The newcomer fell from sight, dropping into the spikes of Marco's tiger trap.

*I'm so glad I had my guys put spikes in that this morning.*

One of the vampires growled, "*Allahu akbar!*"

Marco blinked. "What?"

All three vampires charged.

Marco drew his dual squirt guns and fired, blasting the vampires in the face as they ran at him. They screamed and covered their eyes but didn't slow or stop.

Marco dove between two of the attackers and let them keep running as they charged right into the pit with the wooden spikes.

And he never stopped smiling, even as they fell, screaming, to their deaths.

In the pit, Mister Day growled in frustration. He had been spiked enough to count as a pin cushion. The spear that nailed him through the head was particularly annoying.

A face appeared at the edge of the pit. It was the target.

"Still alive?" He cocked his head to one side, surprised. "Oh well. I can solve that."

Day snarled and tried to calm himself. He could be free with one good roll, breaking the spikes. Then, maybe, if he felt charitable, he would throw Marco down here.

Then he heard the truck backing up.

Day cursed, then held his breath as the cement truck started to pour down on him, burying him alive.

*Aw crap, not again.*

# Chapter 2:

# I'll Get You My Pretty, And Your Little Human, Too

New York City, April 26th

Robert's rules of order would frown on two disputants eating each other, but it was unlikely that the man who wrote the rules of conduct for meetings meant it to apply to vampires. (It certainly didn't apply to werewolves, since packs were less of a democracy, and more of an enlightened dictatorship. Some charitable vampires thought that wolves invented hockey.)

These thoughts drifted through the mind of Amanda Colt as she wandered into the Veterans of Foreign Wars Hall reserved for the meeting of the New York City Vampires Association. Of course, the NYC-VA didn't have even ten percent of New York City's vampire population. This was for the powerful, the affluent, or the really, really troublesome.

Amanda Colt didn't know what category she fell under. She had never been invited to the NYC-VA before.

She wasn't particularly rich. To *normal* people, as she lived in her Upper East Side 70th Street apartment, she was rich. To vampires, she was comfortable. It was an area where the cops had a good response time and people walked the streets at night. Really wealthy vampires (the types that lived in castles and estates, if they could) merely called her type "well invested: the *nouveaux riches* of the vampire world." At the rate her investments were growing, if she broke two hundred (next century), she might be considered part of the club.

Amanda Colt wasn't particularly powerful, either. She was as strong as the average vampire, maybe stronger (she had odd bursts of ability that surprised her, but that didn't count). She didn't have a nest, and her sphere of influence had only recently started. Until last year, her only power was, really, the power to turn heads.

However, Amanda Colt's role as a troublemaker was assured, even though it wasn't her fault. Her friend Marco Catalano was the focus of the trouble.

But these vampires thought of Marco as *her* human, so she was credited with his trail of destruction, including the recently re-killed, the property damage, and generally spreading so much fear through certain ranks of the vampire community that he bordered on being a terrorist.

So, Amanda didn't quite know if she was supposed to be there as a member of the general assembly, or if she was there to be executed as a local troublemaker.

If it was the latter, and they tried to hold even the *semblance* of a trial, she was going to rip them a new one. Maybe a new three or four, while she was at it.

As she looked around the hall, she could recognize a few faces. There was a bar owner from the Blood Bank, an Upper East Side vampire bar not far from Mount Sinai Hospital; he was a gruff, burly fellow who had served as an Irish cop in the nineteenth century. Not far from him was Kalsey, a tall, well-built and well-dressed Anglo-Indian vampire who owned The Platelet.

Well, Kalsey *had* owned the Platelet, before Marco got there. Its replacement was still under construction.

Though it didn't seem like losing his major source of income had hurt Kalsey all that much. He still wore Armani, carried his well-crafted sword cane, and even had a Rolex *Le President*, top of the line gold.

However, for all that, Kalsey didn't seem happy.

Amanda didn't even bother sitting but stood off to the side. The VFW Hall was lined with collapsible chairs, set up in nice neat rows. However, she didn't expect to be sitting much, especially if she was called to defend herself—verbally or physically.

The vampires on the dais were finally starting to file in. Amanda noted them, and she swore she knew some of them, but she couldn't remember from where. The one in the center position was female, blonde, and about Amanda's height, dressed casually in a comfortable leather jacket and blue jeans.

However, vampires were not matriarchal. To get to a position of power, you had to *be* powerful, not to mention manipulative, long-sighted, and willing to stab allies in the back… or whatever angle presented itself.

The blonde *thwacked* the gavel down. "This is the twenty-second meeting of the 235th session of the New York City Vampires Association, President Jennifer Bosley presiding. I hereby call this meeting to order," she said in an upper class British accent that Amanda could narrow down to London. "First order of business. Reading of the minutes from the last meeting? Is there a motion?"

One of the committee members on the dais raised his hands. "Move to waive the reading?"

Three hands went up from the crowd. Jennifer banged the gavel and said, "Moved, and seconded. Is there any old business?"

One person stood up in the back of the room…it was a male vampire in a dress. "Yes," he said in a thick accent. "I would like to object, once again, to acknowledging New York City as it currently stands. This place belongs to the British, and—"

President Jennifer Bosley slammed down the gavel again. "Edward, I said *old* business, not *concluded* business. For the last time, I don't care how old you are, or if you were the royal governor, the entire *continent* has moved on. If you bring this up again, you'll be banned from these meetings for *another* decade. Are we *understood?*" She dismissed the three hundred year old vampire as though he was already dead and dusty. "Next?"

The meeting went on for a while, and it covered a lot of topics one would expect: border disputes, blood supplies, old grudges, territorial haggling due to the latest construction rearranging geographic markers. Vampire bureaucracy was like a regular bureaucracy, but worse, since some topics and situations could drag on for *decades*, if not centuries.

There was even one man complaining that Little Italy should declare war on Chinatown, because

Chinatown was swallowing it whole, and "Back in the days when I was a Centurion in the Roman Empire—"

That one, at least, was cut off by a dozen different groans. Even President Jennifer Bosley seemed weary. She sighed. "Giuseppe, you weren't *part* of an Empire. Mussolini's ability was never as great as him ambition. You were a Sergeant in his army, and we're still telling jokes about *that*. Now, shut up and sit down before we revoke your territory… what little is left of it. As it is, you'll be hiding in your great-grandson's basement in Howard Beach in another two decades. I hope you don't mind swimming when it floods. Now, if that's enough of *old* business…" Jennifer gave the room a glare that told them it was, and if they didn't like it, she had a stake in the back room with their names on it. "New business?"

Kalsey jumped up from his seat so fast, Amanda half-expected him to shoot straight up to the ceiling. "*Yes!*" He thrust his cane at Amanda as though he were stabbing her. "She and her pet human destroyed my bar, slaughtered my most loyal and valuable retainers, then had minions poison me with time-delay release Holy Water capsules. I demand that she, *and* her human, make full restitution."

Jennifer Bosley nodded, then looked to Amanda. "We have had several notifications of this attack. Would anyone else like to add to this?"

"I would like to add something," said Lynch, the Irish cop/bar owner. "My name is Patrick Lynch, I'm the owner of the Blood Bank."

Amanda winced. *This will not be good.*

Jennifer Bosley nodded. "The chair acknowledges you, Proprietor Lynch. You have the floor."

Lynch smiled easily. "That young lady and her man came into my pub the night before Mister Kalsey's place had its unfortunate accident."

Kalsey whirled on Lynch. "Accident! Why you dirty Irish bastard!

Lynch ignored him. "Now, Madam President, you must understand," he continued in a soft, gentle brogue. "Mister Kalsey and I are old competitors, going back a few decades. However, I bear the man no great animosity. When Mistress Colt and her young man came into my place, they merely wanted some information. Marco came in and—"

Jennifer held up a hand. "Who is this Marco?"

"The human in question. Marco Catalano, he called himself," Lynch answered. "A pleasant enough fellow for an Italian, but he's blond, so there must be some Celt, from back in the day when they owned

Northern Italy. Anyway, he wanted some information. One of my customers challenged him directly and tried to kill him."

There was a scattered murmur through the hall. Pet humans were considered private property. A good, reliable human was difficult to come by. It would be like taking a sledgehammer to somebody's Porsche. If there was a problem with someone's human, his or her vampire was the party that should be addressed, and attacked, if need be. Directly going after someone's human was Just Not Done.

"Without any enhancements at all," Lynch said, "he dealt with the troublesome customer himself, with no aid from Mistress Colt. Not even with aid of her bite. He's no minion."

Amanda almost nodded but wanted to maintain an air of cool impassivity. A vampire's bite transferred a slight bit of the metaphysical virus that gave vampires their unique post-resurrection-like status; it helped keep the food stock alive, and it granted the ones they bit temporary preternatural strength. It was something other vampires could sense. Marco had wanted to avoid having any augmentation at all when they went into the Blood Bank, for this very reason.

*He was right again,* she thought. *I hate it when he's right. If I tell him, he'll be insufferable for days.*

President Jennifer Bosley arched a brow. "Indeed?"

Lynch nodded. "So, I contend that Mistress Colt had no hand in the destruction of The Platelet, that Marco Catalano could have done it all by himself."

"Bastard!" Kalsey barked. "What did you do, sic them both on me?"

Lynch merely smiled. "I simply mentioned a few establishments that I knew obtained their blood supply through a less than savory source—like, directly from people."

Jennifer Bosley tapped the gavel twice to cut off another outburst. "Presume for the moment that Amanda Colt's human, Marco Catalano, did indeed act independently in the destruction of The Platelet. What would be the purpose?" She looked at Amanda this time. "What prompted your human's destructive rampage?"

Amanda blinked, and slowly straightened. "Several of his people—by extension, my people—had been murdered by Mikhail the Bear. An issue which I tried to raise before this body and was ignored."

She glared around the room, and everyone went completely and utterly still, as still as only vampires could be. "I sent emails. I made phone calls. I did everything but send smoke signals. No one considered stopping his expansion."

After a moment, Jennifer Bosley cleared her throat. "Mikhail the Bear is an international authority, not bound to our local jurisdiction."

"*Da,*" Amanda said courteously. "That is another way of saying that you were all too terrified to do anything about him when he was rampaging over all of our territories."

Jennifer leaned forward, her dark brown eyes nearly black in the light. "Oh? And why are you using the past tense, young lady?"

Amanda cleared her throat. "Because last week, Mikhail the Bear was assassinated in Greenpoint, on the doorstep of Marco Catalano."

The grave-like quality of the room exploded into a cacophony of ranting. There were expressions of disbelief, objections that Amanda was even still alive, and one thing above all that Amanda found most interesting…

There was an undercurrent of fear. Every vampire in that room was afraid. The President merely hid her fear the best.

"Mikhail was dangerous to *all* of us," Amanda said, her voice rising above the din. She maintained eye contact with President Bosley. "He brought Vatican ninjas to our area. Where were you—all of you—when he was riding roughshod over Greenpoint?

And Howard Beach? And Bensonhurst? And Maspeth, Queens? He killed FBI agents, MI-6 intelligence officers, and mafiosi, attracting attention that none of us want. Through all that time, this body did *nothing*."

Jennifer Bosley rapped the gavel so hard, the crack sounded through the hall like a gunshot. "That aside, what does that have to do with the unwarranted attack on The Platelet?"

"Unwarranted?" Amanda asked. "Marco's territory—my territory—had been invaded, and constantly under siege. Marco attacked any large gathering of less than savory vampires that might be in contact with Mikhail and his people."

Lynch the bar owner stood. "I can vouch for that. That was the exact question I had been asked by her pet human."

Kalsey glared from his seat. "And you gave him *my* bar?"

Lynch grinned at him. "Sure, lad, where else would I send him to find unsavory lowlifes?"

Kalsey smirked. "There are some places in the Village I could name."

"Hey!" barked the male crossdresser from earlier. "What's that supposed to mean?"

Jennifer Bosley rapped the gavel again. "One more outburst, and I am clearing the hall." She looked to Amanda. "You claim that the human Catalano acted in self-defense." She looked to Kalsey. "*Were* you approached by Mikhail the Bear at any time?"

Kalsey winced. "Yes, Madam President, I was."

"And did you join forces with him?"

Kalsey swallowed, and Amanda kept from smiling. He was probably thinking about the holy water poisoning. When the Vatican ninja poisoned Kalsey, the ninja explained that the holy water was encapsulated in nano-capsules that required a secondary agent to unlock them, and flood Kalsey's system with holy water—in case there had been any alliance between him and Mikhail.

Kalsey, probably thinking about all of that, said, "No."

*Though if he is telling the truth,* Amanda thought, *who can tell?*

"Was this due to the threat of retaliation by Amanda and her human?" the President asked.

"Yes, ma'am."

The President looked at him for a long moment, as if wondering if she should believe him. "In that case, I think that Amanda's human has merely adapted himself well to the long-term planning that we vampires take for granted. Now, if there is no other discussion on the topic, I suggest a fifteen-minute recess. Do I have a second?"

Amanda raised her hand. Jennifer Bosley nodded at her. "Motion carried." She looked to Amanda. "Miss Colt, before you leave… "

She reached down, grabbed a pen, and quickly scribbled down a note. She folded it neatly, then ran a letter opener through it.

Then she threw the letter opener at Amanda's head.

# Chapter 3:

# Sitting Targets

New York City, April 26th (4:00 am)

O f course, vampires can dodge throwing knives, and it was made of metal, so it could not hurt me," Amanda explained in the rectory sitting room.

The sitting room was getting crowded. Rodgers sat at the table between Marco and Amanda, while several of the ninjas stood at the other side, drinking from Starbucks mugs bigger than their fists.

Marco Catalano winced at the whole letter opener idea. He knew that she could have, and did, dodge it. But still… "Nice to know she's so confident of your abilities," he drawled. He leaned back in the wooden chair and wondered why they couldn't have this meeting in his family's brownstone only a few miles away.

*Answer: because the Vatican Ninjas in the sitting room would probably not go over well.*

Marco tried not to sigh. He was blond, well built, and moved like a dancer, but social graces were not where his instincts were located. *No, that's more like gutting people.*

Marco tried to get back on track and looked to the priest. Father Rodgers, a black priest who was God-knew how old, was the local contact on all things anti-vampire. "Did she get away clean?"

The priest smiled. "Of course," he said in a booming voice that was trained before churches had microphones. "Hendershot and his men had her covered in the hall, and on the way back. If anyone tried to hurt Amanda, we would be ready for them."

Marco nodded. Hendershot of the Swiss Guard was a humorless Vatican Ninja—the Roman Catholic anti-vampire squad that had been around for longer than Marco wanted to think about. Rodgers was the local contact, and presumably in charge, though Marco had never asked for the exact arrangement of the hierarchy. He looked back to Amanda, "So, the letter?"

Amanda handed it to him. The note read:

*Miss Colt,*

*Obviously, you do not know what depths of trouble you've gotten yourself into, you and your human—if you did, you would never have taken on Mikhail in the first place.*

*Do not think that this verdict has actually gotten you off. Kalsey is a pig. Lynch steered you both in the right direction. And do not think that we don't know about the other two bars Marco destroyed that evening. We do. However, those bar owners are so deep in the mire that they wouldn't dare protest openly. You were lucky there. You are equally fortunate that you acquitted yourself well in the hall. Otherwise, we would have been forced to hang you, whether we wanted to or not. And that was not metaphorical; we would have hung you from a meat hook on a bell tower and waited for morning.*

*You may or may not have surmised from the reaction amongst the crowd that Mikhail was not alone. He was the low man on the food chain, and we're too worried about what's at the top of the pole to go against them directly. However, now that they have lost their primary recruiter, you can rest assured that the others will come and find you.*

*Good luck.*

*Lady Jennifer Bosley*
*President, NYC Vampires Association*


"Well, we *had* theorized that Mikhail had been part of a bigger organization," Marco said, handing it to the priest, "but that clinches it."

"*Da*," Amanda agreed, "but if Mikhail was head of their human resources and recruitment, what does rest of command structure contain?"

Marco smiled at the dropped "the"s in Amanda's speech. Despite being a vampire for over 80 years, she still occasionally reverted to the traditional Russian sentence structure, which had no articles, making her sometimes sound like a villain in *Rocky and Bullwinkle*.

"Not to mention," Rodgers added, "who needs that many vampires?" He finished reading the letter and put it down. "Mikhail was around for centuries, making nests upon nests."

"Sounds like an army," Marco said. "And let's face it, as time goes on, I'm sure that Mikhail's recruiting would have gotten more vigorous, if only because of modern technology."

Amanda nodded. "*Da*. Not every vampire can regulate their heartbeat, respiration, and pulse. Many do not even try, making them all, effectively, room temperature. Any thermal scope could spot them instantly."

"Not to mention incendiary rounds," Marco added. "And automatic arrow-shooters. And if someone else pulls our trick with the forty-gallon drum of holy water and the fire hose, a war of evil vampires versus people would be very, very short."

Rodgers laughed. "True. It would be hard for an army of *good* vampires to wage full-scale war on the land of the living. That would undermine the 'good' in their description."

Marco nodded. As much as he thought the phrase "good vampire" was as strange and as oxymoronic as "good lawyer," Marco had figured out how it worked. As a type of "post-resurrection," vampirism closely intertwined the soul of the vampire with the body; the more actions, good or bad, the more fully formed the soul, and the body, would become. A sinful life, filled with vice and just plain evil, would mar the vampire's body, as well as the soul. While the vampire would travel further and further along the scale of power, it would do the same along the scale of evil. The vampire would gain power but become more restricted in the ability to move—crosses, churches, and the lack of an invitation into a private domicile would be off limits.

Amanda, on the other hand, went to church weekly, sometimes daily, and went through the rosary routinely.

It was one of the many things he loved about her.

Amanda looked to Rodgers and asked, "Have you ever heard of the Council?"

Rodgers blinked behind his coke-bottle glasses. "Rumors, mostly."

Marco raised a finger. "Council? Any Council in particular?"

Amanda and the priest exchanged a glance. Rodgers spoke first. "You haven't run into a master vampire yet, have you?"

"He hasn't," Amanda answered for him.

Marco's amused little smile flickered. "If Mikhail the Bear wasn't a master vampire, then what the hell is one?"

"Think the original Dracula," Rodgers answered. "Only Mister Stoker made it look easier than it really is."

Marco winced. "Ouch."

Amanda nodded. "The council is supposed to be something that even master vampires answer to. Something like that could intimidate the local Vampires Association and could be something Mikhail could work for." She frowned. "If there were any evidence to prove that it ever existed."

Marco shrugged. "True. Anyway, one thing at a time. Your meeting at least gets us off the hook for laying waste to Kalsey's place. I'm not sure if we're going to be safe from *his* retribution, but if he could have taken us out on his own, he would have, but I don't think he'd want to mess with the Vatican Ninjas."

"He also does not know our forces," Amanda said. "Not to mention that Mikhail was killed on your doorstep. No one knows what level of force we brought to bear, nor do they know how he died."

Marco nodded. "I listened to the recording the ninjas made of the meeting. I noticed that you didn't mention how he was taken out. Good idea."

Amanda gave him a smile. "I thought it would be prudent to let them think that we killed him ourselves."

Marco sighed, mostly to himself. He didn't want to think about what had happened last week, when Mikhail beat him half to death at his own front door. Though that had been annoying, it wasn't a problem.

The problem was that Mikhail had been assassinated—and not by anyone allied to Marco and Amanda. Mikhail had been crippled, helpless, and totally at their mercy. If Marco had his way, Mikhail would have spent what little remained of his short life suffering through water torture— an IV of holy water int Mikhail's veins a few units at a time. Mikhail would have talked. Eventually. Marco would have taken his time, and he would have made the vampire tell him *everything*. Someone had killed him to prevent that. Amanda had given chase, but the creature who killed Mikhail had gotten away, only after throwing Amanda off a roof.

That was *also* something Marco didn't want to think about too much.

"I do not think there is any more that we can do," Amanda said. "We have solved one immediate problem, and unless we can find a way to solve the root of it, we would merely be floundering in the dark."

Marco grunted. "True. I hate it, but it's true. Even if it does make us a stationary target."

"You could make it harder on them," Rodgers suggested.

Amanda and Marco looked right at him. "How so?" Marco asked.

"*Da.* Please explain," Amanda concurred.

"Didn't you have an offer lately to go out to San Francisco?" the priest asked.

"That's true," Marco told him. "But what does that have to do with anything?"

"If the two of you are in two different places, that might encourage them to wait until you're both together again," the priest said. "If one of you falls, the other will be put on notice, and considering what happened the last time, the last thing they'd want is to face you while you are prepared."

The two of them went quiet, and the priest waited only a beat before he stood. "I'm going to make some more tea. I think you two need some time to discuss this."

Rodgers left, and the two of them barely noticed.

When Amanda and Marco had faced down Mikhail the Bear's New York army of vampires, they had brought in a new element: Merle Kraft, government expert on "the strange." However, while he had been helpful, he had also figured on there being a problem in his near future: the problem of vampires entering into *his* neighborhood.

Merle had made Marco an offer to go to San Francisco and organize a local anti-vampire squad so Merle could go off and do his "real job," however one could define "real." Merle Kraft had even offered Marco an all-expense paid trip to the University of San Francisco, so Marco could finish his Physician Assistant agree.

"You said it was a good idea," Amanda told Marco.

Marco's smile flickered. "I was beaten half to death at the time. You shouldn't take anything I say at face value."

"That is no denial," Amanda told him.

Marco's smile flickered again. He had no idea what to say. He couldn't tell her what he was thinking, and what he was feeling…that was utterly and completely off-limits. He had secrets of his own…one, really. Going to California, this time last year, would have meant *nothing* to him. And on what was essentially a government grant? Hell yes. It wasn't like people would miss him. The gangs he ran? They were more afraid of him than anything else. His father always wanted him to get out more. There was nothing in the entire world that would keep him from going to California. Not one damn thing…

Then there was Amanda.

*Except for, you know, "By the way, Amanda, I like killing people. That's not a problem for you, is it? Even though you drink blood to survive and don't kill anyone, while I'd happily slaughter some people just to improve the gene pool." That would end well.*

"Yeah. It's not a denial. Let's face it, New York is relatively secure. Merle needs all the help he can get, and these guys are willing to get me away from the schmucks at NYScrew."

Marco smiled, and tried to be as genuine as possible, before she picked up on any signs of deceit.

"But, don't worry," he said, his smile becoming pained. "We'll still be friends."

His words were killing him before he even said them.

Marco's words were killing Amanda, even though she was already dead.

Then again, they had been killing her since she first discovered she was in love with him. One of their first conversations had Marco happily agreeing to being "just friends." Marco had even *said* she was beautiful, and lovely, and he found her attractive… and *of course*, they would just be friends. It had been a pattern he was familiar with all his life, apparently. He had skipped the heartbreak and went straight for the friendship, never expecting or trying for more. And that was *before* he knew she was a vampire.

Now what could she do?

"Yes," she said, "we will always be friends. I am not going anywhere."

Marco gave her one of his easy shrugs. "Yes, but I may be." He reached out and took her hand, giving it a reassuring squeeze. "But no matter where I am, you give me a call, I will come running. And I will kill anyone who gets in my way."

Amanda gave him a little smile and returned the hand squeeze. She cherished the contact, and resisted the urge to pull him closer and embrace him. His hands were surprisingly soft for all the fighting he did, and even a few degrees warmer than her own hand.

Amanda stroked her thumb along the back of his hand. "That's sweet. I think. Do you *want* to go?" she asked, hoping to God that he said no.

Marco gave another little shrug, and leaned back, not releasing her yet. "He seems to think I'm needed there. Though I don't know if I'm the one he's gonna need. It'll be up to him. I guess I should make preparations just in case." He chuckled. "Don't worry, darling, you won't get rid of me quite that easily. Not yet, anyhow. The short version is—I have no idea."

Amanda furrowed her brows. "How can you say so? Merle has offered you an all-expenses-paid scholarship for the rest of your days in college. You can get a Master's in Physician Assistant without spending a dime. Why would you give up all that?"

Marco maintained his grip and stroked her fingers with his thumb… like she had been doing with his hand. "I'm used to New York. It has everything I've ever loved."

Amanda's heart stopped. Literally. She could usually set it to automatically beat and keep all of her vital organs still viable. But, sometimes, there were little moments that could make her forget… and those events lately all seem to be around Marco.

"After all," Marco continued, "it's not like they're going to have sidewalk hotdog vendors in San Francisco."

Amanda had to laugh at that one. "Marco, of all the things to say, really?"

Marco's little smile flickered. She couldn't tell if it flickered up or down, really. "Well, it was one of the first things that came to mind. Ah well. Whatever do you think Merle Kraft would do without us?"

# Chapter 4:

# Welcome To San Francisco

San Francisco, April 27th

If anyone were to know the number of government operations that were actually taken from television, Merle Kraft was fairly certain that most of the general populous would be worried.

Take, for example, the *USS Enterprise*, a space shuttle named after the *Enterprise* of *Star Trek* fame in the 1960s. The first nuclear submarine was named after the *Nautilus*, from *20,000 Leagues Under the Sea*.

As for Merle's subsection of government work, there wasn't much of a name. In fact, the name kept changing every few years.

At the moment, Merle's code name was *Initiative*, named after a government project on *Buffy, the Vampire Slayer*.

*Sometimes, I hate government work,* he thought.

Merle sighed. Generally, he worked with anyone with a problem. He'd hung around Special Forces, the FBI, and Homeland Security, which wasn't bad for a 5'5" Eurasian with midnight blue eyes.

However, as he got back to his place in San Francisco, Merle came to the conclusion that he needed a slightly bigger budget …

*Not to mention a flamethrower, multiple squirt guns, and enough medieval weaponry to launch a crusade.*

Of course, his handlers were no help. Everybody above him in the chain of command were dead silent on the problem. From the moment he learned that vampires were real until he got off the plane in San Francisco, every last text and email he had fired off into the government ethernet had been met with silence.

This only meant one thing: the official *and* the unofficial position of his government overlords was simple, and vampires did not now, or ever, exist. Merle would be expected to handle "whatever" all by himself.

*At least increase my budget, you lousy pricks.*

"You mean the best you can do is throw money at the problem?" said a voice from behind him.

Merle stopped at the door to his magic shop and sighed. It was his half-brother Dalf; and if he wasn't in his traditional top hat and magician's tuxedo and cape, Merle would probably drop dead from shock. "What is it, Dalf?" Merle asked without turning around. "I rid New York of the immediate vampire problem. Can't you leave me in peace for five minutes?"

Dalf smiled, Merle could hear it in his voice. "Immediate, yes, but nothing more."

Merle turned to meet his brother's eyes. His shirt and blood-red tie were the same, and his cape, and his top hat, and his cane topped with the silver wolf's head. The only thing that identified the two of them as brothers were the identical blue eyes. Otherwise, Dalf was Boston Brahman black Irish, and Merle definitely wasn't.

"Funny," Merle said, "it's the afternoon. Are you allowed out in the sunlight?"

His half-brother grinned then waved his hands at the perpetual San Francisco fog.

Merle nodded. "Point taken... actually, I'm surprised that vampires haven't come here yet, the fog all the time, almost no direct sunlight, plenty of bums and freaky weirdos to eat and..." He blinked. "You son of a bitch, there are vampires here."

Dalf smiled – evilly, as usual. "It's not like *I* brought them."

Merle grabbed the door to his store and pushed in. As usual, Tiffany Whitman was there behind the desk.

Tiffany was fated by her name alone and fit the stereotype brilliantly—she was a total and complete blonde, with breasts that should've been implants. The only reason for her employment is that she was great with numbers, as long as they had a dollar sign in front of them. If Merle paid her on commission, she'd haggle with him to the penny, and she'd be right.

Her boyfriend, George Berkeley, was a nice enough fellow. He wasn't that bright, but big, burly, and kind, with brown hair, brown mustache—and sitting off in a side aisle reading a guns-and-ammo magazine. He was the very definition of Neo-Conservative: a Liberal who'd been mugged.

Merle looked over his shoulder. Dalf was still there, mysteriously enough. Merle moved into his well-lit store, certain that Dalf wouldn't follow, preferring instead to stay in the shadows.

"How's business?" Merle asked.

Tiffany looked up from the cash register. "We're making lots and lots of money."

He sighed. "That's nice, Tiffany. Anything happening as of late?"

George looked up from the magazine. "There've been some murders, but that's the only interesting thing in the news lately."

"How're murders interesting?"

"No blood at all," George rumbled, "even though they were kinda gruesome."

"Not to mention that they stole several of the bodies from the morgue just last night," came a new voice. Merle looked over and spotted Yana Rosenburg: slight build, red hair, green eyes, more cute than pretty. She was a bright young woman, which made Merle wonder what she was doing with Tiffany and George half the time.

He looked over at Dalf. The snide smirking son of Satan had vanished. His point had been made, and the message received. *And if I have half a chance, I'd stake him through the heart.* "They stole bodies, huh?" I looked closely at Yana. "Why do you think it's 'they'?"

"Same method on different sides of town around the same time." Yana shrugged. "It's not that hard."

"And when I took out one of them, it didn't stop anything," George added.

Merle cocked his head. "You did what?"

George shrugged. "Some guy jumped me on Grant Street, near one of the knife places—you know, throwing knives and swords? Took his head off. His partners must have taken the body away, because it was gone when the police came back with me."

An idea was starting to form. *Should I bring these people into my little world of strangeness?* "Yana, you said you have a friend who's big on hand-to-hand combat?"

She nodded. "Yup. Sarah. Why?"

"I'm not sure yet. An idea just occurred to me." *I might need eyes and ears if this is going to be more than I expected.* "You think it's the work of a gang?"

Yana nodded thoughtfully. "Maybe. Most of the people dying are all similar: young, healthy, and kinda nasty."

Merle raised an eyebrow at her victimology. She answered the unasked question: "They're all connected to violent crimes."

George glanced up from an article on the latest Glock. "Some of them were mafya…you know, the Russian kind."

Merle frowned. *Great, so there are vampires in town, and already active.* He eyed the three of them closely. *Technically I can bring them into my little secret—just not about the government involvement. But still… And besides, if I do nothing, these kids would probably all get eaten. George was already attacked in a place he hangs out, and Tiffany would be with him one of these days, and Yana was his best friend since they were two.*

Merle turned back to his employee. Tiffany was busy with a customer, and Yana and George were chatting up a short fellow with supernova red hair that had obviously come out of a bottle. He looked sort of like the old actor Barry Fitzgerald, from *The Quiet Man*, if he ever played anything *other* than little old men his entire career. And of course, to fit the image, he came complete with an Irish brogue.

Merle approached with caution. He had wanted to talk with Yana and the others about the vampire problem, and it was already too dark at the moment, so all of Merle's more interesting customers were about to start crawling out of whatever coffin they slept in—and those were just the humans.

*With any luck, I can get rid of Mister Potatohead and start the very strange conversation I have in mind.* "Ah, Yana... maybe I should hire you, you're already so friendly with the customers." Merle looked at Tiffany, who was busy eyeing the cash handed to her by the latest customer. "Unlike some people," he muttered.

"Actually, this is a friend of ours," Yana explained. "We met him on campus not too long ago. Transfer student to the university. Rory."

"Pleased to meetcha, lad," he said in a thick brogue, extending a hand.

Merle nodded thoughtfully. It wasn't unusual for people to start on their education later in life, but this man was easily in his forties, and the smile lines along his face looked older, and his eyes looked older still… in fact, Merle had some idea of where he knew them.

He'd seen a similar look in Amanda Colt's eyes back in New York.

Merle reached forward and grabbed Rory's hand. It was cold… about room temperature.

Merle's eyes narrowed, and he glanced over to the other customer, just departing. His grip tightened and with a simple move, Merle flipped Rory to the other side of the room, slamming him against a wall. Merle slid into a combat stance without a thought.

Rory was, unsurprisingly, on his feet in a split second, and, without taking his eyes off him, Merle said, "Tiffany, close the door."

The blonde stood there, blinking for a moment, then quickly moved to flip over the sign to "Closed." She then stood at the door, checking for any potential customers who were turned away by the sign—*Undoubtedly to tell me how much speculative cash we lost with this hiatus.*

"Might I ask what yer problem is, sir?" Rory asked.

"Your body temperature, bloodsucker."

Rory paused a moment, then he smiled. "Ah, and he's one of the hard men, is he?" He looked at Yana, then George. "You're right, he is a quick one. Quicker than they say. But then again, who knew that was possible, eh?"

Merle quickly checked his peripheral vision. Both George and Yana were still seated. They hadn't even been surprised by Rory being thrown about. "You know what he is?"

Yana nodded. "I did… George, um, not so much."

George looked up from his magazine. "Did I miss something?"

"Your friend over there is a vampire," Merle explained.

Rory smiled. "At least I'm not an IRS agent, yeah?"

Merle arched a brow. "You're not from around here, right?

Rory blinked a moment, probably wondering if Merle hadn't noticed his red hair, green eyes, or Irish brogue. "Good guess."

"Next time you eat someone, take a dose of mouthwash, you have blood breath."

Yana took a step forward. "Um, Mister Kraft, it's kinda like this… we've known Rory for a year now, and he hasn't eaten us, um, yet, so we thought we could introduce you to him." She leaned forward, and her voice dropped to an innocent whisper. "It's about the recent murders. It's not about gang violence."

"Yes, it is," he corrected her. "Only the gangs are bloodsuckers."

George looked around with his normal, easy going style. "Wow, this is like a Hammer film. Which one is Dracula?"

"Christopher Lee, isn't he always?" Merle muttered. He grabbed the back of a wooden chair and lifted it so he could grab one of the legs. With a flick of his wrist, he broke off the leg, creating a handy stake. "Now, start talking."

Rory nodded. "I came here a bit back, befriended this lot to get close to you, Mister Kraft. There's trouble brewing, and from what I hear, you're the one to talk to about it."

Merle sighed, and lowered the stake, visibly relaxing so Rory could take a swing if he thought his guard was down. "Sure, I'm Nero Wolfe for the supernaturally inclined."

Tiffany let out a breath. "Thank God."

Merle laid the stake against the counter. "Yes, it could've been bad."

Tiffany: "No, it was bad, that's why it's good!"

He rolled his eyes, knowing that it would be useless to play twenty questions. "Explain."

"You broke the chair with the bad leg," Tiffany cheered, "and that means we don't have to fix it, yay! You saved us money! Are you finally getting money sense?"

He looked at the wooden stake, then reconsidered… *If I staked Tiffany, there would still be a body left over. Nuts.*

George closed the magazine and put it aside. "So, we've got a vampire, a magician, and a werewolf. I think we have enough for a D&D campaign."

Merle kept his eyes on the vampire. "We have a vampire, a magic store owner, and a *what* now?"

"Werewolf." George shrugged, as placid as ever. "My last girlfriend was a biter."

"Not a wolf!" Tiffany called over his shoulder. "Wolf*hound*. You're not a problem, honey!"

Merle looked back to the vampire. "You're a dog?"

"He's really a gentleman. No. Really," Tiffany corrected, almost sadly. "He's a gentleman."

George sighed. "I guess I'm too laid back to be a wolf?"

Merle frowned. "So, vampire—"

The redhead held up a hand. "To start with, my name at the moment is Rory, and I'd prefer it," the vampire said. "It would raise fewer questions than my real name."

"Which is?"

# Chapter 5:

# Enter Darkness

San Francisco, May 20th

Marco Catalano's first thought, looking at the University of San Francisco, was, *Wow, they have a nice field of fire here.*

Marco looked on with approval. The campus wasn't very large. If it topped out at a dozen acres, he would be surprised, and he hoped that the campus before him was merely a main campus. So far, it seemed to be a really nice, green lawn, closed in on three sides, leaving the open side to the main street and facing Golden Gate Park, which Marco had already dismissed as a cheap imitation of New York's Central Park (even though the same man designed both).

*Heck,* he thought, *this central park has a windmill, what do they think this is?* Don Quixote? *New York has a friggin'* castle, *take that, you dirty hippies!*

Marco sighed. That was his third hippie thought today, and he hadn't even been near the more hipster part of the city yet. He was going to explode if he even got near Haight-Ashbury.

*What the Hell am I doing here? I'm ready to set this city on fire if I stay here five more minutes, and I'm actually considering a whole regimen of Physician Assistant studies here? Four more years for a Master's? Yeesh.*

Of course, the answer came to him fast enough. Amanda.

His problem was less with Amanda and more with himself. He loved her, there was no question, but he was a bit of a monster. More along the lines of "Oh, you're mugging me? Good, I wanted to kill something."

There were also other things to consider. He was a genius. The problem with being a genius is being easily bored, as any true genius can tell you…in his case, he would also insist that he was annoying; the student body of his university agreed with this assessment. He wasn't welcome there. There was a possible solution in going to a nice, quiet little town to attend classes in—though "little" was relative, considering the size of New York City. Thus far, San Francisco offered a full scholarship and hinted at offers of sex, drugs, and rock and roll if they could only get him and his 4.0 GPA there.

"Can we help you?"

Marco glanced over at a trio of female college students. None of them were much taller than five-foot, and they were an odd set of two blondes and a redhead. The taller blonde (topping out at 5'5") was a dirty blonde who wasn't excessively pretty; she had muddy brown eyes and a square face, a stout figure, and leaned towards butch without falling into it.

Marco's brain automatically compared them each to Amanda. It was like comparing candles to the sun.

*Next.*

Marco's omnipresent little smile flickered, widened for a split second, then he offered his hand. "Marco Catalano, prospective student."

The redhead reached forward and took it. "I'm Yana Rosenburg." She nodded to the taller blonde, and said, "This is Tara. And this is Buffy."

Marco blinked. "I'm sorry, what?"

The athletic blonde rolled her eyes and looked to Marco. "Sarah Bell. They're just being funny."

Tara shrugged. "She complains when we call her the Chosen One," she said in a soft, almost childlike whisper.

Sarah looked at her taller friend and said, "That's because I am *so* much cooler than Keanu Reeves."

"True," Marco said, his voice deadpan, "but would that really be hard?"

Sarah gave him a look he was familiar with—sizing him up, trying to fit him for potential dating material.

He couldn't figure out what her conclusions were when she said, "Hope to see you around, should you come around, I mean."

Marco shrugged. "Perhaps."

Marco looked at the storefront for the Art of Kraft, the magic shop run by Merle Kraft. It was on the Embarcadero, the closest San Francisco had to a Rodeo Drive, or a Fifth Avenue.

*Meh, I suppose it'll do.* He walked up to the front door, and hesitated. He knew it was good manners to at least talk to Merle Kraft. After all, the government employee and magician had paid for Marco's trip out here and *had* even offered to pay for the rest of his academic career, as long as he came to San Francisco. Politeness dictated that Marco at least stop by.

"The last thing I need is another problem," Merle Kraft muttered as he shoved a box onto the shelf. He turned back to the front door and stopped. "Damn it, of course you show up now."

Marco arched a brow. "Well, if that's your attitude about it, I'll go back to New York."

Merle Kraft sighed. "Come on in. Have a look around." He waved a hand at the rest of the store layout.

Marco glanced around and shrugged. There wasn't much to see. "Been there, done that. You sure the University of San Francisco even *has* a PA program?"

Merle smiled tiredly. "Yup. If it didn't, I would have found somewhere else."

He nodded, then looked over the shorter man. "You look like hell."

Merle chuckled. "Gee, thanks." He rubbed his eyes and sighed. "I've been training my own local task force."

"Oh? With what? You have a SWAT team? A Delta unit? More Vatican Ninjas?"

Merle really laughed aloud this time. "Thanks, I needed that." He shook his head. "No, I couldn't even begin to try and convince the people I work for that vampires are a real threat. I'd be sent to the nearest funny farm. And then I'd have to escape." He bent over and picked up another box. "So I've been stuck using local college kids, because they've already fallen into the whole routine. They've already taken to using call signs out of *Buffy the Vampire Slayer.*"

A minor alarm bell went off in Marco's head. "Yeah, you're right, you're in trouble."

Merle's mouth bunched up in one corner as he slid the box onto the counter. "Gee, thanks for letting me know. You're such a *mensch*."

He blinked, still not used to Merle throwing out the occasional Yiddish. "I've already met several of your Buffy crowd. You're going to have an interesting training program."

Merle opened the box with a boxcutter that Marco hadn't seen a split-second before. It had come from nowhere. Literally nowhere. Marco searched his memory twice. It… appeared while Marco was somehow not paying attention. He filed this away for later in case he had to kill Merle at some point down the line.

"Well," Marco said, "in some cases, I'm already ahead of the game with one of my kids. Though you may not have noticed her. Sarah Bell is already a professional-level martial artist." He cut away the final bit of tape, and just like that, the boxcutter was gone again. "She's good," Merle continued, as though nothing interesting happened, "even by my standards, and I don't even meet my own standards. The others make some good support staff, and some of them can even aim. But I need someone who can take all of them and form them into a coherent, cohesive fighting force. You made street gangs act like military units, and you can at least keep people alive. I need you. Heck, I'll even take some of your street gangs out here."

Marco chuckled. "Yeah, I suppose. The problem is manpower. I can keep your people alive, but for how long? I've got *dozens* at my command out in New York. How many do you have?"

Merle looked into the box, and reached in, coming out with boxes of flash paper. "Seven, if you count me."

Marco growled to himself. "Of course I don't. You said you needed people to hold the fort while you're out of town. I can't count you. Is six the best you can do?"

Merle yawned, then shook his head. "Listen, it's not like I came prepared with a small army in my back pocket. Nor do I have a lot of people in the area who are interested in fighting vampires—assuming they're even aware. If this were LA, we would at least have the Crips or the Bloods as a recruiting pool." He shoved the flash paper onto the shelf behind the counter. Each box thumped as he rammed it in. "But this is *San Francisco*, where everyone stays in their nice, neat little communities, and no one *bothers* anyone else, because several of these communities spend their time getting high and screwing their brains out. Except for the homeless, who aren't mentally ill, they want to be out on the street and what they do is less pan-handling, and more extortion."

Marco arched an eyebrow. "Don't be shy," he muttered, "tell me what you really think."

"And," Merle continued, as though Marco hadn't spoken, "then when someone *gets* eaten, no one sees anything… again, because they're busy getting high and screwing their brains out."

Marco rolled his eyes and leaned against the counter. "You've gotta be kidding me. I can just imagine some poor vampire biting one of your hippies. He'd be stoned out of his mind after the first sip, and then an addict within a week. I'd start to feel sorry for the vampires."

"Yeah, well, don't bet on it," Merle said, turning back. "Would that be the case. We're not that lucky. But we've got two heavy hitters, three shooters, and someone to do a lot of screaming and waving a cross around. And there's me. And the lycanthrope."

Marco shook his head to clear it. He knew he had the advantage with the time difference, but he felt like he had fallen asleep. "Did you say lycanthrope? As in werewolf?"

Merle waved him off. "He's more like a weredog. Wolfhound, in fact."

Marco opened his mouth, paused, thought a moment, raised a finger, and paused again, looking like a Daffy Duck cartoon. "Wait. Hold it. You've got a weredog problem?"

Merle chuckled. "Not a problem. George is nice enough and makes for a good pet. He's well trained as a wolfhound, and he remembers enough afterward that he's cognizant of what's going on when he's a dog."

Marco rubbed his temple, feeling a headache coming on. "Okay, lemme get this straight. You've got vampires, and one of your people is a werepuppy. Great. Does he have a pack?"

"Not that we know of." Merle took the empty box off of the counter, dropping it on the ground.

Marco looked at the box, then back to the shelves. "How did you do that?"

Merle blinked. "Do what?"

"Stock the shelf fully? I swear you put three boxes there, but the package is too big for it, and the shelf is full."

Merle shook his head and sighed. "Jet lag. Oh well. As for the lycanthrope thing, it's not a problem. George got bitten by his ex-girlfriend, and she's some kind of cat, so, lycanthropy has a few more variables than most original stories would imply."

Marco sighed, closed his eyes, and said nothing for a moment. "Does George at least have something like a superpower?"

"He's very laid back, and he's good as a shooter. We haven't really tried him at hand-to-hand combat, but we know he cut off someone's head."

"That's something. How bad is the vampire problem, though?" Marco asked. "Seriously. Are we talking full scale Armageddon, or merely a few roaming packs of street gangs?"

A shrug. "We can't tell yet. The major problem is San Francisco itself. During the spring to summer months, the fog around here is so thick, the sun can't shine through for half of daylight hours. Basically, it's a vampire playground. Not to mention that you can't even pick out the ones who are pale and pasty because they're dead and tell them apart from the ones who look that way due to a lifestyle choice. Unless, of course, they've read too many books about vampires."

Marco growled. "Yeah, well, someone should tell them that real vampires don't sparkle."

"Speaking of which, how is Amanda?"

Marco smiled. "She's okay. Still breathing."

"So to speak."

Marco gave Merle a glare that caused him to shiver. "*Anyway*," Marco continued, "Amanda is doing quite well, thank you, and she is currently negotiating our current arrangement between our various factions."

Merle arched a brow, wondering what sort of arrangement could be brokered between Vatican Ninjas, mafiosi, and the NYPD. "How's that going?"

Marco chuckled. "Why do you think I chose this week to come out to San Francisco?"

Merle flinched, obviously surprised. "You abandoned her to deal with politics?"

Marco's gaze went back to daggers. "I did *not* abandon her. She *wanted* me out of the neighborhood so I wouldn't screw anything up."

"How did she figure you would do that?"

Marco cocked his head. "Setting people on fire doesn't help anything."

"I thought that fire was a great way to kill vampires."

"Who said anything about *vampires*?"

"Oh, yeah, that'd do it. I wonder how she's getting along without you."

Marco shrugged. "Perfectly well, I imagine. She's quite charming. There's a reason she's over a hundred years old without turning evil."

New York City

Amanda Colt was thirty seconds away from becoming allergic to any crosses, churches, or synagogues. That's the sort of thing that happened after a vampire committed mass murder.

And she was so very, very close to doing that just now.

The fragile alliance that she and Marco had put together only weeks ago, was already starting to fall apart. These people had no problem slaughtering vampires together, but the issue became very different when they had to sit down and deal with each other face to face.

Officer Donald "Duck" Tolbert of the New York City Police Department was next to her, in full-dress uniform. He was a tall, light-skinned officer of Jamaican heritage, two generations back. And he looked ready to draw his sidearm.

Yet another reasons why Amanda refused to let anyone have guns in the room.

On the other side of him was the Mafia wiseguy known only as "Enrico." He was tall, but more elegant than the standard thug. When Amanda first met him, he was relaxing at Doctor Catalano's desk like he was there for a business meeting, instead of holding Marco's father hostage. He was of medium build, with thick cheekbones, and an easy, conman smile... when he wasn't threatening to kill someone.

In between the two of them was a generally colorless man named Robert Hendershot, Vatican Ninja. Hendershot was definitely Germanic in background, and he talked with a light German accent; he said he was Swiss, and one of *the Guards*. He was blond and blue-eyed, and his expression was so neutral, he might as well have been a block of cheese. He also had quick muscle, not gym muscle... though Hendershot usually had enough heavy weapons on him that it had to have added a hundred pounds.

And the fourth person in the room was the host for this evening - Monsignor Rodgers, the black, Roman Catholic pastor of Greenpoint's Church of Saints Anthony-Alphonsus.

When one considered that a major issue with vampires going over to the dark side bore with it a penalty of *all* the things that hurt Dracula, including religious items, Amanda's thoughts of hurting these people only showed her just how much they were wearing on her patience.

She briefly wondered if the church had to be reconsecrated if there was a murder in the rectory.

"Enrico," Amanda said, slowly, keeping her fangs in, "you cannot ask for total police immunity. You are not bringing your entire Mafia into fighting the vampires, and we can't even bring in the entire police department. This is a demand that is impossible to enforce, you know that. If you prefer, we can let your people be eaten, and leave you out entirely."

The priest cleared his throat. "Before we get carried away, we should stick to the main point. Now that we have stopped the creation of more vampires—we hope—how do we break down the areas protected by each group?"

Enrico sighed. "Fine. How about this - we will take up most of the areas around our fields of influence, and you know where those are, we all do. And we'll add another half-mile."

Tolbert sighed and nodded. "We'll be happy to let you do that, and we'll see about putting as many of our guys on the borders of your areas as is possible, so your people don't get pulled over for carrying lots of sharp pointy sticks."

Enrico scoffed. "To heck with that. We carry Mac-10s with incendiary rounds."

And the yelling started again.

*I so miss Marco.*

# Chapter 6:

# I Am Coming Home

New York City

Amanda Colt looked at Marco as he got off the plane, and her undead heart stopped for a few seconds too long. As a vampire, she could regulate her own bodily functions, and much like a "real person," had most of their organs operate without too much thought (she had yet to meet the human being who gave large amounts of thought to how many times they had to blink… though, come to think of it, Marco just might. He was that sort of scary-smart).

In Amanda's case, her heart seemed to completely reset when she saw Marco. She didn't know why, exactly. Certainly, she had feelings for him, and it occasionally caused her some problems when she thought too hard about them, or him. But why it would have a direct effect on her cardiovascular regulation, that was beyond her.

Marco hadn't even gotten off of the escalator of LaGuardia Airport's arrivals area when she spotted him, and he saw her as soon as the moving stairs sank low enough.

"Hey there, beautiful," he whispered, knowing she would hear it. "Have fun with the league of extraordinary cops and criminals?"

Amanda smiled and shook her head slightly from side to side–he couldn't hear her from there and shouting like a madwoman across an airport in a post-9/11 universe was a really, really bad idea.

Marco merely sighed, and waited until he got off the escalator with his travel bag. He had packed for a four-day excursion, and a briefcase was more than enough to handle everything he needed. The novels he packed took up most of the room.

Marco stepped off and walked over to her, and she gave him a bear hug that would have lifted most people off the ground. But someone would have noticed if *she* was the one who picked *him* off the ground. It was a nice, comforting sensation. He was so refreshingly… *solid*, a firm hold on the reality her life sorely needed for decades.

"So, how was your stay?" she asked, holding in her trepidation.

On the one hand, she wanted Marco to stay… she also just *wanted* him. On the other hand, she wanted Marco as far away from her as possible. Ignoring the "just friends," disclaimer, there were other issues. Namely all of the usual complications of being immortal and saw human beings as a daily meal.

Having Marco away in San Francisco would be a Godsend, leading her from temptation, and delivering him from her urges.

On the other hand, it felt like someone was *already* pulling her heart out through her sternum, and he hadn't even told her if he was going to stay in San Francisco.

Marco shrugged. "Meh. I've had worse. I've also had better." His ever-present smile flickered just a bit wider. "I've had nights in Central Park with you."

Amanda's heart warmed… and she hoped it wasn't literally, otherwise she would start glowing any minute. "Well, it could have been worse. You could have had my days."

Marco nodded. "Let's get in the car, and you can tell me all about it."

"Your father drove me."

"Really? Dad drove?"

Amanda couldn't help but smile. "Of course. I live in Manhattan; I do not need a car. How else could I come in and get you?"

He grinned. "Gotcha."

Marco settled into the passenger seat of his car and gave his father a kiss on the cheek. "Hey, Dad, how was life?"

Robert Catalano, a tall, slender man with salt-and-pepper hair, gave a little shrug that Marco utilized so often. "Not bad. No drive-bys, no major traumas. Overall, a slow week. It's like the vampires have taken vacation, and your gangs have actually learned to protect themselves."

Marco laughed. "Well, they better have learned *something* by now. I can't keep saving them forever."

Amanda smiled. It was nice to see someone who got along well with family. And the two Catalano men were very much alike. She tried to remember her family and didn't succeed very well. Between becoming a vampire, and then the Soviet Union turned Imperial Russia into a vast police state she couldn't recognize, she had spent more time penetrating the Soviet Union's political and military hierarchy than she had visiting her parents…

So Marco and his father were quite refreshing.

"So, Amanda," Marco said, "tell me what the problem was with the Mafia?"

Amanda rolled her amber eyes. "What is not problem?" she replied, her accent thickening, her speech patterns slipping into what Marco called "Boris and Natasha." "They are pain in backside. They want full immunity from *every* police officer. Even when we can accommodate them, they must take more. It is at point where we will even have trouble getting them to acknowledge our own limits. I suspect they will want City Hall next."

Marco cleared his throat and furrowed his brow. "That's just plain *strange*. Wasn't all this cleared up after they held Dad hostage for a few hours?"

Amanda shook her head. "*Nyet*. For that, we sent Father Rodgers and his Vatican Ninjas. Then, they did not know we were also in collusion with police officers. And, now that they *do* know, they are attempting to take… liberties."

Doctor Catalano 'hmmed' and said, "Have you explained to them that you don't *need* the mob? After all, it's not like they're all over the place; they're limited in where they can go, and what they can do. This isn't 1920s Chicago or anything."

"They believe themselves indispensable," Amanda explained. "They push no matter what we do or say. We have yet to formally cut ties with them, but that is, in practice, what has happened."

Marco blinked hard and shook his head to clear it. "What does that mean in standard English?"

Amanda blushed, and composed herself, her speech changing with it, and her accent becoming less pronounced. "We've stopped helping them, even though we will occasionally talk to them. In short, everything has fallen apart as far as the Mafia are concerned."

Marco growled. "Fine. As you said, we don't need them. They're nice support and a little extra firepower, but that's all. If they can't be content to accept the small legal protection that I'm sure you offered, then they get nothing at all from us."

Amanda nodded. "Precisely."

"What protection?" Robert Catalano asked.

"Immunity for all people carrying weapons, as long as they're on the vampire hunting detail," Marco answered. "Assigning all of the NYPD officers who are in on the vampire situation to Mafia-controlled parts of New York so that they can recognize each other and try to not get in each other's way. That sort of thing." He glanced back at Amanda. "You did that, right?"

Amanda nodded. "But of course."

"In other words, it's basic politics," Robert muttered. "Lovely. I'm surprised that you haven't eaten them all yet, Amanda."

The vampire grinned. "It wouldn't do me much good in the long run, Doctor Catalano."

"Please, call me Robert," he objected. "You're older than I am, you're allowed."

Amanda blushed again and continued. "If I were to eat the Mafia, it would be utterly selfish. I can kill people in self-defense, but not for simple negotiation. Otherwise, it would be immoral, and I would risk going over to the dark side… and I like going to church. Thank you."

"Ah, that's right. Religious artifacts only hurt you if you're leaning on the evil scale." Robert swerved around yet another curve, and a double-parked car. They *still* weren't out of the airport yet. "It's hard to keep track of which of the various and sundry vampire myths are real anymore. They keep rewriting it."

"Usually to write out the religious parts of it," Marco said. "It's all *Blade* and Ann Rice, and The Mormon."

Robert blinked. "The Mormon?"

"Sparkle-pyres?" Marco prompted.

Doctor Catalano made a face. "Oh, yes. *Her.*"

Amanda laughed. "It is so nice to know I am not the only one who dislikes that series."

"Like Marco, I draw the line at a female protagonist who has no self-esteem and doesn't mind being stalked." Robert glanced at his son. "So, what did you think of San Francisco?"

Marco hesitated, caught flat-footed by the sudden shift in topics. He half-expected his father and Amanda to banter for a bit before getting onto the topic. In fact, if he had waited until Amanda was back in Manhattan, and he was back in Brooklyn, Marco wouldn't have been at all surprised.

Instead, he had to go straight to it. *Oh well, good old dad. Always right to the point. So refreshing…usually.*

"It was okay," Marco answered. "They're not bad. There are some nice attributes, but nothing that makes me want to go there, or utterly discount it."

He made certain to look at his father the entire time as he said this. It wasn't so much to make certain he maintained eye contact to establish the truth of his statement, but it was to make certain that Amanda didn't catch on to the lie of the matter. It wouldn't have gone over well to say he was *looking* for reasons to stay home because he wanted to stay close to Amanda.

Marco smiled, and described the campus, and the area, and the park that was such an obvious rip-off of *his* park (it was New York, the park was *his*, dammit). And for some reason, it had a windmill in the middle of it. All very strange.

As for a skyline, the most impressive building they had was the Pyramid Building, in the "good" part of town, near the piers and the Embarcadero—a strip of stores that was almost an outdoor mall. And it looked like just that—a pyramid. It was a jewel of the city, the peak of San Francisco 20th-century construction. Beyond that was the Bay, and there, Alcatraz.

Down the road from Chinatown, within walking distance through a more Italian part of town, was the large, square-shaped, marble visage of Saint Peter's-Saint Paul's. It was a pure-white church, immaculate and unyielding. Set in front of Grant Park, it was a great, traditional church that had stood against the ages and ravages of time and modern architecture.

As Marco let his mouth run off without his brain, he tried very hard *not* to think about Amanda. While he had been in San Francisco, he had managed to *not* think about her quite well. He could *not* think about the feel of her body as he hugged her; or her scent (which was a light, vanilla spice that apparently needed no perfume to generate), or her smile, or her lovely full lips.

Basically, had Marco *not* had the mind of a supercomputer, most of his brain cells would have been dedicated to the pure pleasure of seeing Amanda again. From the instant he had seen her, his heart practically leapt his in chest, despite the amount of breathing and meditation exercises he had gone through in order to hide his attraction. By the time he was down the escalator, he had already gotten himself under control. But it had taken a huge hunk of his brain matter to get his breathing and heart rate from giving him away.

It was bad enough Marco was in love with Amanda. He couldn't begin to imagine her reaction if his pulse shot up every time he saw her. She might take it the wrong way.

Or worse, she would take it the *right* way.

Looking at it objectively, Marco couldn't *begin* to imagine putting Amanda in the uncomfortable position of being lusted after by a semi-sociopath. He had no problem killing people he thought needed killing; he rather enjoyed it.

*Groucho Marx once said, "I wouldn't join any club that would allow me as a member." Since all of the good clubs didn't allow Jews, he was too good for any club that would allow him to join. In my case, I wouldn't date any woman I loved, because I'd care too much to have her date a crazy person… hmm, I think I'm more screwed up than I thought.*

"All in all," Marco concluded, "I can think of worse places to get a free ride. It's a very… pretty city," he said, making it sound like an insult. But then again, he would be the first to admit that he was a New York chauvinist. He finally gave Amanda a glance, and his little smile, and felt conflicted. He knew he really should go, but seriously didn't want to. "It's a nice place to visit, but I wouldn't want to live there."

Amanda gave him a broad smile. "Good. I would miss you if you went."

"Same here," Marco said. "Same here."

# Chapter 7:

# Death In The Family

San Francisco, August 1st

Merle Kraft looked around his magic store at his small crew of vampire hunters and winced. Three women of relatively healthy build, one athlete. There was George, built like a brick wall, and Rory, whose major achievement was that he was a vampire.

*Do I trust these people enough to leave them alone for a few days?*

Tiffany Whitman didn't even bother to look out from behind the cash register. "Go, have fun, boss. We promise not to steal anything from the cash register." She looked up, and her perfectly clear blue eyes were as sincere and as vacant as her head. "Honest. I mean it."

Merle rolled his eyes. "Thanks, Tiffany, that's oh so reassuring."

"What? I meant it!"

"He knows that," Yana told her, putting her hand on Tiffany's shoulder. "He trusts you."

"Oh. Well. Good." Tiffany looked back to the cash register.

George chuckled, amused by his girlfriend—and Merle couldn't even think of Tiffany as George's girlfriend. *Damn, she is such a blonde.* "Don't worry, Merle, we'll be fine."

Rory leaned up against a wall and grinned. "Aye, what could happen?" He lit up a cigarette and inhaled. "You're going out for, what? A day or two?"

Merle nodded. "Right. I'm going to help my wife and…" he caught himself, cleared his throat, and said, "my ex-wife and son move to San Francisco. It shouldn't take long. Can y'all try not to get yourself killed in the meantime?"

Several of them exchanged a glance at the blue eyed-California Asian saying *y'all* like a Texan. Sarah "Buffy" Bell laughed, and nodded, then slapped him on the arm. "Sure, chief, whatever you say."

Merle sighed, and walked out the door, before he could talk himself out of leaving. He wanted to keep his people safe, but he wanted his son and his ex-wife closer to him, and farther from the resting place of Dalf Kraft. Dalf had been the one who prompted the entire move. He had visited his nephew recently, a visit that had even prompted the tough NYPD Detective Kristen Kelly into leaving the east coast.

Though he did wonder if there could have been another issue…

Six people moved through some of the darker ends of Haight-Ashbury—San Francisco's traditionally "hippie" district. Also home to a number of marijuana plants left so long they had tipped over and seemed to be heading towards street level like hanging vines.

"So, what are we doing here?" George Berkeley rumbled. His deep bass voice sounded like it came from the inside of a tank.

"Multiple vampire attacks have been listed here in the past week," Sarah "Buffy" Bell said casually. "Merle said it was probably nothing, but I want to check it out anyway."

Rory rolled his eyes. "Aye? Is that so? Why is that, then?"

Yana Rosenburg gave the other redhead a glance. "Because this is our test run. We all know that Merle has a business outside of San Francisco. This is him letting us out on our own. He can get back to his business, and we can kick ass and take names all on our own."

Tiffany looked around like a nervous cat. "Does anyone else know where the hell we're going?"

"Yup," Yana said, pointing, "that's where I get my herbs for my spells."

Rory sighed. "Ye say ye're a witch, lass, but do you actually make any spells that work?"

"Um, no, but I'm still working on it. I'll get it right, really."

Rory sighed and said nothing for a long moment. "Whatever ye say, dearie. Whatever you say. Wiccans."

Sarah looked over her shoulder. "Don't vampires have super-sensitive hearing? Then how about you all shut up before somebody hears—"

Sarah was cut off by the sound of screaming, and she looked around, trying to narrow down the location. Rory pointed and said, "I think it's over there. But—"

Before he could finish speaking, Sarah had taken off, with Yana and George right next to her. Tiffany and Tara were right behind them.

Rory sighed. "Kids."

He chased after the five of them, hoping to get to them before they could do something really stupid.

Five normal college students were more than a match for a mediocre vampire. Unless he was the sort who committed murder on a semi-regular basis, the sheer numbers were enough to overpower him. So, by the time Rory had gotten there, there was already a dead vampire.

However, the person they had come to save was also dead. A hippie-type with long blond braids and bulging eyes, her neck had been broken, probably when she was tossed aside like a rag doll against the solid brick wall.

Rory shrugged, lit a cigarette, and said, "Well, that's nice of ye. Can we go and find a real vampire threat n—?"

Rory cut himself off and looked around. This was a standard alley. There was a fire escape, a garbage bin, and two ends of the alleyway.

And there was also the strong, sudden sense of vampires. Lots of vampires.

"Under the fire escape! Now!" he bellowed and leapt for his cohorts. He grabbed Yana and Tara, throwing them under the fire escape. He had just reached Tiffany and George when the sky started to rain vampires.

Demons Are Forever

They were suddenly everywhere. They had been dropping from the rooftops and coming in from both ends of the alley.

Three had landed on Sarah Bell, pressing her down to the ground.

New York City, August 2nd, 7:00am.

A 5'3" athletic, golden-haired blonde (leaning heavily on the gold) stood in the arrivals section of LaGuardia Airport in New York City, with strands falling smoothly to the nape of her neck. Rich blue eyes set over smooth Celtic cheekbones locked onto Merle Kraft immediately once he was down the escalator stairs. She wore a lightweight black sweatshirt with a zipper in front, opened partly at the neck, revealing creamy skin he knew so very well, with a pair of black jeans.

Merle smiled instinctively at the first sight of her. He wanted to run into her arms, and hold her for all he was worth …

Then he remembered they were divorced. And that his job was the reason; middle of the night calls and secrets he couldn't divulge would doom any marriage.

"So, how's Arthur?" he asked politely.

She shrugged. "Asleep at home. There wasn't anything on today's agenda, and I thought it would be nice if we all had breakfast together before we finished the packing."

Merle smiled. "That sounds like a great idea."

They went straight to the parking lot, since all Merle carried was a backpack, just in case the return flight was screwed up somehow.

"How much is left?" he asked.

"Not too much," she said with a smile. "But enough to keep you busy."

Merle chuckled and stopped at the car door. He slipped his phone out of his pocket, and he turned it on. "Sorry, but I really should be in contact at all—"

His iPhone went off like a Fourth of July fireworks display. Alarms for voice mail, text, email, and an incoming call all went off at the same time—which meant that a *Star Trek* phaser fired, a bomb exploded, and the theme to *The Sorcerer's Apprentice* went off at the same time.

Even Kristen jumped back from the car, reaching for her sidearm. "What the hell?"

"My cell phone," Merle said, confused. "I wonder what blew up while I was away." He frowned, confused, and slid into the seat as he answered the phone call.

"Hi," he said, buckling up, "who is this, and why are you trying to shut down my iPhone?"

"It's Yana," the redhead sobbed, "something has—has hap-hap-*happeeeeeennnnned.*"

Merle jerked the phone away from his ear. "What the hell?" he muttered. He looked at Kristen as she slipped in, and he shrugged. "Get the car moving. I suspect I'm going to be on the phone for a while."

Kristen rolled her eyes and started the car, while Merle tentatively moved the phone back to his ear. "*What's* happened? Hello?"

"Yeah," came the deep, gruff voice of George Berkeley, Tiffany's boyfriend, the one built like a linebacker. "Yana can't handle this right now…she held together until she got on the phone with you. You see she's…um…well, she's… " George took a deep breath. "She's dead."

Merle blinked. *Yana was dead? But she was just talking to me. Does that means she's a vampire now?* "Who's dead?"

Kristen looked over. She put the car into drive and pulled out.

This went on for a while as Merle tried to calm down almost everyone in turn. In the end, Rory had to tell him the story. The century-old vampire was the only one who could get through the tale without breaking down into tears. But, as Rory had told Merle, he had lost everyone in his life at least twice.

However, even Rory seemed to hesitate at moments as he told the story of the night before.

Merle sat and listened as Kristen drove. He had to fight to keep his face impassive. Because, it had been the night that the vampires had come to San Francisco to kill Merle Kraft.

These vampires had been well trained. Very well trained. Rory had said that they were all as good as Merle Kraft was. Considering that Merle knew who Rory had been when he still had a pulse, that meant something.

These people had been well-trained, meaning full military-level training.

Unfortunately, there was only one person that Merle could think of who had that many vampires like that, and he was already dead.

*But that doesn't mean everyone else dies off too, now does it? All of Mikhail's friends, and followers, and everyone who he had ever trained. Someone had assassinated him to keep him from talking. And they're apparently not happy that they had to do that.*

The tale Rory told was somewhere between the most horrid thing that had ever happened in Merle's life, and the most glorious act of heroism unseen by a civilian in years.

But the night of August 1st was the night they came—a group of vampires spawned and trained by Mikhail the Bear himself.

It was one hundred of them versus some humans and Rory.

Merle's people had been led into a trap, blocked in an alley in the back end of Haight Ashbury. Vampires were at both ends of the alley, Sarah and Rory at either end, the others for support. There was only one way out, and it involved climbing atop a dumpster to get up to a fire escape. Sarah ended up holding off the hordes, and she cut down forty of the best-trained vampires in the world—in Rory's opinion.

The rest were finished off long-range by arrow, holy water, fire, and crucifix.

But not before Sarah Bell was herself torn apart and eaten.

Rory hadn't been able to say *that*, but he drifted off into silence, leaving all sorts of horrible implications in Merle's brain.

Merle hadn't even noticed when the car had stopped. "Merle?" Kristen said. "We're at the house."

He glanced at his wife… *Ex-wife, dammit.* "Sorry about that." He said into the phone, "I'll see what I can do. As soon as possible. I'll give you guys a ring back when I can, okay?"

After Merle heard about the nightmare of last night's slaughter in San Francisco, he had to endure hours of working with his ex-wife and son, working together to pack up the rest of their valuables.

He had to do it without telling them a single thing. What would he tell them? That he had sent college kids not six years older than their son out to fight vampires while he went gallivanting off to "safety"?

Granted, that was only because they didn't know what he did while he gallivanted.

Making an excuse that he had to run an errand, he managed to break away, and found himself at the 42nd Street New York Public Library. It was easy enough to find an empty darkened room, and he merely sat for a while.

*I brought her into this,* he thought. *But in all likelihood, she would have been killed by a vampire sooner or later, as vampires swarmed the city. Only she wouldn't have been prepared for the end…only now I'd like to kill them all.*

Merle sat in the dark and waited for the inevitable.

"I didn't have anything to do with it," Dalf hissed behind him.

"If I thought you did," Merle said, low and dangerously, "we'd have a long discussion involving you, me, and a car battery."

"She served her purpose," he said, in a tone that bordered on reassuring. "Don't worry, you already have a replacement, someone who's lethality itself."

Merle looked over his shoulder to make sure he'd disappeared into the shadows. *I wonder where Marco Catalano is.*

# Chapter 8:

# Welcome To The Jungle

August 2nd, New York City

Amanda Colt opened her eyes in New York City and looked around her bed, and then her room in general. It was a nice place up in the East 70s, almost nothing to disturb her.

*Blackout curtains in place, check. Duct tape still secure, check. Time…nine in the morning? What in God's name is the problem?*

She rose from her bed, thankful she had abandoned the age-old habit of sleeping in coffins. Did anyone know what it did to their backs? Dear God, it was like sleeping on a bed of nails… and she had been thrown on a set of those once.

She stretched, cat like, and fell down on the mattress, feeling the Ziploc bags of Russian soil. The myth said that they needed home soil; they never said how much was required.

Everything was secure… it wasn't like this was a bad neighborhood, and it wasn't like anyone could harm her anyway… Burglars were truly up to date, with metal knives, plastic guns. Ironic that if they just stuck to wooden clubs, they would live longer, at least against her.

*What a quandary. Get eaten by me, or easily gunned down by…well, anyone else in New York…the odds are on their side, I suppose.*

But no one was there, that was certain. It was less a sense of someone in the room, and more a matter of feeling a very hard thump and then…

Amanda opened her eyes and smiled. Marco was at the door. "I've made my decision?"

"Are you going to fight vampires in San Francisco?" Amanda Colt asked. Her golden-red hair flowed down her back, neat as always, and lights of amusement danced in her brown eyes.

Marco mentally frowned, comparing it with his blue eyes and blond hair, which made him look like a Nazi stormtrooper, especially with a crew cut. "The middle of nowhere, San Francisco? Just a few vampires here and there." He rolled his eyes. "If it were worth the trouble, maybe I'd go. But no. I'm not going to go."

Amanda smiled at him with a tender look that melted his heart and stiffened his spine—yes, spine. "Are you sure?"

"I'm sure. If they were really a problem, I'd be happy to go. They don't exactly scare me."

"I know."

"I carry silver cross," he said in a bad impersonation of a Russian sentence structure. "I don't attend parties at night." He smirked, paused, and said normally, "Especially not in Hashbury. Granted, if I went, I'd probably just stay in my dorm room where I shall invite no vampire or anything else. I'd nail a crucifix to my door so vamps couldn't even knock. And… now that I think of it, none of ours flew, did they?"

"Not unless they were bats," Amanda agreed. "Or mist."

"Besides," Marco continued, "why would I want to go to San Francisco? It's not New York, and it's not even Hell-A."

Amanda rolled her eyes at the nickname of the largest vampire population on the West coast. "You can't see living there at all?"

"Meh. The dorm rooms are nice," Marco continued, "most of the people are friendly…though I even met this cute little redhead."

"*Really?*" she teased.

He sighed deeply. "I didn't go there to check out the female population. She was polite, intelligent, and pretty. Hung around with a blonde who wasn't exactly my type, and another one who was athletic."

Marco's little smile flickered a little wider, then, went back to normal. "It's too suburby for me." He turned his head and stretched a muscle. He examined the door noting that it had a lock like a bank vault—metal bars that would interlock with the doorframe if needed.

"But, if you're going to go, you're going soon, *da?*" she asked.

He looked back at her. "Eh. They take people at the last moment—and literally in the middle of September, if I so wanted." A shrug. "So…"

She nodded. "*Da*… so…"

They looked at each other for a long moment, and he couldn't put a laser pointer on it, but something was…there. She looked at him with such… such…

*Oh, stop it,* he thought, *you're being sentimental.*

He stepped forward and hugged her furiously, and she hugged back so hard, ribs creaked. After a moment, he slowly stepped away from her, hands trailing down her arms as they parted.

He smiled and stepped away, moving for the door. However, when he reached back to grab the doorknob, he caught hold of someone's wrist. Marco looked over his shoulder. There stood a short, funny little man with a midnight blue windbreaker and a set of matching eyes placed in a thoroughly Asian face.

"Merle," Marco muttered, "how nice. What brings you by?"

Merlin Kraft smiled and looked to the vampire. "Good to see he hasn't been eaten yet. How are you, Miss Colt?"

"Amanda," she corrected him. "Helping your family move out to California?"

Merle smiled slightly. "You have a good intelligence system. Your gangs?"

Amanda nodded. "In part. Marco works that part of it, and we both deal with the vampire world." She was being polite about the matter, since handling vampires involved lots of coercion and a slow drip of holy water, sometimes.

Kraft nodded thoughtfully. "Right." He studied us a moment. "Are you up on San Francisco vampires?"

Colt nodded. "How recent do you want us to be?"

"Last night."

Marco smirked. "We're good, but not that good."

Amanda shrugged. "San Francisco is such a small community of vampires, there aren't even enough in the area to form their own Vampire's association. There just aren't that many of them. They prefer Los Angeles, probably because they don't have to worry about exceptionally cool summers."

Marco chuckled. "Also, LA has more gang-bangers that won't be missed. Do they still have the highest murder-by-drive-by rate in the country? But that's getting off topic. Why do you ask about San Francisco."

Merle glided over to the couch and sat, crossing his legs at the knees. "Some of Mikhail's boys decided to pay me a visit. But I'm here, helping Kristen and Arthur pack. I want a country between my family and my brother Dalf."

Amanda growled slightly. "They hurt your people," she stated. "How many did they get?"

His eyes flickered for a moment, revealing the pain inside. "Just one, but that's enough to set me back *months*. I'm too busy cutting down vampires to do my job—you know, the one I'm *paid for*. If I can't secure my home base, I'm not going to be much good to anyone."

Amanda nodded thoughtfully. "Have you found who killed your FBI agent yet?" she asked, referring to the case that had first brought Merle to New York.

"No, and that's the biggest problem," Merle said. "This is my first time back to the East coast since our shootout in April, and already I'm down someone. I need help, and my government resources don't allow for expansion, you can imagine why—I'm too weird, and this is too out there for anyone else to justify the expense."

"Even after the death of an FBI agent?" Marco asked.

"Several FBI agents?" Amanda added. "And MI-6 allies? This is strange. Why has no one else investigated?"

"Probably because I killed the assassin who murdered the FBI agent," Merle answered. "One dead bad guy is sufficient, apparently. Fine, he's a vampire whose body disintegrated—but I can't say that, so 'associates and co-conspirators' carried off his body. But apparently, having my word that the killer was decapitated is enough to file away the report and move on."

Marco's amused little smile was fixed, even as he rolled his eyes. "Since we killed off his boss and a lot of his minions, there's probably been nothing for future spies to *find*."

"And," Amanda continued, "if there is nothing further to find, there is no reason to kill other FBI agents and spies who look around the United Nations."

"In short," Merle said, "they're laying low."

"Until they kill off the people who are already onto them," Marco said. He looked to Merle. "So they're after you for certain."

"And us," Amanda added. She glanced at Merle. "There was an entire meeting of the New York City Vampires Association about killing Mikhail the Bear. They know that Marco and I were involved. And if the ruling body of the local vampires knows of our involvement—"

"Then everyone in the vampire community knows," Marco concluded.

Merle looked from Marco to Amanda and back. "Have you ever noticed that you two complete each other's sentences a lot?"

"No," Marco answered, as Amanda said, "*Nyet.*"

Merle arched a brow, nodded, and said, "Right. Anyway. Marco, I need you sooner than I thought. If Amanda stays here with your gangs and Vatican Ninjas, you can come with me to San Francisco, to my little team, then both of you should be as protected as possible from any possible reprisal."

Marco and Amanda merely exchanged a glance, and the genial mood shifted. Merle had said the magic word, whether he knew it or not. Marco was *needed.*

Someone *had* to go to San Francisco.

Amanda knew this. She loved that he'd run to the rescue but hated that it would mean dragging him away from her.

Marco Catalano chuckled. "Sure, I might be able to help."

Amanda smiled at Marco warmly, then, turned to Merle. "Have you brought your anti-Vampire squad in on your government work?"

Merle looked at them and smiled. "I have no idea what you mean."

"I see," and Amanda did, without fail. "Lucky for you, most vampires only know you're dangerous, and nothing more than that"

One of Merle's eyebrows did a vertical lift. "Me in the vampire underground? *Oy*, I don't like the sound of that *mischegas*."

*Yiddish…Asiatic face…da…* Amanda smiled reassuringly. "Don't worry, you and your brother Dalf are mentioned most prominently. If they knew you were involved with government, you would be hunted by everyone."

"Goody." He looked to Marco. "So, when can you come?"

"Next week," Marco told Amanda and Father Rodgers, seated at the rectory table again.

The other two at the table didn't answer. At one side of the circular table was Father Rodgers. A double shot of Sambuca Romana on the rocks in hand, he said, "I think that if it be done, it would best be done quickly. And frankly, I could think of worse things. You get extra ties to the government. This might eventually translate into additional support down the line. Tactically, it's a good move. At the end of the day, it will make a big difference in reference to hunting down and suppressing vampires."

Marco nodded, his little amused smiled frozen in place, though not quite as amused as usual. "Any other concerns?"

Rodgers looked to Amanda. "Will the gangs follow you?"

Amanda nodded. "Yes, they will. Even if they did not respect me to start with, Marco gave them a good talking to shortly after the battle in front of his house."

The priest cringed. Marco had actually taken on his Vatican Ninjas, in his own church. The street gangs must have been terrified of him, if they had enough brain cells to rub together.

Marco smiled and said, "Well, Amanda, if it makes you feel better," at the next vampire meeting, tell them you banished me from New York for the school year. That might make them feel more at ease."

Amanda gave him a slight smile. "Maybe."

# Chapter 9:

# Politics Bite

August 10th, San Francisco

A week later, Marco finished moving into the dorms of the University of San Francisco and found himself located down the hall from two women he had spotted on his last visit— the redhead's name was Yana Rosenburg, he remembered. Both were friendly and amicable, and looked slightly like the living dead—Marco chalked it up to a recent murder of an undergrad he had heard about. *I wonder if that undergrad was Merle's dead colleague.*

"So, Marco, you're from New York?" Yana asked. Her hair was the color of a pale fire, eyes light green, and while she wasn't an athlete, she was on the light side.

Marco didn't look at her as he lifted another box into place. *"Certo, bella donna,"* he said in Italian, without looking over his shoulder.

"So, what's it like?" she asked, as though eager to hear about some great and majestic foreign land.

Marco chuckled. "Oh, it's nice enough. Easy to get lost there if you don't know what you're doing, which, of course, I never do. I prefer leaving a trail of string behind me."

She giggled, hanging back on the threshold of the door, like a vampire waiting to be invited in. *I hate thinking like that,* he thought. "I'm not exactly sure how I would describe New York City for a foreigner." She didn't reply, or even make a noise, but he looked at her, and chuckled at her slight, confused frown. "New Yorkers tend to think their home is a different country from mainland— remember, we're on an island. Which means someone around here is going to have to help me through culture shock… or I'm going to have to do that for the rest of the town."

The pale blonde, Tara, ducked her head in. As he remembered, she was a dirty blonde who wasn't excessively pretty. She had muddy brown eyes and a square face, and a stout figure.

"Um, San Francisco is a *city*."

Marco shook his head and turned back to unpacking his books. "I can't call San Francisco a city… a city has a skyline, a subway, a high violent crime rate."

"Why come here then?" Tara asked.

Marco had a perfect lie already ready—mainly because he it wasn't really a lie. "Because I was tired of the even more obnoxious, stuck up, perfect…*people* at NY…U."

Both of them knew he wasn't going to say either "people" or "U." But the words "bastards" and "NYScrew" didn't seem like the right thing to say. They seemed too…nice.

"But to come all the way out here?" Tara asked.

*Because I had to come this far to get away from someone I love too much to inflict my psycho-ass on.* "Because I would hate to miss out on all the nice quiet people you have hanging out around here," Marco said with such a straight face that they had to laugh.

New York, August 12th

Lady Jennifer Bosley, President of the New York City Vampire's Association, was not only powerful, but very, very rich. Not Bernie Madoff rich, or Bill Gates rich, but she was *rich*, as in "old world, old money, I can buy and sell China ten times" *rich*. She was not "the 1%" but the 0.0001%. If anyone had known she existed, or if she had all of her money in the same place under one name, she would have been one of the top ten richest entities on the planet, including nations.

Like many other wealthy vampires, she bought an entire apartment complex, and left the outside alone, turning the inside into a luxurious palace. On the outside, it looked like a gang-ridden neighborhood had declared war on her building. Inside, it looked like a modern-day palace. Her office was the size of a large living room. The carpet was Persian, the tapestries were European, the paintings were by old masters, some of which Amanda knew as having gone missing during World War II, and the bookcases had nothing but first editions.

But Jennifer Bosley herself was surprisingly relaxed. She came in wearing dark green jogging pants and top, as though she had just come in from a run. Her basic attitude was such that she knew she was rich, and she didn't need to prove it to anyone. Her form was curvy, and she moved with effortless grace. Her blonde hair terminated at the base of her neck, with her hair at the sides tucked behind her ears. Her full lips were unadorned, and her brown eyes seemed to just cut through whatever she saw.

"Don't worry about the paintings," she said in her London accent. "I ate the ones who stole them, and their original owners weren't alive to file any complaints."

"Understood."

Amanda Colt stood before President Bosley in a simple but good-looking sweater and jeans. Marco, and every other person who had ever talked about her appearance, would be the first to say that it would be hard for anyone who met her to say that she *didn't* look good in everything she wore.

Though Marco had suggested testing the theory by dressing her in a burlap bag and see how many people stop and stare at her down the street. Amanda had laughed it off, but Marco's little smile didn't move, and his eyes hadn't twitched from her gaze… she didn't feel like testing his hypothesis.

"Now," Bosley continued as she sat behind her 19th-century oak desk, "what's the purpose of today's visit, Miss Colt? You haven't been letting Marco off his leash again, have you? I haven't heard of any reports of massive property damage, but the night is young, after all."

Amanda took a deep breath—more out of habit than necessity. "Lady Bosley—"

The President waved a hand, cutting Amanda off. "Oh, please, call me Jen. It's not like I *care* for all that formality. I suspect that you won't abuse the privilege."

Amanda smiled a little bit. "I sent Marco away."

Bosley blinked. It was obvious that she hadn't been expecting that. "Really? Where, exactly? Siberia?"

"San Francisco."

Bosley arched a brow, and grinned broadly, letting out a short laugh. "Really? Oh, Miss Colt, I suspect you and I think alike. You're going to be *fun*." She leaned back in the chair and shook her head, letting out an amused sigh. "There's a new band of hunters in San Francisco, who only recently got ambushed by a small horde of vampires—*Mikhail the Bear's* vampires. Not long after, you 'send Marco away.' Simple genius. Though I must ask, who suggested coming to me with this cheerful news of your seeming capitulation?"

Amanda cocked her head. She didn't think it would be quite *that* easy for Jennifer Bosley to have figured it out. "Marco."

Her grin got even broader, showing most of her teeth, and a hint of fang. "He's good for you, isn't he?" She let out a pleased sigh, and casually asked, "Are you doing him?"

Amanda flinched, taken aback. "*Nyet*, of course not."

Bosley chuckled, as though Amanda's shock and indignation pleased her. "That's all right. I believe you. Do you love him?"

Amanda's mouth fell open. "What?"

Bosley shrugged. "It happens with our pets. We get attached, we forget *our* place."

Amanda laughed at that. "Trust me, Marco is not a pet. Try to throw him in a cage sometime, I suspect he would work his way out with a toothpick and garrote whatever guards are put on him with a shoelace."

Bosley laughed. A great belly laugh. "Ah. Well, I'll be sure to remember that should we ever need to throw him in a cage. Keep in mind, I could probably tear your head off without a problem right here and now."

Amanda tried not to smile. The last time Marco had looked deeply into her eyes—which was a vampire's way into the human brain—he had used it to hack into *her* brain. *I wonder what would happen if Lady Bosley tried it.*

"I dun'na, that's a good question," President Bosley answered, her London accent slipping into the conversation as she relaxed more.

"Did I say that out loud?"

She grinned, baring her bright white teeth. "No. Do you know how I'm as powerful as I am? Not by being very good or very evil, but purely pragmatic. And I am *very* pragmatic."

"I thought that virtues or vices contributed to that."

Bosley stared at her a moment. "I keep forgetting that you're young. I can only presume that your mentor was one of those who just sort of bit and ran, inn'it he?"

Amanda gave the President a smile of her own. "I bit him back."

"Good for you. You'd be surprised how many people we 'ave in the association who were made that way. Virtues and vices only effect whether or not religious artifacts will kill me. Though you'd be surprised how much following a path to power leads to the dark side. At the end of the day, the path to power is much like the path to sainthood—you have to find your path and take it. However, I find that being practical, while it mightn't lead me to virtue, it'll at least land me on God's good side."

Amanda raised a brow. "Would I be surprised how much being pragmatic is being good?"

Bosley nodded. "If you look at things in the long view. And I am very, very good at that."

Amanda said nothing for a moment. *If she plans as much as she says, how much is she trying to tell me without telling me anything?* "You said in the letter that Mikhail the Bear was the low man on a totem pole. Who would be on top of it?"

Bosley shook her head. "Now, now. You should know better." Better came out as *beh'er.*

Amanda nodded. She made eye contact with Bosley and thought intently: *What about a tall, redheaded female vampire who has no difficulty assassinating one of their own within Mikhail's organization?*

Bosley nodded with approval. "Well, that's better, inn'it? The answer is… we have no idea. There've been some rumors, but aside from that." She gave a little shrug. "So…if you're not sleeping with Marco, are you becoming attached to him?"

Amanda balked. "Why do you have these questions?"

Bosley gave another little wave of her hand. "Oh, please. These things happen. A lot. I've been 'round the block a few times, I've seen 'em." She smiled wryly. "A good human is 'ard to find, Amanda. And yours sounds like he'll come in 'andy one day."

# Chapter 10:

# War

September 6th San Francisco

The first weeks of classes went by, and Marco found them easy enough. San Francisco, as far as he was concerned, seemed quieter the longer he stayed. The color also came back into Yana's cheeks by the second week of September, and Tara had had no color in her cheeks to begin with.

That Thursday, Marco had locked himself in his single-person dorm room and heard screams out the window. Being from New York, his first reaction should have been to ignore it, but he figured that it was yet another opportunity to piss someone off. Ever since he arrived, he'd been charming, polite, courteous, and anything but annoying.

It was time for a change.

He looked out the window to see what looked like a couple "necking" in the courtyard below. However, the creature pulled back and decided to terrorize his midnight snack, by showing off his vampire face, a design practically stolen from the old silent film *Nosferatu.*

Marco casually picked up a heavy wooden paperweight, calculated that a six-story drop would at least honk the vampire off, and simply dropped it on its skull before it could move in again. The vampire stood there for a moment, dazed, then crumpled. The woman he'd been attacking ran for the hills. The vampire took a moment before he slowly rose to its feet and looked up at Marco.

The human gave a smile meant to annoy a saint. "If you're so annoyed, why don't you come and get me?"

The vampire rammed his fingers between the bricks and started climbing. Marco pulled his head back into the room and waited for it to come to the window. He reached the window and tried to climb through, stuck at the frame.

"Poor baby," he taunted. "Can't tell the difference between being mocked and being invited in?" Marco grabbed the lapels of his jacket, dragging the jacket past the window, slamming the vampire's face against the invisible barrier that kept it outside. He snarled and tried to lash out but failed.

Someone knocked on the door. "Yes?"

"Hey, Marco, it's me, Yana. Can I come in a moment?" she asked, even though it was unlocked.

*So polite, these people… eh, I need an extra set of hands anyway.* "Sure, why not?"

The vampire's eyes went wild, and he tried to slip out of his jacket, but Marco pulled the lapels one over the other, trapping him in the high-quality leather duster.

*What is it with vampires and dusters? Can't they just stay with a damn cape and be done with it? And, really, leather? Wouldn't you want something easy to break out of? I blame Joss Whedon. At least he doesn't sparkle. Well, unless I set him on fire.*

Yana came in and her very pretty eyes widened at the thing he held. Marco slammed the vampire against the barrier several more times. "Do you think you can take over for a moment? I need to get something…or you do want to stake it?"

The thing snarled again, and he slammed him a little more. "Shut *up*, will you? Can't you see I'm talking with the lady? I thought vampires were only rude in New York. Can't you people read *Dracula* or something? Learn some manners?" He looked back to Yana. "Don't worry, he won't bite… as long as you stay on this side."

She blinked, a little unsure about Marco, not the vampire. "What are you doing?"

He smiled politely. "I'm either going to hold onto this guy until he's staked, or until about sunrise, whichever comes first. So would you please hand me a stake or do it yourself?"

She handed him a stake. He raised it, then noticed it didn't reek of turpentine.

*Good girl, you carry your own. You really are one of Merle's band of merry vampire slayers.* He dusted the vampire, and then sat back on the bed. He looked at Yana, noting cute little bunny slippers and button-down pajamas. "I hope I didn't ruin your sleep."

"No, I was about to get up… in about six hours or so."

"Okay. Thanks. I thought I wouldn't need to carry stakes up my sleeve while in my own room, but apparently, I was wrong…and if you knew me, you'd know that's a heck of an admission."

"How did you… did you…?"

"Know it was a vampire?" Marco asked. "There aren't too many creatures of the night that drink blood, although I may be wrong on that."

She opened her mouth, as though ready to go into all those creatures that drank blood, then became terribly shy again.

"By the way," Marco explained, "I do know about vampires, you apparently know about them, and deal with them regularly. Any *other* questions?"

She blinked a few more times, then said, "Oh."

"Yeah. Oh… And we should both be getting to bed about now, we have class in the morning. Is there anything else you'd like to know?"

"Um… Could we start again?"

"Sure. My name is Marco Catalano, nice to meet you."

"No, about the—"

"Vampire?" He shrugged. "Oh, we had a few problems with them in Brooklyn. No big deal, more like a nasty infestation of cockroaches. In fact, we have nastier roaches. Heck, I even have a bottle of holy water I had my friend the priest bless for me—water from the Gowanus Canal, the worst EPA site in America, so if the holiness doesn't kill a vampire, the chemicals probably will. My preferred weapon of choice, however, is a stake doused in turpentine, which is—"

"Is the most flammable substance!" Yana cheered.

"Bingo." *What is the likelihood that she's part of a different pack of vampire hunters?* "Might you be a friend of Merle Kraft's?"

"How did you know?"

Marco gave another small shrug. "Lucky guess."

She smiled shyly, then tottered off.

*I wonder how things are in New York.*

Demons Are Forever

New York City

Underneath New York City is an estimated nine hundred miles of subway tunnels. There are more beneath that. Hundreds of miles of track that had been lost to time. Personal train stations of millionaires who didn't want to ride with the common people, but didn't want to drive, either. A veritable maze of subway tunnels formed a labyrinth that would have confounded any balls of twine, and could certainly hide a whole herd of minotaurs.

Of course, a minotaur wasn't the only thing it could hide. Hundreds of New York's homeless had taken up residence below the city. Some were crazy, some just poor, others declared it "freedom," but they all needed shelter, and a few hundred feet beneath the sidewalks of New York was a good place to start.

However, it was also a gathering place for people who were "non-persons," who had fallen off the grid, with no firm ties to anyone or anything.

Or, in the vampire Wikipedia(vykipedia.vmp), "a buffet."

The horde descended en masse. Three dozen vampires who were out on the hunt, but weren't picky enough to choose their prey in the wilds of Central Park or singles' bars. They preferred a land of eternal dark, where they had all the advantages.

Normally, vampires didn't tend to frequent the homeless. The pungent body odor that irritated humans nearly acted like tear gas to heightened vampiric olfactory nerves. These vampires weren't all that picky.

The area that they chose for their ambush was routine. It was a deep, dark, secluded portion of the subway system, over 150 feet below the street, out of the way even by the standards of the homeless who lived there. And it was a reusable trap, since no one caught inside it once ever made it out again to warn the next unsuspecting visitors.

They burst into the darkened tunnel at three in the morning, charging through the battery of odors left behind by visitors past. They simply turned off their sense of smell, refusing to enjoy the nasal assault.

They surrounded the center of the room, where they had left enough pizzas to signal the entire homeless population of New York. There were rolls of sleeping bags and a fire burning to provide warmth in the cavernous concrete womb.

The vampires tore into the sleeping bags, slashing, biting, and diving down, expecting fountains of blood to follow…

And they stopped, almost as one, noticing the vile, harsh taste overwhelming their senses.

Kerosene.

"With night vision," came a light, pleasant voice, tinged slightly with a Russian accent, "couldn't you be more observant?"

A Bic lighter hit the floor, and a sea of fire flowed from one end of the room and spread across it like a flood.

Amanda Colt smiled in the white-hot glow of burning vampires. Being vampires, they burnt like flash paper - hot and bright and over in a moment. The temperature in the room flared, and Amanda was hit with a wave of heat like stepping out of an over-air-air conditioned mall into a humid August F train. Each vampire turned into a burst of white fire, and were gone shortly thereafter.

Hector Vega stepped out of the shadows just behind her. The leader of the local Hispanic gang smiled and looked at the ashes of their adversaries. "Nice cookout, babe. Why'd you even bring us along?"

Amanda shrugged. "It's sometimes nice to have the company."

He sauntered up next to her and pressed against her side. "I'm always good for that."

The vampire looked at him, and then to the rest of the team who ringed the room. She had brought both gangs with her, and made certain to mix and match persons and personalities and specialties. And for some reason, she could practically smell the pheromones.

She sighed. "Don't make me eat you."

Miguel smiled. "No, you'll want to before long."

Amanda turned her gaze on him, and made her eyes glow red, and deliberately extended her teeth. Now he took a step back. While he had been fighting vampires for a while, and he was relatively certain that she wouldn't eat him, he had seen enough of what she was capable of that he didn't feel like testing the hypothesis.

Amanda was about to follow it up with a suitably witty threat that would have made James Bond proud, but before she could, she heard something rustle in the dark. For a fraction of a nanosecond, she thought it might have been a rat pack…

And then concluded that rats didn't tend to wear size-twelve Nikes.

She thought a curse in Russian and pivoted towards the one entrance to the room. There was only one way out, and the gang members she'd brought with her were only going to hamper her progress. "I also bring you along because it's good to have the backup when things go to Hell. Combat positions. We have company!"

The first vampires that burst through ran straight into Amanda as they would a wall. Her arms were spread out, and her feet braced in a classic fencing stance for balance. The vampires had charged in recklessly, and her counterattack looked like one lineman holding back the entire offensive line.

One vampire tried biting her, and recoiled as though he had swallowed acid. The organisms that allowed for vampirism didn't react well to each other. They had become so used to their hosts' DNA that they would attack any similar microbe, almost as though the microbe were afraid that another microbe would take over. That vampire had effectively bitten off more than he could chew.

The others were too packed in for normal attacks. None of them had enough room to swing a punch, and barely enough room to knee her.

The vampires in front did knee her, however, and the two closest to her head-butted her viciously.

These were basic petty thugs on the scale of vice, probably using their powers for nothing more than the basic biker gang rowdiness, and the occasional human snack. Individually, none of them were a match for her, but collectively, the hits crashed against her body continuously, taking their toll.

She endured all of five seconds of this, which was all she had to.

The pike-men from the gangs behind her had been at the ready since before the last group of vampires had been toasted. Most of the effective combat had been at long distance—Amanda preferred to give the fragile humans longer reach whenever possible. The only reason there were no incendiary rounds was that the enclosed space of the sewers would lead to suffocation in no time.

The pike-men charged in, ramming their wooden pikes under Amanda's arms and into the crowd of vampires. Behind them, the other gang members pushed as well, ramming over a ton of pressure into a few square inches of space. The wood split right through the bodies ahead of them, crunching through bone and flesh.

Six feet of wood penetrated deep into the vampire horde. Several vampires on the skewer disintegrated along the way, letting the six feet of pike stab through ten feet of vampire.

The vampires directly in front of Amanda grinned viciously, protected by Colt's body.

And then another row of pikes came from the side, stabbing through and between the rib cages. The pike drove through one side of the remaining front ranks and out the other side.

With the vampires locked into a grid pattern of pikes, Amanda took a step back before the inevitable happened—five bottles of Molotov cocktails arced overhead, the flaming rags bright in the darkness below.

The firebombs splashed over the vampires, and the flames consumed them as fast as the group dowsed in kerosene, turning into one bright white fireball.

Three of the men on the pikes had not followed the hint when Amanda fell back, and were burned, badly.

All that was left of the three closest to the fireball were carbonized.

Colt didn't even hesitate long enough to call out what she was doing, merely picked up the three who were still alive and bolted. Two were under one arm, and a third under the other.

San Francisco, September 7th

The next morning, Marco took a brief jog in the post-dawn hours (he *used* to do predawn), through the cemetery. He went past a mausoleum, and made a double take—it was open. He stopped, turned, and closed the door tightly, locking it.

"Eh, what the bloody hell do you think you're doing out there!" someone barked from inside. He stepped back, knowing only two types of people who'd live in someplace like this.

The door imploded as someone inside pulled it open, breaking the outside lock. The man inside glared like he wanted to tear Marco's arms off. His ugly red hair stuck up in all directions. He wore a black T-shirt and jeans with a pair of combat boots. His eyes were dark green, which either corresponded with the contents of his skull or his soul, maybe both. His cheekbones looked so sharp they could cut through the *Titanic.*

"Damn bugger! What're you doing to my home?"

"Sorry, I figured most people around here could afford their own homes. My mistake."

"Eh? Well why don't you come here, and we'll settle this, laddie."

Marco raised a brow. With the level of malevolence mounting, there was only one possible reason this guy didn't step outside and attack. "Better plan, why don't you come here? You seem like the type who'd want to take this outside." Catalano slipped the crucifix out of his shirt and his opponent flinched. "Unless you'd *really* want me to come in there and stake your undead ass…Don't you people ever adapt to modern day speech? Even Bella Lugosi had better English!"

His faced morphed into that of a vampire. Marco sighed. "Please, I've seen TV shows with better makeup. Go to Jim Henson's Creature Shop and get some improvements."

VmpBytr1917: So, Marco, enjoying classes?
TaliesinMS911: Classes aren't boring yet, Amanda. Met with members of Merle's stake-out crew. They don't seem to have recovered just yet from their friend being eaten.

VmpBytr1917: Oh dear, afraid of that. Any sign of vampires?

TaliesinMS911: One, outside my dorm. Decided coming after me might be good idea and climbed the side of the building to window. He didn't get far.

VmpBytr1917: (cocked eyebrow) I'm sure he didn't.

VmpBytr1917: The locals say 'hi' and 'be careful', not in that order.

TaliesinMS911: oy…. How are the lizards and the kitty cats?

VmpBytr1917: Both gangs are doing well… sort of.

TaliesinMS911: Sort of?

VmpBytr1917: We lost three yesterday.

TaliesinMS911: How bad?

VmpBytr1917: Rodriquez, Vega, Hiaro dead. Noriega, Diego and Vaan are in the hospital. They may not be getting out, we do not know yet.

TaliesinMS911: Crap.

VmpBytr1917: Ironically, I think that was the last group. We have more or less burned out the local vampyre population.

TaliesinMS911: I guess they are playing well with you?

VmpBytr1917: Yes, but not as much as they would like, I am sure.

TaliesinMS911: \`:( Indeed?

VmpBytr1917: What is \`:(?

TaliesinMS911: [cocked brow, disapproving frown]

VmpBytr1917: Ah. As for the gangs, some seem to think because I am undead, I am therefore immune to STDs, therefore promiscuous. Where do they get these ideas?

TaliesinMS911: Ann Rice, *Buffy*, and the 101 vampire romance books.

VmpBytr1917: There are days that eating them looks like a good idea.

TaliesinMS911: Good vampire, nice vampire.

VmpBytr1917: :) Is this the point where you start stroking me?

TaliesinMS911: Only if I want to lose a hand.

VmpBytr1917: You certain?

TaliesinMS911: (blink) Um… .

VmpBytr1917: :) Loosen up, Marco. You're in California.

TaliesinMS911: I'm not in California. I'm in a suburb, they don't count.

VmpBytr1917: You're in San Francisco, Marco.

TaliesinMS911: Amanda, I'm from NYC. By me, this is a suburb. Anyway, gtg see Merle now about the wonderful world of San Fran vamps. Keep me apprised of the 3 in hospital.

VmpBytr1917: OK. See you on later.

# Chapter 11:

# Bankrupt

September 7th New York City

Amanda watched Marco sign off from the inside of her apartment. The Internet was a wonderful thing for one of her kind. Anonymity, long distance communication, and the ability to socialize with humans without constantly keeping an eye on the time.

Colt sighed to herself and sat back in the computer chair. There were times the entire human race had changed on her. Back in the Old Country, they had feared her. When they discovered she was vampyre, they would flee, wetting themselves. The situation had been intolerable until she had found the Americans on her soil. They did not know what she was, even after she explained it, and they had not cared. They only understood that she could cut a bloody swath through those trying to kill them, and could you get us *out* of this frozen Hellhole of a country, please, ma'am?

Now, it was almost a hundred years later, and they were trying to get into her crypt...

*Or is the phrase "get into my pants?" Hmm.*

Except, of course, for Marco, who just wanted to be freaking *friends*, dammit. He was just so *frustrating*.

Amanda paused, took a deep, slow breath, and let it out as calmly as she could.

Colt frowned thoughtfully, and considered what she was going to do next. She could not visit anyone in the hospital, unless the hospital had underground access. And she was more tired than she had any right to be, under the circumstances. She had survived as long as she had by being, to a certain extent, quite powerful, and if not stronger, then certainly smarter than many of her adversaries. This level of exhaustion was disproportionate to the work she had done that evening. She had fed, she had been well rested the night before, she had everything that she had always had…

Except for Marco, of course.

It was starting to become annoying. He had been gone for only a few weeks. They talked every night online – or almost every night. Between instant messaging, email and the telephone, she could probably trace Marco's every footstep without GPS.

She sighed, then moved toward her bed. She had enough soil there for a good night's rest, but she would have to exchange it after a while. She didn't know if it was her own imagination, or if the soil almost wore out on her after a time.

Amanda slid under the covers, her current supply of soil freshly wrapped in Ziploc bags under her mattress.

She closed her eyes, falling into a deep, dreamless sleep.

San Francisco

After classes, Marco walked into Artful Krafts, figuring it was about time to check in with Merle Kraft and begin integration into Merle's little vampire killer squad.

"Ah, customer person. Can I help you with giving us money today?"

He turned to note a *Baywatch* blond, whom Merle had mentioned before… Oh yes, Tiffany Whitman. His permanent smile met her semi-vacant gaze.

"Oh!" she exclaimed. "It's you! Annoying New York person! Mark O'Catty-something."

"Marco Catalano."

"Hey! Marco! What's up?" came Yana's cheery voice from the table tucked off to the side. She trotted up, a bounce in her step.

"I'm here to see Merle, actually."

"Okey dokey."

*Okey dokey?* "So, where is the proprietor?"

"Right here." The short Asian fellow with the deep blue eyes wore his eternal windbreaker—and given that this was San Francisco, Marco couldn't blame him. The eternal night and fog made the clothing a must…it also made carrying weapons in daylight a must.

Marco was about to greet him, when his eye caught sight of the vampire from that morning, wearing a leather coat. *What was it with these people; did they all read Anne Rice novels?* Why couldn't they even think of Bram Stoker? "Excuse me, I just need to stake a vampire."

Yana followed his gaze and noted the vamp with the bright, flaming red hair. She turned back to say, "Oh, that's just Rory. Don't worry, he's a good guy."

*Hmm…maybe he had flinched only after the sun glinted off of my crucifix.* He raised a brow at Merle. "Your hiring requirements are this low?"

Kraft shrugged slightly, giving an enigmatic little smile. "He has his uses."

"And if all else fails, you can use him for a flare. And I meant his hair."

"I heard that!" Rory called.

Merle Kraft nodded towards the back room, which turned out to be a nice little training center—swords, knives, etc. for decoration on the wall, and a punching bag in the middle. The bag was being pounded by a tall burly fellow with dark hair and eyes—George Berkeley.

"So, anything else about this hunting club that doesn't operate within seasonal guidelines?" Marco asked.

Merle shook his head, and murmured, letting the sounds of the punching bag cover his words. "I'll need to introduce you, but that's about it. No one's going to be happy if they think of you as Sarah's replacement. And if I tell them that I invited you into this, that's exactly what they'll think."

Marco arched a brow. "And would they be wrong?" He frowned. *That would be a problem. The last thing I need is for that to get in the way, not to mention dying. Dying isn't high on my list of priorities—it's at the bottom, below "be canonized." Right. St. Marco the vampire slayer.* "Well, I'll think of something. I—"

"Hey, Marco!" Yana called from the front. "You want to come to an off-campus party tonight? Everyone's invited."

Marco glanced at Yana with incredulity. *An off-campus party in vampire-plagued San Francisco, where "all are invited"—I call that a buffet.*

Marco was about to say no, and Yana saw it coming and pouted…

"Um, sure."

Merle lightly punched him on the arm. "Look at it as an opportunity."

*Ah well, I could at least ingratiate myself into the group. Though the phrase "all are invited" ensures that I'm carrying a stake up each leg, two on each side of my chest in shoulder holsters, one up each sleeve, a squirt gun at the small of my back, and a holy water atomizer on a key chain. Never in the Boy Scouts, but I like to be prepared. And I don't like to lose… And I don't like the Boy Scouts. I at least liked the girl scouts, but I couldn't exactly pass the physical.*

Marco entered the dance hall and almost immediately took up position in a corner, smiling an absurd little smile, and basically enjoying the entire ludicrousness of modern dancing… or foreplay, in some cases.

*Call me a Puritan, but when you're dancing consists of gliding up against each other, that's foreplay.*

"You're not dancing?" Yana asked.

He looked over at her and smiled. "Not if I can help it…" he gestured out to those in the midst of foreplay. "At least, not like that."

"Oh. I see." She looked over his body. "Um… is that a stake in your pocket or are you happy to see me?" she asked awkwardly.

Marco smirked. "I'm always happy to see a pretty face."

Yana blushed again. The music changed to the theme music from *Ghost*. "Unchained Melody." It was simple and slow. Most of the floor dissipated except for a few couples who were more interested in dancing than fornicating.

He gestured to the speakers with an open left hand. *"This* I can dance to."

His hand dangled a moment longer than necessary, and Yana grabbed it and moved onto the dance floor. As opposed to everyone else, he danced with Yana the old-fashioned way: one hand clasped in another, a hand respectfully at her waist, and her hand on his shoulder.

"So, why all the sharp, pointy wooden thingies?" she asked.

Marco's ever-present smile never even flickered. "I'm from New York, ergo I am paranoid—which isn't paranoia, if they really are out to get you. Besides, I also believe in Murphy's Law, so I live my life ready to combat anything short of Armageddon."

"Oh, that's bad…I mean, that's good, in a bad sort of way."

He kinked a brow. "What do you mean?"

"I mean, you know, you can't go out at night without…."

"The sharp, pointy wooden thingies?" he teased. "Oh, it's not fear, it's just a job. There are bloodsuckers out there that can give hematologists a run for their money—someone has to be ready for them."

When the tempo picked up slightly at "Lonely rivers flow, to the sea, to the sea," Marco smiled. He liked Yana. She was likable, and friendly. She wasn't Amanda, but good company.

*Should I even try an approach? Tempting. I don't like her too* much. *She can be good company… eh. Step one, send out a feeler.* "I hope your significant other isn't the jealous type."

"Oh, no," she said innocently. "She's not."

A laugh escaped his lips. *Of course she's gay! It's San Francisco! Ha! Murphy knows me so very well.*

Yana furrowed her brows. "What?"

His smile mirrored his amusement. "I'm sorry. It's just… I find my luck with women is somewhat lacking. For example, I've found a beautiful young woman, friendly and sociable, and unable to find interest in me even if I were Apollo."

"Oh… *Oh*," she said, catching his meaning. "I—"

"Don't give it another thought; I'm the only male on the planet you can tell 'let's be friends' and I'll take you at face value. And so"—he whirled her out—"nothing has changed except I don't make passes at you." He pulled her back in, and, hoping to get off the topic, said, "So, who does patrols in your little monster squad?"

"Depends on the day. You wanna help?" Yana furrowed her brows and stiffened her lips to make a face that attempted to be serious, but dissolved into her soft features as she continued. "I mean, you're big and strong, and prepared, and all that."

*In the words of the eminently quotable Darth Vader, this is all too easy. What would happen if I just jumped right in? It would be obviously too eager, even to the San Francisco flakes. But if I play hard to get…?*

"You do realize that I'm insane, and neurotic, somewhat mean, vicious and out of my mind with paranoia."

"Oh, that too," she said casually.

*Really? Are these people not used to New Yorkers, or is this just my wild imagination?* "Yana, you're sweet, you're kind, and you're pretty. I won't say adorable because I hate that word. But I can't think of why you'd need me hanging around. I'd get in the way. I'm reckless and I don't play well with others… Including vampires with *bad* taste in hairstyles. And couldn't he get a better dye job?"

She giggled. *How anyone manages to stay so young in this place is beyond me. Vampires are bad enough, but this is San Francisco, where Catholics and Satanists live side-by-side. I arrive a week ago, and already she trusts me enough to stay in such close proximity? Is this the world outside New York, or is it just her? And if it's just her, I want to move to whatever planet she's from.*

Marco gave a deep sigh, as though her offer was really such a heavy burden on him. "You know what, I'll be happy to join, though. Just to see what happens."

Yana froze in mid-sway. Her eyes were frozen open in fear.

"What is it?"

"It's them," she whispered. "The ones who killed Sarah."

Marco didn't look around for a moment, but tried to keep moving with a dance partner who was rotted to the floor. "How many?"

"Five."

"I thought there was a legion of them."

"These were the guys in front."

He turned around, and spotted them instantly. Five men, all in black, looking like they were twenty-year veterans in their mid-twenties. "Right. Find out if the DJ has any *Nightwish* in the playlist. Something heavy and loud."

Marco studied the vampires as he approached them. He did some math. He had small, airplane-serving size soda bottles on him, made of glass. Except that the bottles were filled with holy water – some with gasoline, but he wanted to hold off on those for a bit. He had more stakes on him than he knew what to do with.

The plan needed to take out the front-runners. A leader and a second in command. Then, he needed to kill the others. Unless the five of them were here to lead a massacre, they wanted to keep a low-profile – seduce, or mind control victims into a place of privacy.

*Holy water the first two… Water the faces of the two farthest away…*

*Kill the closest near me with fire / water / stake… stake.*

*Stab for the head… he blocks, rips my arm out. The heart… he blocks faster, throws me across the room. Abdomen, he blocks… he attacks, I block his attack, then kill him. Three down.*

*Watered face #1 should still be feeling the effects. Dispatch him instantly. The second might be operational. Deal with him using fire stake.*

By the time he reached the vampires, he had developed a slight, purposeful and drunken stagger. He held up two of his soda bottles with holy water in them, the caps already open.

"Drinks, guys?" he asked, slurring the words.

The vampires closest to him looked at him with disdain. The other three didn't even look at him – too busy checking out prey.

One vampire laughed.

One of the others said, "We do not drink –"

Marco's fists shot forward, jamming the soda bottles into their mouths, open-parts first. His hands dropped down and slammed into their chins, forcing their teeth to crush the bottles, spilling holy water everywhere.

Marco shot between the two dying vampires as he suddenly had the attention of the other three vampires. He already had two other bottles of holy water in his hands and hurled off to either side, striking the vampires at either side of the formation. He flicked his twist, releasing a stake into his hand and whirled to his right, at the nearest healthy vampire.

The vampire swept his arm down like a pendulum swing, blocking the attack wrist-to-wrist. At the same time, the vampire punched for Marco's face.

Just like Marco had planned.

Marco intercepted the strike, redirecting it with an open palm. The punch went right by his head. Marco stabbed into the vampire's arm, driving the stake all the way through.

This was one of Marco's special stakes. He had a firecracker taped to one side of it. This wouldn't have impacted the vampire… except that the stake had been soaked in turpentine.

Marco kicked the vampire away as his arm burst into flame, dismissing him as dead already. Marco leapt upon the next vampire, who was still blinded by holy water to the face. Three good stabs to the chest, and it was dead and dusted in seconds.

Marco whirled on the last vampire standing, the second one he had hit with holy water.

That vampire was still blinded by the holy water, but reached inside his coat anyway.

Marco spotted the H&K MP5K submachinegun.

That math was even easier.

*I run at him, he cuts me down with blind-fire.*

*I run away from him, he sprays and prays, and cuts down bystanders.*

*One move.*

Marco reached into his jacket and drew two more glass soda bottles, and hurled them for the vampire.

The vampire did exactly as Marco expected, and swatted them both out of the air with no problem, moving with the speed and ferocity of a bullet. Had the vampire moved slower, it would have lived.

Instead, the impact activated the blasting caps on the inside of the bottlecaps.

The blasting caps ignited the volatile mix of Styrofoam, soap powder, and gasoline in the bottles.

This mix is commonly known as homemade napalm.

When all was said and done, from the opening salvo to the second the final vampire burned to dust took all of ten seconds. The sounds had been covered by the opening chords of Nightwish's

"Everdream," and the crowd had mostly been blinded by the flashing lights that Marco had so hated of modern dance halls.

By the time Yana had found Marco, he was already leaning up against the wall, eyes closed, as though taking a nap. She threw herself at him, hugging him.

"You were awesome," she shouted, barely heard over the music.

Marco smiled. *Well. I'm in, just as Merle Kraft wanted me to be.*

Merle Kraft wasn't entirely certain what he wanted to do next.

Over the months since he first encountered the entire strangeness of the United Nations case, his life had been frantic. He hadn't been bored once—fight vampires in one's backyard on one hand, and fight them abroad with the other, and suddenly, one's life becomes quite eventful.

*Mine certainly has.*

Merle looked into the mirror that evening and wondered when his dark blue eyes had become framed by red. He'd been protecting his people, and the citizens of San Francisco, by night, researching, locating, and burning out vampires by day, and in the down time, he had been Googling his little heart out about the United Nations and Saddam Hussein and the food-for-oil program.

For most people, it was old news. Saddam was dead, Iraq had management and new problems. But there were several dead intelligence officers, including a few FBI agents, who would severely disagree that it was irrelevant.

Merle's mouth bunched up at one corner as he looked over the research. *For the most part, it's rather plain that Something Was Not Right. Oil was purchased from Iraq, with the expressed purpose of purchasing food from the United States. They weren't purchasing food from the United States, and about eighty thousand people starved to death in Iraq every year from the first Gulf War to 2001. Nearly a million people died, and most of them children, since they're always the first to go in times of hunger.*

*Now, if they weren't buying food, where was the money going?*

*We know the answer now, don't we?* Merle thought. *It went into kickbacks. Lots of kickbacks, mostly to the French, and the Russians, and the Chinese, and everyone else who didn't want to go into Iraq in 2003. They had all been bought and paid for via the very same program they were in charge of.*

*I'm sure the pocket change is what Saddam used for suicide bomber life insurance in Israel.*

*Part of the money went to buy off Secretary General Kofi Annon's son, Kojo. But oil is a billion-dollar enterprise.* Merle frowned at his cellular phone and muttered a curse before dialing out to a friend at The Farm—the Central Intelligence Agency.

"DDI Patrick Cochran," came the sleepy voice of a Harvard man, his voice thick with the sound of New England salt air and clam chowder.

"Pat, it's Merle. How are you?"

"Mmm?" he grunted. There was the rustle of sheets at the other end. "Merle, what do you want?"

"I want some information that you haven't given the FBI."

There was a harsh chuckle at the other end. "Please, Kraft, be more specific than that."

Merle arched a brow, even though he couldn't see it, and closed his eyes, leaning back on his bed. His eyes burned like they had a bad rash. "Do I look like FBI to you?"

"Well, it's true that I have yet to see you in a suit …"

*The Deputy Director for Intelligence of the CIA thinks he's funny. This is why I have him on speed dial… and he's one of the few people who know I exist. Maybe I should have talked to the DDO.* "Patrick, I'm serious. Where did the food-for-oil money go?"

Cochran paused a moment. "Forgive me for asking, but why do you want to know?"

"Because an FBI agent got eaten in an alleyway a few months ago while investigating the UN, and I heard that Kujo got kickbacks."

"You mean Kojo. Right, and?"

Merle squeezed his eyes harder, forcing the burn to sting him awake. "There are billions of dollars kicking around, and the Israelis never had enough suicide bombers knocking down their doors for Saddam to burn through *all* the cash."

"Saddam had dozens of Presidential palaces, Merle," Cochran answered, "where do you think? That, and paying off the United Nations, of course." Cochran hesitated a moment, thinking. "Didn't you catch that killer? Some scarred monstrosity in the middle of Brooklyn. I recall something about you taking his head."

Merle almost laughed. *Lucky that I did, otherwise the vampire probably would have eaten me.* "My dead fed had a laser microphone pointed at Kofi's old window while he was looking into food-for-oil. The guy who ate him? I found him destroying the laser mic."

There was a pause as long as the California coastline. "You said he was eaten?"

Merle winced at the choice of words. "He had his throat ripped out and his blood drained. I live in the land of San Francisco vampires. Think about it."

"Oh… point taken." Pat cleared his throat. "Now, if you're wondering if this were enough to kill the man over, definitely. One man for billions? Certainly murder is possible. Just don't expect anyone from the UN to be involved, you understand. Not directly. They may have many undesirable qualities, but murder is not one of them…that's what the savages running two-thirds of the nations on the planet are for. They make good muscle when their interests are threatened. And you can *always* find someone whose interests are threatened."

After a moment, Pat said, "Merle, are you there?"

Merle's eyes flashed open. He had fallen asleep. *Damn, that isn't good.* "Hey, Pat, I'm here. So, what you're thinking is that someone from, what, the UN was the killer?"

"Not impossible. It could also be someone from Iraq who pocketed some money."

*Yes, but would an old Saddam crony have sent a vampire? And if he had, how bad can this get?* "If that's the case, then why did the FBI send an agent to look, if we know where all the money is going? *Just* so they could prove it?"

"Of course, why not? They're the FBI, it's what they do."

However, there was a problem. The United States never did *anything* when the UN screwed up. *Ever.* The only one to ever really complain about it was New York's mayor over parking tickets. As part of Merle's investigation, he could write a small history of the United Nations, from when it had been designed by the Soviet double agent Alger Hiss, to how it helped to create the 1967 war between Egypt and Israel, and other miscellaneous idiocies. And, while the Unites States held the purse strings, it never, *ever*, yanked them.

So, the question became, "But if the FBI proved all of this, what would happen then?"

Another long pause. Nothing on his end.

*Exactly. Nothing.* "Patrick, what aren't you telling me?"

"Well… while it is certain where the money is going, some of it… we can't account for it with absolute certainty. We keep losing the money around Switzerland."

Merle sighed. "Of course. Bankers for the world's fascists since 1933."

"Yes, well, it was a trifle hard for them to release any of their records during the initial food-for-oil project. We're not even certain where Arafat's money is, and the old bastard had millions squirreled away somewhere before he died."

Merle nodded to himself. "So, money goes into a bank account in Geneva, but no one knows who it belongs to, whether or not it's still there, or where it goes. How much is unaccounted for?"

"About ten billion dollars, possibly more. Not to mention the money our government lost when we went in."

Merle winced. *The UN lost about a billion a year for the length of the program. Just great.* "Now we're talking real money. All right, thanks Pat."

*Missing money, vampires, the UN, Saddam Hussein, Switzerland, oil …*

He was asleep before he could finish the list piling up in his head.

# Chapter 12:

## Bloodstained

September 10th, 10:00 pm, New York

Amanda walked out of the hospital chapel, feeling like death warmed over, which she supposed she was, technically. The night had started for her as it always did—exercise to keep the muscles fresh, a visit to church—and then, to the hospital.

Since visiting hours and her waking hours never overlapped, she had slipped into a hall closet, hung up her clothes and changed into a rat, covertly visiting each of the men wounded in the previous night's assault.

Once upon a time, she might have felt slightly disturbed about reforming naked into someone's hospital room. But, after the first five decades of men hitting on her while abroad, she was darned certain of her body, and, in this case, none of the patients were conscious.

The three of them were in the same ICU wing. They were better than they had been, but not by much. They were stable, but whether or not they would live was another quandary.

She quickly checked the area around her before reforming as a person, then did exactly as she had the night before.

She bent down and she bit each of them.

Her teeth drained only milliliters of blood, but it didn't matter. The microbes in her saliva were mingling with the blood of each of the burned gang members, making him stronger. When she and Marco spent the next week after Kraft's visit to New York explaining what she was, they had left out the fact that a small bite from her could make a person stronger. Marco had argued that it would be annoying if they kept asking for her to charge them up, or relied on it too much.

Though, given the big deal that novels about her kind that made blood draining like unto sex, she suspected that Marco had other reasons. Had he foreseen those other problems, too?

Having had a quick bite with all three of them, she had gone back, changed into her clothes, and then moved out of the hospital as quickly as possible.

*To what, though? Where in Hell am I going?*

That was a problem. She had spent decades alone, but she did have jobs, plenty of them. That had ended over twenty years ago, though.

But then, she had found Marco. Which, amazingly, had been a surprise at a point in her unlife where she thought she had run out of them. He was even mentally stimulating, and never boring. And he was certainly...

She stopped in her tracks. She hadn't even noticed that she was walking down that far. Technically, she was walking the wrong way, she needed to go due north, but she didn't even need to do that directly, since she wasn't exactly going to be slowing down anytime soon.

Somehow, Amanda had walked straight to Marco's college.

*No, we're not being Freudian or anything,* she thought, even her own brain reflecting sarcasm.

She shook her head and sighed, looking down Manhattan Island. The new World Trade Center stood there, twinkling in the night. The "Freedom Tower" looked like the entire building was still alight with people working, a strange green quartz shape in the middle of her beloved island.

Colt smiled and shook her head. She had been in the City when they had built the first World Trade

Center. She thought they were…inoffensive, despite the critique that the towers disrupted "the gentle slope to the sea" of the other buildings. They were nicknamed the butter sticks, bread boxes, and generally every nasty name in the books. Then, twenty-six years later, they were just… there, taken completely for granted, until one day, they were just gone.

*Sort of like Marco.*

Amanda shook her head again. Marco was smart. Hell, he was brilliant. He didn't think it was a big deal, and he wouldn't hesitate to tell anyone—mainly *because* he didn't think it was a big deal. He would usually state it the same way he would tell someone that he was "just fine" that day, or that the weather looked "not bad."

Marco's problem was that most of the people he met resented him for it. Something about the general attitude of the university that disagreed with him. Possibly because he was a Catholic in an aggressively anti-theist institution. Most of his friends had moved away, and much of his time was spent with her and the gangs, and even the gangs were just purely business.

*In fact, when was the last time he had a girlfriend? Or just a date? Or… ?* She shook her head. There was something niggling in the back of her head. Something was just *wrong* with that particular bit of information. Marco was smart, physically fit, and while not personable, he was certainly not unattractive.

*Heck, I deal with him often enough... dealt with, anyway... Did Lily hurt him that badly? Or did Marco merely throw himself into hunting vampires?*

Colt turned away from the World Trade Center and started making her way home. It wasn't like she had any place to go, or anything in particular to do.

Why had I never noticed that Marco consumed all of my nights, and some of my days? Maybe I really should try getting an afterlife.

Greenpoint

The concrete floor of the unfinished building vibrated, as though a T-Rex stomped around outside. There was even a glass of water on a desk that vibrated, the surface of the water rippling as though a pebble had hit.

The next strike was audible, shaking the floor, as though a truck had struck the building.

The blows came fast and furious now. They came with the speed of a jackhammer, and the force of a bomb. Across Brooklyn, there were military veterans who hit the deck, thinking that mortar fire was incoming. In Queens, there were people who thought that there were gunshots. In the Bronx, they this it was a few backfires.

When the fist finally came through the floor, half the floor exploded away.

The creature that emerged from the floor was covered in concrete dust. It was slight and almost scrawny. As it took the first breath of air in months, it let out the most terrifying sound it knew.

It laughed.

The rats scurried away in fear at the sound.

Mister Day was back.

# Chapter 13:

# Hunting Party

San Francisco, September 10th

Marco Catalano looked around the Artful Krafts and said, "Did you steal this design from the store on *Buffy the Vampire Slayer* or something?"

Merle's face was buried in folded arms, down on the table in the center of the main room. A cup of coffee was clutched in one hand, and it had long ago been mostly drained, and completely cooled.

Merle looked up and glared. "Do you have something interesting to say, or should I just kill you now for even *joking* about that?"

Marco grunted a laugh. He grabbed a chair and sat across from Merle. "So, what's up? You look like hell."

Blink. "No kidding." Blink. "I've been trying to keep up with the various and sundry disasters of my life. My job is to find the terminally weird and run a stake through its heart…"

Catalano grinned. "Metaphorically, of course."

"Or at least until lately. Most of my cases tend to end with some kind of cult, or some kind of strange and wondrous insanity that is, thankfully, mostly human. Now, it's just… " Merle blinked again. "Don't you have *classes* to go to?"

He shook his head. "You think I would be able to organize an effective resistance against the vampires of Brooklyn *and* handle my training without being smart enough to generally write off the whole educational experience?"

*Damn, I'm useless this morning.* "What do you mean?"

Marco gave him a *look*. "I mean I have an eidetic memory, and an IQ somewhere around a hundred and sixty-plus. I bore *really* easily."

Merle shook his head. "So, go out and find, oh, I don't know, *friends*, leave the rest of us alone. Get a social life."

Marco smiled. "You think I'd fit in well in San Francisco? I'm a somewhat Conservative, ultramontane Catholic who thinks that if Haight Ashbury burnt down, it wouldn't be that bad an idea... except that the rest of the city high for the next week."

The government agent had to smile. "You're at least right about that last part. But, no, seriously, can't you waste time talking on the phone to friends in New York or something?"

"Friends? What is this concept you speak of?" He grinned and shook his head. "Most of my friends moved out of New York a while ago. Trust me, if they hadn't, I probably would have recruited them into my own personal vampire killing army. But keep in mind, they were far more tolerant and tolerable people. Then I met Amanda and the vampire problem and… well, meeting new, other, friends wouldn't have fit very well."

Merle cocked a brow. "With the vampires, or with Amanda?"

Marco, for once, didn't come up with a smart retort.

Merle smiled a little. "Are you in love with her?"

Marco merely stared a moment. "What the heck are you talking about? Me? Amanda? She has… a few years on me, at least."

*Wow, for a smart guy, he doesn't lie very well. He couldn't even come up with a better reason than that?* "I'm sure after the first few hundred years, a fifty-year age difference isn't going to matter much to her." Merle took a sip of coffee. It wasn't even lukewarm, but caffeine was caffeine. "So, are you telling me, basically, that you spent all of your time either with school, or killing vampires with Amanda?"

"Well, I didn't spend *all* that time killing vampires," he said defensively.

Merle smiled. "Sure. So, are you in?"

He nodded. "Aye, I'm in. I'm going on a hunt tonight."

"Wonderful." He raised the mug to him and said, "Mazel tov."

There was something about Yiddish coming out of a face like Merle's that threw people. "By the way, what exactly do you want me to do?"

Merle shrugged. "Be yourself."

"I thought you said that you wanted me to integrate myself with them, not tempt them to kill me."

Merle rolled his eyes. "Here's the short version: I won't be there."

Marco arched a blond eyebrow. "Oh? Really?"

"The sole purpose of this endeavor was to see how they cope without me. And, more importantly, how they handle you. Yes, Yana invited you in, but having a member join is already going to feel like a replacement."

"And while I'm out doing this, what party will you be throwing?"

"A slumber party, so I can get some damn sleep."

New York City

The creature that had called itself Mister Day had studied Marco Catalano's brownstone from the shadows ever since it had escaped. It was quiet as the grave. No one resembling Marco came in or out.

Day was patient.

It stretched its muscles again, rolling its shoulders. Spending months encased in concrete had made the joints stiff. Day had just barely managed to hold his breath before the concrete landed, and was seriously lucky. There were drawbacks to being what he was, but the perks certainly outweighed them.

Day slid a cigarette into his mouth, and lit it casually. *It would have been odd to be murdered after walking the Earth for as long as I've been around.*

Day sucked down half the cigarette in a single pull, then flicked the ashes away, careful not to get any on his latest suit. This one was Gucci, and the shoes were Manolo. He wasn't going to let this one get ruined like the last.

Day chuckled to himself, a sound that made the roaches scurry in terror. Taken out by luck. The worst luck he had ever faced. To be kicked into a tiger trap at a construction site. Had it been any other place, or any other trap made for a vampire, Day could have killed Marco and have been feasting in midtown in an hour.

*But no. Marco really does have the luck of the Devil. Heh. I guess I should know, shouldn't I?*

*But then, fortune favors the prepared mind, and whatever I can say about Marco, he is prepared. A lot. Heh. Just wait until he gets a load of me.*

Day let out a stream of smoke. *I guess Marco has moved on in the past few months. It's time for me to get Marco's attention.*

Day grinned. It was time to change outfits. He needed different clothing for what he had in mind. It might take a while to find the right matching suit.

San Francisco

That evening, Marco walked out of his dorm room, wearing a rosary around his neck. While it was not supposed to be worn as an article of clothing or as a necklace, he didn't think anyone would mind if it used it to ward off vampires. Since it came down to his chest, it meant the beads would protect his neck from being bitten, and the crucifix would prevent his heart from being torn out.

It wasn't much, but it couldn't hurt.

According to the "patrols", many of the vampires in the area were former Goths, so they imitated being a vampire from the only source they knew—media.

*It's sort of like the Mafia using the* Godfather *films as their guidelines on culture.*

Merle Kraft wasn't with them that evening in order to see how they would be without him—more specifically, how they would handle Marco.

Marco stopped in mid-step at the sound of a scream, then shot off towards the source. He tacked to the right, and twisted around a large stone angel. He sighed and dropped his crossbow, walking up to the couple.

The woman's blouse had been forcibly torn open, and the man smiled as he held her wrists.

Marco's eyes narrowed, and his blood went cool.

Her screams covered Marco's advance. He casually punched the rapist's kidney, making his back cringe, then kicked sideways into his kneecap, making him twist. Marco grabbed him by the hair, tossing him backwards.

"Go," Marco snapped. She ran.

Marco turned to the assailant, and ground a heel into his crotch. The rapist screamed louder than his intended victim, and an octave higher.

Marco continued to grind his heel, almost like a cigarette. "Listen to me, pal–" The rapist simply whimpered. Marco lifted his foot long enough to bring it up and stomp down again. "I said *listen!*"

The rapist curled up into a fetal position. Marco lowered himself to one knee, patted down the rapist, and pulled out his wallet. Marco pocketed the cash, because why not, and pulled out the driver's license.

He grabbed the rapist's hair, and yanked it back. "Are. You. Listening?"

The rapist, his face clenched shut with pain, nodded slightly.

"Good. You will not come back here. You will be a good little boy, and you will turn yourself in to the local police station. You will confess every last crime you've ever committed—and don't tell me this is your only crime ever—and you will go to jail for as

long as they'll send you away. Otherwise, Mister—"
he glanced at the driver's license card "—Otto Evert,
I will find you. And your balls will never hurt you
ever again, because I will remove them, and
everything else down there. Am I understood?"

Otto muttered and whimpered and nodded.

Marco slammed his head against a rock, and left
him there, unconscious.

Marco turned on his heel and walked back to the
gang, running into them as they sought the source of
the screams.

"What happened?" Yana said immediately.

A shrug right before he scooped up his crossbow.
"No big deal. Would-be rapist. Broke his knee and
procreation tool. We were heading that way, weren't
we?"

He continued along, and George Berkeley—the
big, burly fellow sleeping with Tiffany—stepped in
front of him and put a hand on his chest. "Hey, wait,
you said rape? Shouldn't we call the cops?"

"Nah. She's gone, and he won't be doing this
again."

"But how—?"

Marco grabbed the hand, straightened his arm, and
stepped forward, putting a leg behind his. Marco
bent sideways, then slammed his arm against

George's chest, tossing him over Marco's hip. The maneuver took less than a second.

"As easy as that." Marco stepped over him and continued moving onward.

*So what if I lied to Amanda about not being able to take a human being.*

Yana moved in front of him, almost like George did. "Later, please," Marco murmured. He glanced at his watch. It was well past one in the morning. "Anyone really think we're going to find anyone out here for vampires to feed on, never mind vampires to attack? At the moment, we're the only living things out here."

"That's right, you are," came a voice to the right.

Marco twisted to one knee and brought up the crossbow in a two-handed grip. He fired, making it the last night of one vampire's life. Three others had been with him, one on either side and one behind. Marco swept from left to right. A second one died, then the New Yorker fired for the middle one while in mid leap, nailing him through the forehead. Rory had jumped onto a mausoleum and leapt off again, landing on another one. Marco let the crossbow fall back on its strap and pulled two stakes from a holster, holding them points-up like knives in Brooklyn on a Saturday night.

The vampire with an arrow sticking out of its skull rolled to its feet in front of a tree, but Yana and Tara knocked him down. Marco leapt on him with both stakes driving into his chest. Rory held onto his vampire, head-butting him, as George jabbed a stake into its back.

Marco stood, smiling. "Is that all?" Two arms wrapped around his chest, pinning his arms to his sides.

"Don't move, or he dies," the thing behind him ordered.

Catalano rolled his eyes as he reversed the stakes he held. "Will someone shoot this over actor? He can't bite me and can't move his arms lest I get away." He rammed both stakes into his assailant's legs, and vampire tightened his grip.

George looked at Marco, rubbing his back, sore from having been thrown on it. "Go ahead."

"Ever try baked Alaska?" Marco asked as he slipped twin lighters from his sleeves into his palms, then to his fingers. He flicked the lighters at the stakes, letting the turpentine catch fire. The blaze quickly moved up the vampire's legs and onto the shirt, traveling up its sides. He ground his jaw together, trying to bear the pain.

Marco sighed and slammed his skull back into the vampire's nose. He finally let go, throwing the human away as he tried to put out the fire. It was more resilient than he was, and he lit up like a candle as Marco leapt away. After that, all was quiet.

A bit of movement caught his eye, and Marco focused in on a tall, elegant man across the graveyard, shrouded in mist—which wasn't surprising, it was always foggy in San Francisco. He was dressed in a classical magician's costume, if Dracula were the magician.

Marco knew the man only from a single photo, and from the odd, midnight blue eyes which he could somehow see from a distance of thirty yards. He was looking directly at Catalano, with a small, amused smile on his face that made him look like he was about to start laughing. The New Yorker knew the man by reputation only and didn't like what he'd heard.

Dalf Kraft had come to San Francisco, and he had taken a very strange interest in Marco.

*Merle, this isn't what I signed up for.*

"Dalf, stop scaring my people, would you?"

Dalf turned, and, for once, looked like he was startled at Merle's appearance. *It's a nice change.*

Any shock didn't last long. His stance slid easily into a posture of stage magician meets Jack the Ripper. A lazy smile and drooping eyelids, as though he wasn't worried about anything.

*Maybe I should introduce him to Marco on a bad day. I suspected that would involve lots of fire. Then again, Dalf would probably respond with sulfur.*

"You want to stop jerking me around now?" Merle asked. "Or should I just get cranky now and save time?"

Dalf merely raised a brow. "Don't you mean that I wouldn't like you when you're angry?"

"Do I look like Bill Bixby?"

"No, but you are looking rather green. Not sleeping well?"

Merle narrowed his eyes. Dalf was… Dalf, and somewhat predictable, which was why Merle had lied to Marco about actually getting some sleep that evening. Dalf liked screwing with people just for the fun of it.

It was Merle's turn. "I've been busy. Now, you can either explain yourself, or I can have someone report that your place in Boston is a base for terrorists."

"Don't make such idle threats, Merlin. You may regret it."

Merle stepped closer, despite that their height discrepancies wouldn't make Merle look at all intimidating. "I regret even being *related* to scum like you, Dalf, my brother. Anything else is secondary."

Dalf simply nodded and stepped back into the fog. Merle was tempted to follow after, but he was certain Dalf would be gone. Of all the odd things he had ever had to chase down and kill, he had never, once, found one quite as odd as Dalf.

Which seriously made Merle wonder what exactly he himself was.

New York

Amanda Colt watched over the three members of the vampire hunting crew and nodded slowly at the progress. After only two treatments of her biting them, they were already out of the intensive care unit.

She drifted back to the closet as a light fog. No one had noticed a fog rolling down the hallways, and she wasn't at all surprised. Most of the night shift at St. Vincent's Hospital was asleep on their feet. There had to be some way to put more life into these people.

*But I'd be darned if I knew what to do.*

Amanda reformed quickly and dressed just as fast. She didn't much enjoy the sensation as floating about as mist, but it had its uses—especially since tonight the halls were filled with mousetraps. She could only assume that someone had seen her the night before and had decided to prepare for an infestation. And if someone had decided to throw something at her in rat form…well, there were too many heavy wooden objects around for her taste. One good solid wooden chair hurled at her, and she would be crushed to death, or suffering from a broken back for a good long time.

Colt walked out, and this time knew exactly where to go—BCC Bar.

BCC for Blood Cell Count.

Amanda walked into the bar cautiously. It was obviously a dive to the outside world. The moment she stepped inside, the smell of stale beer and hints of blood hit her nose—and that wasn't with her keen senses, just normal human ones. The entire main room looked like it had been made from the wood of a wrecked Spanish galleon. The three tables matched the floors, walls, and ceilings, made of thick wood, and the benches were haphazardly lined up with them. The mirror behind the bar had been long removed, for obvious reasons. Even if it had been there, it probably would have been covered by the alcohol in front of it.

*Basically, a 19th-century Irish bar in the Village, which probably turns away scores of NYU students.*

She smiled at the bartender, a bald bloodsucker who looked like he had been a retired cop or fireman before he had been turned. He merely nodded in her general direction after taking in her appearance.

Unfortunately, she could almost tell by his glance what he was thinking: *An uptown vampyre who's slumming.*

She looked down at her outfit and shrugged. It was a simple blouse and blue jeans. She never quite thought of Levi's as upper-class snobbery.

Amanda was almost to the bar when she noticed something off. People around her started to go silent. She paused in mid-step. Had she really walked into the wrong bar?

A vampyre whose sexuality had obviously been in question—if the Eddie Izzard outfit was any indication—glared at her. "Hey, lady, don't you want to be somewhere north of Forty-Seventh Street?"

She shrugged. "Have you met vampyres within sight of Central Park? They are so obnoxious it makes my fangs hurt. They think their blood never cools, but most of them are just mid-level vamps like everyone else. They just invested their money better. Not to mention that they seem to get their idea of vampyre life from movies and bad novels. And worse television."

Another vampyre stepped in front of her. He was either around for the Byronic period, or was simply "emo" and read too many Anne Rice novels. He stared at her with disdain. "You stink of power. How could you think you could ever move through without us picking up on it?"

She shrugged. "I go to Church. That does not make me powerful." She looked him up and down. "That might just mean that you are a wuss who has not updated his wardrobe since Mary Shelly."

"Byron" blinked. Definitely less Byron, more Anne Rice.

A hand landed on her shoulder. She was tempted to break it off, but she simply looked over her shoulder. It was the bartender, holding a shotgun.

"Maybe you bozos haven't been paying attention," he said in a rather thick brogue that marked him as an 1850s police officer, possibly recruited straight off the boat by a Tammany Hall recruiter. Amanda's eyes flicked to the name over the bar. The bartender's last name was Lynch. *Another one? How many of them are there?* "But this is my bar. Chasing out my customers is my priority, and who you socialize with is yours. And, not to mention, laddies, that this lady has been keeping the worst of you knuckleheads in line."

She sighed and shook her head. This was definitely a bad idea. "Thank you, but…" Amanda looked around her, at all the stares and the glares, at faces of stone around her. *How ironic that I have humans trying to hit on me daily, but I should be looked upon as a freak by people I technically have more in common with.*

Amanda's eyes focused on the door, and only on the door. She didn't see the people between her and the exit, only the path to take around them. Her hands were balled into fists, and she didn't even speak. She could feel her sinuses contract, as though she were about to break into tears, and her chest felt empty.

She moved with quick, controlled steps. A fast walk. She stepped around, between, and across anyone in her way. Only one person tried getting in her way, and she barely noticed him as she drove her palm straight into his nose, snapping his head back with the force of the blow.

She was out into the night air before she even noticed.

And she kept walking.

Somehow. There was nothing left for her. Humans who knew what she was wanted only sex from her, the vampyres down here held her in contempt, and the ones uptown treated her no differently.

*Maybe I should try Brooklyn, see if any of them have Marco's sense of apathy about the superficial.*

*When did I become an outcast?*

San Francisco

Marco looked at his textbooks as his hands slowly and carefully whittled away. Every other page, he looked down at his progress. His hands had become so adept at this, he had finished the project in thirty pages.

He lifted the oblong shape with one finger, balancing it there. The balance was dead center. Perfect.

He had another wooden throwing knife.

He grabbed another leg from another wrecked chair he had found in the hallway. The things colleges threw away was just awful.

Another throwing knife later, a brief knock at the door started him away from the reading. "*Ja?*"

"Can I come in?" the redhead asked. Yana was so obviously timid, it even showed in her knock. *Probably why she prefers crossbows—less personal contact that way.*

"*Jawohl.*"

The door opened and she walked in, as though creeping in by stealth.

He smiled. "Don't worry. No one will hear you, honest. Everyone's dead by now… asleep." He gestured to the foot of the bed. "Would you like to sit?" Once she was seated, he asked, "You want to talk about what you saw, don't you?"

"Um, yeah…if you're cool with it and all, about me butting my big nose into your life and everything; I mean, you only arrived here a week or two ago, you barely know me and—"

Marco held up a hand to break into her endless sentence. "I find your cute little nose to be quite endearing, and we've already discussed enough for you to enter my personal life. As long as it stays between us…" He lowered the hand, noticed it still held the knife he was working on, and slid it into the textbook as a bookmark. "What do you want to know?"

"Why did you move so… ?" She frowned, uncertain. "You didn't even wait for us. You were our guy with the big gun thingy who backs us up."

"The heavy weapons specialist… I've never worked well in groups."

"How could you hurt that guy so calmly?"

*Ah, she means the rapist.* "The same way I handle vamps: monsters are monsters no matter the form. I've trained myself to handle all sorts of predators. He was nothing."

Yana looked at him. "I saw something in your eyes when you did it. I saw…"

"You saw in my eyes the echo of…" He drifted off a bit, staring past Yana. "I killed someone once. A mugger." Catalano smiled to himself. "Human…after a fashion, I suppose. I hurt him. A lot." His eyes locked onto her once more. "Predators are predators, Yana. No difference between the two. Be it a vampire or a back alley rapist, they only differ in degree."

"But…he was a human being," she insisted.

He arched a brow. *San Franciscans…oy.* "Was the rapist I maimed tonight human? If so, you have a very broad, not to mention exceedingly generous, definition of what's human, Yana. There are as many evils in the real world as there are in the world you specialize in." Marco leaned over and touched the back of his fingers along her cheek. "I'm just so glad that you don't seem to know of them."

His fingertips glided behind her ear, down her neck, and off her shoulder, landing on the bed. "You're such a sweet person, Yana, and I'm a little glad you're not straight." He gave a lopsided grin. "I'd ask you out, and probably propose on the third date. They don't have women like you where I come from." *Well, there is Amanda…always Amanda…* He patted her arm. "Get home, wouldn't want Tara to get any ideas."

"Okie dokey. G'night."

She made it to the door when she turned and asked, "Do you ever think about it?"

"About?" He replied, not looking up from his textbook.

"About killing the guy."

This time, he met her eyes. "The mugger? Yana, I killed a man in self-defense. I don't dwell on it, nor have I given a first thought to it since. As for guilt…"

Marco grinned. "In all honesty, I sort of enjoyed it. Sleep well."

# Chapter 14:

# Remember, Remember…

September 11th, 12:06 am

Doctor Robert Catalano opened his door to Amanda Colt standing on his doorstep. "Hi. How are you?"

Amanda gave him a weary smile. "Do you really wish to ask?"

Robert stood to one side to let her in, and said, "Wouldn't have asked if I didn't. Parlor or living room?"

Amanda moved inside. "Living room. I don't have fond memories of the parlor. Marco killed Lily there."

Robert shrugged and closed the door. *I don't know. Isn't it every girlfriend's dream to see her boyfriend's ex set on fire?* "Can I get you anything? We don't have blood, but I recall you ingest food."

Amanda shook her head. "No thank you." She slid into one of the living room chairs and slunk down. She looked almost boneless.

Robert sat down behind his desk in the corner. "What can I do for you?"

"It has been difficult without Marco here. His gangs eye me like I am a party favor, and many vampires do not want to be seen with me, given all the trouble my 'pet human' has caused."

Robert suddenly had an image of Marco on a leash. It didn't really work, though, not with his son's temperament. "As far as the gangs are concerned, you do realize that one phone call from Marco would have them all keeping a respectful distance."

One of Amanda's eyebrows went up, and a wry smile crept across her face. "I am vampyre. If I want them scared, I do it myself." She sighed.

"Amanda, why did you come here? I can't imagine it's to complain about something you're eminently qualified to handle yourself."

"I don't have anything else to do. I have nowhere to go. I have already fixed the gang members at the hospital."

Robert blinked. "How does that work?"

Amanda paused and forgot that she had not explained. "The microbes that are part of my condition are transferred to any blood donor, enabling them to survive the donation. In the case of actively healing someone, I prolong the contact of saliva and blood, without the actual blood-drinking."

Robert furrowed his brow, thought it over a moment, and nodded, accepting it as reasonable. "Makes sense. When are the gang members going to get out of the hospital?"

"If I continue with the treatments, maybe a week."

Robert leaned back in his chair, his brow still furrowed. He stared off at a point on the wall next to Amanda's head, and he said, "When this first started, Marco swabbed a wound on one of the victims. Basically, I sent samples of vampire saliva to the CDC. Strangely enough, I never heard back from them."

Amanda thought, *Oooh, that will come back and bite me later. I wonder if they have already sent those test results up the chain of command, or if they're still running the tests?* "It may be interesting."

"Have you ever considered growing the microorganisms? That way you don't have to be bothered with the biting?"

Amanda arched a brow. "You realize that we would have to quantify the amount of microbes in the blood that turns someone into a vampire before we did that."

Robert smiled slightly. "I figured. Nothing's ever easy. Though I do wonder if the CDC people might be experimenting."

Amanda made sure to not smile. *They tried that once. I had to kill the resulting horde. I'm not sure what's worse, vampyres or government-sponsored mad scientists.*

"Let us hope that they don't try too hard." *Or that they learned their lesson from last time.*

"Indeed. I would hate to see what they do with vampire white mice."

Amanda laughed. There may still have been one or two of those scurrying around somewhere. "True. By the way, have you heard from Marco lately?"

Robert shrugged. "He sends me an email every once in a while."

"Me too. I wonder if he is carbon copying us?"

He chuckled. "Maybe." He leaned forward. "Amanda, I once asked you what your intentions were towards my son. Your reaction then makes me curious about your *lack* of reaction when Marco decided to leave."

Amanda studied him for a long moment. "Tell me what you really think."

Robert sighed. "Fine. Sure. I think you're in love with my son. I'm damn certain he's in love with you. My only real question is why the hell the both of you have been dancing around it for months. I can't imagine it's being a vampire, it doesn't seem to bother him."

Amanda wasn't even slightly surprised at the doctor's perceptiveness. "Have you ever eaten at the CIA?"

"I presume you mean the Culinary Institute of America. Yes. Once or twice."

"The dishes look nice."

"They're beautiful. They're art."

She nodded. "Exactly. But you still eat them. I may love Marco. But he is also an especially attractive hamburger. Marco *might* have been able to get past the vampire part of me. But it does not mean that I have as well."

Robert laughed. "You know what, Amanda? Sure." He was still chuckling even as he said, "I've been a doctor for a while. I've seen hungry patients, especially when they were on hospital food a month. You don't look like you're going to …" He paused, frowned. "You know, everything I was about to say just sounds like a double entendre."

Amanda opened her mouth to supply the rest of the sentence and paused. *Eat Marco… bite him… devour him… drain him dry… suck him…* "Rip his throat out?"

Robert sighed, even sagged, with relief. "Thank you."

"If that's so, why would Marco not say something?"

The doctor grinned. "Have you ever seen him openly express an emotion that wasn't sarcastic or angry?"

She thought for a moment. "Rarely."

"Exactly. Give him time. He'll come around. You monopolized his days and his nights for nearly a year. I can't wait to see what he's like after a single semester without you." He glanced to his watch. "Listen, I have to get to the clinic. Probably only there for an hour, but if you'd like to come along, I'll live." He glanced at the time. "If you're certain that you'll be able to make it back in time. I don't want you to get a sunburn or anything."

She gave him a smile. "Certainly." *I could use the company.*

The clinic was just a small subsection of the hospital that Doctor Catalano worked in, but he seemed to enjoy it.

Amanda looked around, trying not to breathe too deeply. If the average human thought that the antiseptic smells of a hospital were bad, they should have spent a day with her senses. Not only could she smell the antiseptic, she could smell each and every piece of gauze, every chemical, every bedpan.

Amanda grabbed a bedpan off of a stack and thrust it at an orderly, "Scrub this again, I can still smell it."

The man looked back at her. "You've got to be kidding me."

Amanda's eyes narrowed. "Do it or wear it as a necklace."

He took it away, muttering constantly, at least until she finally tuned him out.

Amanda rolled her eyes and kept scanning the halls. No one bothered looking at her more than twice, which is what she was used to. No one challenged her, probably because Marco had had a "talk" with them.

*Come to think of it, Marco has had a talk with a lot of people. I'm wondering if I shouldn't have a talk with* him? *If he's busy playing lord protector, how many think that I'm too weak to defend myself? Or does he think he's merely making life easier on me by making certain I don't have to? Either is possible. There are days I don't think I know how his mind works. It could be some of each from column A and B.*

Amanda kept scanning the hall. If she was lucky, maybe she could get a line on a new vampyre attack.

*Can't be that lucky, Marco's men have done well at driving them underground. Literally.*

She blinked. She had a moment that was very rare in her long life. She had only developed a proper name for it in 1977. At first, she thought it was like someone had walked over her grave, but she knew that feeling (literally), and then she was able to call it by its proper name: A disturbance in the force.

The first time she felt it, it was like a ripple in time, space, a wrinkle in the air. That first time coincided with the creation of the first Gulag. Then the first Nazi death camp. Bhopal. Chernobyl.

It was the sense that something evil had been born.

*Just breathe. It could be anywhere. There aren't even vampyres here. In fact, the only blood I really smell here is…*

Amanda took a deep breath. Instead of the smells of the hospital, it had all been replaced by three scents: blood, sand, and corruption. It was a combination that she hadn't smelled since… *Oh darn.*

Afghanistan.

Amanda's eyes cast about quickly. The decay was something she could never explain, or really understand. She had smelled it on a Soviet agent once, long ago.

*How could he have survived?*

She turned, making a full three-sixty, then spun back ninety degrees.

There he was, as bland and as ordinary as the first day she'd seen him. He was, once again, physically unremarkable. He was thin and slender, with brown hair and eyes, and that was about it. He had not aged a day.

That was odd. When she'd seen him, he was busy being horribly, horribly murdered. Not even she could have survived what had been done to the mysterious creature she had known only as "Mister Day."

Day smiled at her and waved his spider-leg fingers at her with his left hand and raised his right. She could clearly see the small detonator, and his small, playful smile. He whispered, "Allahu akbar."

The only true thought that went through Amanda's head was *God, let me be fast enough.*

Time slowed to a crawl as she pushed her abilities to the utmost. As she moved, she threw two stakes simultaneously. One went for the fire alarm, and the other went for the detonator wire.

Day didn't blink. He didn't flinch. He was so deliberately still, he might have been stone.

As she reached him, Day struck with his left hand, punching her right in the face, and rocked her back.

*Obviously, not a normal human,* she thought as she crashed through a wall. *A normal human hand would have been crushed at the velocity I was going.*

Amanda slid across the floor, past some patient beds, and was back up on her feet in the blink of an eye.

Day stepped through the hole in the wall. He smoothed his black leather coat—was that Armani?—perfectly casual. "Madam Colt, how nice it is to see you again," he purred. His accent was vaguely, almost generically Russian. It wasn't from any area she could remember. "It's been so long. Afghanistan, wasn't it?"

Amanda's eyes narrowed. "I preferred the gunship that opened you up like a zipper."

Day rolled his eyes. "Yes, yes. I'm sure you're nostalgic for the old days, when you had air support."

"Weren't they your people?"

"A slight failure in target identification. It wasn't like they had friend-or-foe systems for infantry."

"Is that your excuse?"

"That isn't an ex—"

Amanda flicked her wrist, and three razor discs went straight for Day's face and neck.

Day simply cocked his head to one side, then another, and the first two discs flew past, trimming only a few hairs from his head. The third disc was suddenly in his hand, caught between his thumb and forefinger.

She hadn't even seen his hand move. The hand was faster than the human eye, but never the vampyre eye.

"—cuse, if it's true," Day finished. He rolled the disc from one finger to the other and tossed it aside. "Do you wish to talk, or do you wish to fight? Because if you want me to kill you, I can arrange for that."

Amanda smiled. She slowly, raised her hand, and pointed at her hip pocket. She carefully reached into the pocket and slipped out her iPhone. "Do you know my friend Marco?"

Day's eyes flared. "Oh, yes. I know Marco. Your little boyfriend. He's the reason I'm here."

Amanda started. "Really? Marco? You want Marco?" She chuckled. "You must be kidding. Marco will very much hurt you if he got his hands on you."

Day took a deep breath and let out a heavy sigh. "Truly? You've seen what I do with hurt. Your little friend couldn't hurt me with anything short of a nuclear bomb. And I would love to see what happens then." He furrowed his brows. "Come to think of it, I never thought to give Los Alamos a whirl, or the

Nevada desert. I should have. No one is doing any *quality* nuclear testing these days. Oh well. I'll have to wait for Iran to get its act together."

Amanda's face didn't change. "Here is thing about Marco." She raised her hand and showed Day the face of her iPhone. It was the icon of a big red shiny button. "He plans ahead. For everything."

Day arched a brow, decidedly unimpressed. "Really, Amanda? What are you going to do? Blow up the entire hospital? Bring it down upon us? I intend to do that anyway."

"He plans for emergencies. Including full-on, vampyre invasion." She pressed the button. "There is app for that."

The program on the phone did two things. First, it turned on all of the fire sprinklers in the hospital.

Secondly, it redirected the flow of the water tank on the roof through a fifty-gallon drum of holy water, making every fire sprinkler rain holy water throughout the hospital.

Day blanched before the first burst of water even reached the pipes, as though he felt what was coming. He leapt to the ceiling, and punched a hole in the wall, and he hung there like a spider as the sprinklers kicked in, dousing everything on the floor.

Amanda leapt straight for him. This time, she could see his attack coming, and deflected it with her own parry, and used her other arm to wrap around his neck. Amanda pulled her knees to her chest and kicked out against the wall, yanking Day from his perch and into the spray, splashing into the river developing on the floor.

Day suddenly roared with the bellow of a dozen angry Godzillas. Though the volume threatened to shatter her eardrums, Amanda maintained her hold on his neck. The arm nearest Amanda came up, over her shoulder, and smacked her in the face with an open palm, snapping her head back so far, she felt vertebrae crunch, if not quite breaking. Amanda's body bent backwards, almost in half, breaking her grip.

Day hammer-fisted her chest, shattering her sternum. He cocked his fist again and collapsed her ribcage.

The hospital shook as Day roared, and he hurled Amanda back through the wall she came through, and she distinctly felt her broken body smash through at least two more walls before she hit an MRI.

Amanda flipped the wet hair out of her eyes and saw Day slowly stalking towards her. His eyes were burning with rage, and it wasn't a metaphor. His eyes were literal flame. The water dripped down off his coat, his head the only visible part of him that was wet. She expected to see burns on him, or something like the kind of damage a vampire would take from being exposed to holiness.

Day raised his hands, gesturing to the holy precipitation. "You think all of *this* will stop me? At the most, it will slow me down."

Day grabbed a phone from his pocket. This time, she could track his movements, even though he was going at supernatural speeds. The holy water had literally slowed him down.

"I saved the patients."

"Heh. You think this had anything to do with killing meaningless peasants? No. We wish to hurt Marco. That's why I waited until you arrived. You'll be dead, and he'll light up like a beacon." Day raised his phone. "Remember, remember, that day in September."

Amanda went cold. The date, and its significance to Marco, hit her at once.

"There's an app for *this*, too," he gloated

Amanda leapt as he hit the dial button.

The entire world disappeared in fire.

# Chapter 15:

# Reflections of The Way Life Used to Be

San Francisco

Marco blinked awake at the blare of his phone. It was 5:00 am on a Tuesday. Now, what was he supposed to care about *this* early?

On the fifth ring, he rolled over and picked up the phone with eyes closed and brain shut off. "Voice identification disengaged, please identify yourself."

"It's me, Yana. Marco, something's happened in New York."

He blinked. Yana's voice was wrong. Shaky? Scared? Of what? His mouth was on autopilot. "My lovely redhead, how are you? Wait… *My* New York? What about it?"

She told him.

"Hm?"

She told him *again.*

Marco's eyes snapped open. "WHAT!!"

Merle Kraft woke up at six. He didn't want to wake up today. He was surprised that he'd allowed himself to sleep after meeting with Dalf.

He sighed and turned on the television, straight to the news, and while it played in the background, he went to his computer. Now that he had Marco in the neighborhood, it was time to pick up on his United Nations investigation again.

Kraft went to work while CNN played across the room. The first vampire Merle had killed had been meeting with someone at the United Nations, so the first step was to find out exactly who that vampire had been met with the night the FBI used a laser-mic to bug the UN. Unless… What if that vampire had not been the one *in* the UN? What if *his* boss had heard the laser mic?

Merle shook his head. *Why would el jefe condescend to meet someone at the UN? For negotiations, you don't go in person—vampires are not micromanaging senators, are they?*

*Unless… Damn Dalf… oh, wait, it's far, far too late for that… What if the number-one vampire killed in Brooklyn wasn't THE number-one guy? What if he were just a point man? Someone to lay the groundwork for negotiations?*

*I think it's time for me to go back to New York.*

Merle grimaced and looked up at the television. It looked like someone was replaying footage of 9/11.

Then he turned on the volume.

Doctor Robert Catalano blinked. Why was his head buzzing? Why was his world blurry, and… was he in an ambulance? It a cross between a hospital and a garage with an undercurrent of burnt – hair, plastic and flesh.

Robert rolled his head from one side to the other. He was on a gurney? Why? Had he inhaled smoke? The sprinklers had all gone off, he had been getting people out, he got out, and then…?

*Short-term memory loss. Physical trauma? My vision is still blurry, so I have a concussion, and not one of the "take two Advil" variety.*

Robert coughed, said, "Hello?"

After a moment of no response, he slowly sat up. *Second opinion on the vision…it would help if I had my glasses.*

Robert gently put his feet on the floor and tried to rise. When the world went sideways, he sat back down.

"Robert!" came a booming voice that didn't need a microphone.

He smiled. He didn't need eyes to know who that was. "Bill! How are you?"

The dark brown and black blur that was Robert's friend Father Rodgers appeared at the open door of the ambulance. "Good doctor! How are you?"

Robert held his head. "Advil would be nice. What happened? First the building was on fire, then I'm… here. What's going on out there?"

Rodgers sighed deeply. "You're not going to like this."

Robert chuckled. "Best case scenario is a faulty fire alarm. Worst case…" Robert squinted. He seemed to still be in the same area. "Well, the block hasn't blown up, so it wasn't nuclear."

"Come and see."

The priest helped the doctor hobble out of the back of the ambulance.

Robert looked over what was left of the hospital. It was gone. Well, more than half of it was standing, but there was a wing gone, taking at least a third of the building.

*Still trying to figure out how all of the patients got evacuated in time,* he thought, remembering that he was the last one out. *How does a terrorist attack happen, and no one die?*

Robert winced. He couldn't exactly say no one, could he? There was still someone missing in action, he was afraid. If she had gotten out, she would have been the first person he saw, he was certain. Pity, he had been hoping that she would consider being his daughter-in-law one day. Then again, she was technically sort of dead, though she was still breathing, with a pulse, and he still wasn't certain how *that* worked.

Now… "Amanda was in there."

Rodgers blinked. "Amanda Colt?" He looked to the sky. The sun was already over the horizon. "We'll have to watch the clearance of the rubble closely. If she's found before sunset—"

"It would be bad," Robert concluded.

The doctor felt the buzzing once more. Only this time it came from his pocket. He grabbed his phone, looking at the caller ID.

"It's Marco."

Demons Are Forever

San Francisco

Marco Catalano paced back and forth in his dorm room, waiting for someone to pick up the *damn phone*. Somebody had to pick up. Eventually. Didn't they? Right now, he had two people waiting on the phone—he had dialed his father with one phone, and he had dialed Amanda from the land line in the dorm.

And as it happened before, ever since he heard That Song, every time he thought about that fateful day, the song just kept being stuck in his head. Phrases in the song discussed walls falling down in a beloved city, with clouds bringing darkness from above.

Marco had been so put off, he was no longer smiling. The television was on, though he didn't need to see it. In the last hour, he had seen the hospital explode almost on a loop. Somehow, the news had gotten video clips from security cameras across the street. The giant fireball came up from the hospital, and nearly half the building went down like a Las Vegas hotel implosion.

However, there was already an evacuation going on as the hospital went up. The problem there was simple: someone knew it was coming. There hadn't even been a whisper of smoke before the fireball, which meant that someone knew that *something* was going to happen.

Of the people that Marco knew who frequented that hospital, all of them could have seen something, pulled the fire alarm, and delayed the bomber long enough to let the evacuation happen. If it were a human threat, that could be anyone *but* Amanda—humans would have been lunch in a matter of seconds, literally. But if it was someone or something otherworldly, something demonic, then everyone Marco knew could be lying dead in that rubble, right now.

The fireball played again on the television, and Marco winced. He reacted less to the flash of fire, and more to the memory. When he was younger, he had seen something similar, and while it, too, had been replayed over and over on the television, he hadn't needed to see it played. He had seen it live. He had seen the ashes and the dust, the fireballs, the impacts. Marco could still remember the dust cloud that covered the Island of Manhattan, and the ash that covered the Brooklyn bridge. He vividly remembered that day.

Marco didn't even need to be told what day it was. It was The Anniversary. It was why he rarely called the police. He had issues about 9/11. He was one of the rare witnesses to have seen 9/11 live, and in person, from the first airplane to the last tower.

Marco had been six.

From that point on, Marco had done everything he could to be ready to join military service when it came time. He had let himself sleepwalk through "normal" classes instead of jump straight to college, because he couldn't be allowed to join ROTC at age twelve. He did his schoolwork in his free time, and studied the best ways to kill people, and whatever else he thought would be useful. Being sidetracked by vampires and other miscellaneous crap hadn't helped.

But now, as he looked on, watching the hospital he all but grew up in blow up, over and over again, probably killing everyone he knew, over and over again, Marco knew one thing. It was the very thing he knew all those years ago.

There would be death. There would fire. Marco would see to it, if he had to kill all of them himself. He didn't care what color they were. Didn't care where they were from, what they believed, or what language they spoke. Didn't care if they prayed to Thor, Kali, Shiva, Allah, or Satan. Anyone who was behind this attack would die screaming as he personally sent them each to Hell. He'd make them scream for each person who died. Just as soon as he had the body count.

*Speaking of which—* "Will one of you pick up the damn phone!" Marco screamed at both of the phones.

"Marco, I'm okay," Robert Catalano answered.

Something in Marco shifted. It was a surprising wave of relief. Heck, it was Easter morning. Someone Marco thought was dead was alive. It was a miracle. It was …

The relief faded. The relief took him out of his reverie of death and murder, and into his senses. "Who's dead?"

"No one I know. None of your gangs were in, the cops that were there are on the street right now, no ninjas were in residence… did I miss anybody?"

*Yes, Dad, you missed the most important one. You know you missed her, because you know what's important to me better than I do. But you didn't mention her, because… she's in there. She was in the great big freaking fireball. And whatever it is, it's big and it's mean, and it may have taken her out, because that's the only way she would have let anything blow up the hospital.*

"You don't know if she's alive or dead, do you?"

"Right."

Marco furrowed his brow. Whatever it was had killed—or tried to kill—Amanda and blew up the hospital in order to do it. Which meant that something had been most unhappy with *him*. He had sincerely pissed off the forces of darkness. It wanted to send him a message. Maybe make him reveal his position.

Good. He *wanted* them to find him. It would save him time.

Marco's smile returned. Had his father seen the smile, he would have known what would happen next.

Whoever had blown up the hospital had to get past Amanda. They were stronger in either power, or in numbers.

Marco's free hand clenched as his eyes went dark. *Good. I would hate for them to die before I'm done beating them to death. And it's gotta be vampiric or demonic in nature. Good. Human wreckage is so much harder to clean up.*

"But Marco," Robert continued, "we still don't know. You're aware that she could have survived all of this. You know that. Don't do anything until then, okay?"

Marco's right eye twitched, though the smile remained. "Okay, Dad. I hear ya. I promise not to do anything stupid."

"Of course not," Robert said wryly. "You never do anything stupid. How about crazy?"

"Come now, I'm a conservative Catholic in San Francisco. I'm crazy just to breathe the air here."

"How are you doing, Marco?"

"Me?" *Don't bite his head off. Don't bite his head off.* "I'm fine. I didn't have my place of work blown out from under me. I'll live Dad. Make sure you stay that way, too."

A random college student grabbed Marco on the shoulder.

Marco twisted, grabbed the wrist, rammed a palm into the attached elbow, and leveraged the dumbass into a wall.

"*What the hell do you want?*" Marco roared, stopping everyone in the hallway dead in their tracks.

The hennaed, dread-locked hippie gasped, sputtered, and finally stuttered out. "I'm – I'm just so sorry to hear about New York."

Marco's eyes narrowed. *Who are you, and why are you—oh, never mind.* "Oh. Right."

Marco let him go, then turned, seeing the entire hallway staring at him.

"What the *hell* are all of *you* people look at? Of all the freaks in San Francisco, I can't be the most interesting thing here."

The students scattered, like cockroaches when the lights came on.

Marco spent a moment panting, growling.

Marco's phone vibrated with another text. Marco checked his phone. Seven condolences and three updates from New York. According to Don Tolbert, NYPD officer, the mob was behaving perfectly well with the others, now that a terrorist strike has happened in their neck of the woods once again.

Marco nodded. *Good mobsters. You get a cookie. And I don't rip your lungs out.*

The next texts were from his two "gang" leaders, who reported situation normal, as far as everything else was concerned.

Another one came in, this one from an unknown number. This text said *Friend of Amanda would like to chat.*

"And just who are you?" Marco muttered to himself. He noted the number, moved outside, out of the way, and dialed it back.

"Hello?" came a proper British voice. "Is this Marco?"

"Correct." *I don't know many Brits.* "May I presume that I am speaking with Lady Jennifer Bosley?"

"Correct," she parroted, amused. "Have we met?"

"No, but Amanda hasn't talked to me about any other British friends of hers, so, tag, you're it."

"I had heard that you were a smart one."

Marco restrained a growl. *Don't alienate someone who might actually be genuine – or valuable.* "How can I help you, Milady?"

"Ooo, how formal," she cooed. "If there has been a problem with Mistress Colt, I will be happy to adopt you."

Marco felt a spike of anger at her even suggesting that Amanda was anything than perfectly fine.

*Be calm. Be polite. Be formal.* "I do not think so, Lady Bosley. Amanda will be fine. As far as her ownership of me goes, I assure you, there will be no problem. I expect she'll be turning into mist as soon as the sun goes down, get through the wreckage, and come out alive."

"And if she doesn't? You must at least suspect that whatever attacked her was coming after you."

*How dare she —… think strategy. Think strategy. Kill her later. If you feel like it.* "Tell me something I don't already know."

"His name is Mister Day," she told him primly. "He dresses well, and kills whoever he likes, whenever he likes."

Marco's smile came back. Something to latch onto. Something to be angry at. Something to hunt down, maim, and simply *hurt*. "Sounds charming. Can't wait to kill him."

"Good luck with that," Bosley answered. "I saw him once across the front lines in World War I. He took mortar fire and bounced back faster than any vampire I've ever seen. Be grateful if you can slow him down."

"When in doubt, Lady Bosley, kill it with fire."

"Perhaps. Though I believe there might have been a flame thrower involved during the same fracas."

Marco frowned. *That could be odd.* "Mister Day, huh? Good to know. May I ask why you're being so helpful, Milady?"

"Because there are some creatures of the night who deserve to have their heads cut off and mounted on a pike as a warning to the next ten generations that some things should not be done. You're not the only one who was in town on 9/11, love."

Marco blinked. *Oh. Dear. Well then, you get to live.* "I didn't think you folks would have cared."

Bosley's voice darkened. "There were *four* thousand people who died that day, not three. No one knew because they were using fake identities, and there were no bodies because they couldn't even try to leave the building." Bosley was silent for another moment. "You know that if she's dead, there won't be a body."

Marco took a deep, angry breath. Through gritted teeth, he said, "She. Is. *Not. DEAD.*"

Bosley let out a breath. "As you say, love."

"So long, Milady Bosley. If I see Mister Day, I'll be sure to tell him goodbye from you."

Once more, the song came unbidden, asking if it felt as though he had been there before. Because yes, he did.

Merle Kraft leapt for the telephone, and it rang before he even came near the phone. He scooped it up and said, "Who is it? Make it quick, I need to call New York."

"Merle, turn off your reflexes. I'm in San Francisco now, remember?" Kristen answered. He sighed, relieved that his ex-wife could call. He then remembered that he had personally helped her pack. He had been so used to her being on the other end of the country that his automatic responses didn't realize she was only a few miles away. "I'm fine," she continued.

Merle sat back and relaxed slightly. This was going to be nightmarish. "I know, Kris, but we're going to get these bastards. *I'll* get them, if need be."

She sighed lightly, on the other end of the phone. "Merle, you can't. They're not in your area." She took a moment to laugh. "After all, they're not vampires," she joked.

He smiled evilly, even though she couldn't see it, but he let her hear it. "Oops, so I cut their heads off for nothing. My mistake." He hesitated. "Listen, are they going to want you in the office today?"

"Probably, yeah. I can't see what they're going to want me to do about it, but they're talking about closing the city. So, I expect the entire SFPD will be put onto enforcing it."

"Why would they do that?"

"They closed down the country for days after 9/11, too, LA, Vegas. Even Idaho. Because, you know, terrorists would be going after potato crops. It's SOP against more attacks now."

Kraft nodded, even though she couldn't see him. "I'll take Arthur for the day if you want."

Detective Kelly's voice grew lighter. "Thanks, Merle, but I've already arranged something for today. I think there's going to be a small kiddie convention over at a friend's house. He'll be fine."

"Would you mind if I visited anyway?"

He could hear the smile in her voice as she said, "Of course not. But what happened to your mission to hunt down terrorists out of your jurisdiction?"

Merle could hear the attempt at amusement in her voice and smiled. "I'm going to spend an hour or two finding out who to kill first."

"Well, the guys who blew the place up are probably dead."

"I know. I'll kill the guys who helped with the logistics, then I'm going to kill the guys who planned it, and then I'm going to kill everyone who was happy about it."

"It's a start."

Marco stomped forward, moving around obstacles without really seeing them. His eyes focused on his target, and only on the graveyard – the only place on earth where the locals wouldn't give him condolences. He didn't see people between him and the cemetery, only the path to take around them. His hands were balled into fists, and he didn't even speak to people who called out his name. He could feel his sinuses contract, as though he were about to break into tears, and his chest felt hollow.

*What if Amanda really was gone?*

Catalano moved with quick, controlled steps. A fast walk. He stepped around, between, and across anyone in his way. He was at the cemetery for five minutes before he even noticed.

And he kept walking.

Terrorists had decided to take it upon themselves to trash *his* city, *his* home, *AGAIN*. Someone wished to bring death and chaos to the country…

So, logically, he decided to bring death and chaos in his own fashion.

Marco stopped at his dorm, very briefly. He collected all of his equipment, and an iPod. And one cut. There was only one song for the day. Something to cut out the song of cities falling, and clouds of darkness.

*This* song was called *"March of Cambreadth."* It had only one refrain: *How many of them can we make die?*

Marco picked up his phone, ringing one more time. Another text. Another condolence call.

Marco growled, threw it across the room, and stormed out.

If there was good news, it could wait.

If there was bad news about Amanda…

Marco didn't want to know.

# Chapter 16:

# Fun And Games

Robert Catalano looked over the ruins of his hospital building. He grimaced and wondered what he was going to do with the rest of his patients, now that he no longer had someplace to treat them.

*At least I've confirmed the evacuation of damned near everybody. Except Amanda. Marco's going to hurt after this. I almost feel sorry for whatever tried to do it to him.*

"Doctor Catalano?" came a voice to one side.

Robert looked over. There was Enrico, the suave mobster. He reached forward with an open hand, as though he *hadn't* held the doctor at gunpoint only a few months before.

Robert took the offered hand. "Enrico. What can I do for you?"

Enrico smiled. "Not the question today. What can I do for *you*, sir?" He nodded towards the wreckage. "Anything I can do to help? Anyone in there?"

"No, not today." Robert frowned. "Not unless you can block out the sun."

Enrico's eyebrows went up. "Is one of our mutual friends still in there?"

"You could say that." He looked to one side, at Father Rodgers, still on the phone, still dialing, hoping to get an answer. "We're working on it."

"Ah. Indeed. Well, I think I can help with that."

Robert arched a brow. "Really? You can get rid of the sun?"

Enrico pulled out a cell phone of his own and started typing. "You could say that," he murmured. "I'm going to need an hour or so. I have some of my construction guys already en route. Meanwhile, I think you should talk to someone. Follow me."

Robert frowned thoughtfully and followed. He figured he had nothing to lose, and the mobster had nothing to gain from hurting him.

Robert followed Enrico to a long black limousine. Enrico knocked on the door, and it opened. Enrico waved him in. Robert shrugged and entered. The door was closed behind him, and Robert found himself face to face with a lovely blonde woman. She was dressed in an elegant white power suit with a skirt that showed off her well-toned legs.

"Hello, Doctor Catalano," she said in a pleasant British accent. "I wondered if I couldn't help you dig up a mutual acquaintance of ours."

Robert cocked his head and studied her but made certain to avoid her gaze. If he had learned anything lately, it was that making eye contact with someone he don't know personally could end badly for all concerned.

"Friend of Amanda Colt's, I presume?"

"You could say that. My name is Jennifer Bosley. Has Amanda told you anything about the New York City Vampires Association?"

Robert smiled slightly. "She may have mentioned it here or there."

"I'll bet." She made certain to flash her teeth and show a bit of fang. "Obviously, I can't come outside and help you with your operation, but I would like to offer some assistance."

Robert frowned to himself. "You? Really? From what I've heard, while you yourself have been largely an ally, your association hasn't been part of Amanda's fan club. Or my son's."

"Understood. However, I have talked to your son rather recently. As I explained to him," she pointed outside at the rubble, "*this* is unacceptable. I will not put up with it, and neither will anyone else." She paused, then shrugged, throwing the hand with the pointing finger in the air. "Publicly, anyway. There are some who think that any harm to humans is a benefit to us. I don't. This sort of unfocused aggression and destruction doesn't help anyone, except maybe a select element. And I don't play with that sort. They're bad for business. I will not have it in my city."

"And what do you intend to do?"

"I can't do anything directly to help you confront this," Bosley said. "Direct confrontation would require unanimity, and I couldn't guarantee that. If I can't guarantee it, it's not worth bringing up. You understand me?"

Robert nodded. "Sounds like basic politics. If you bring it up and you're thwarted, you lose position and power."

"Precisely." Bosley gave him a broad, genuine grin. "I like you. I can see where Marco gets it from." She spared a glance outside, and the smile faded. "When Enrico puts up the tent—similar to a circus big top—you can be certain that Amanda will be found in short order."

"You can do that? Even with the sun up?"

"We have our ways. If she is alive, a group of us, put together, could pinpoint her location. And that of anyone else still breathing. Mister Enrico's construction crews can help us clear away whatever might be in the way."

"Should I ask where you dug him up?"

"I have connections in this town that go back longer than you've been alive. You don't think that I would have a few friends in low places?

Robert opened his mouth, hesitated, then shut it, saying nothing.

Bosley laughed. "I really do like you."

There was a knock at the door. It was Father Rodgers. Robert tensed. It could only mean one thing.

He had news.

Amanda Colt opened her eyes, and it felt like an entire building had fallen on her.

*Apparently, it has.*

Amanda could feel parts of her body trying to knit itself back together, and sometimes failing. She tried moving her fingers, or her toes, and while they would respond, they were buried under too much rubble. In fact, she was relatively certain that if she hadn't been a vampire, she would be so much bloody paste.

Though now wasn't that much better. *Maybe I can turn to mist?*

Amanda focused on making her hand transform and found she couldn't. *So, the sun is up. I'm sure I would have noticed... if there wasn't a building on top of me.*

Amanda sighed and concentrated on the sun. It felt like it was after noon. One? Two? Two felt right.

*But it's early September. Sundown is still hours away. And I have to hope they* don't *find me before then. Lovely.*

She closed her eyes and thought it over. What could she possibly do? It wasn't like her phone would be intact after all of this. And even if it wasn't, it wasn't like she could even get to her phone, and—

Then the phone rang.

Amanda wondered how that happened, then dismissed it. She didn't care how it was still intact. The next question was how to get to it.

Amanda shifted her hips, so her pocket was lower down her body, pulled her shoulder up, pulling her hand farther up, and slowly worked her hand into the pocket. She reversed the process to get it out again, swiped the lock, and hit what she hoped was speakerphone.

"Yes?" she shouted.

"Madam Colt!" came the billowing voice she knew so well. "How are you?"

"Father Rodgers, I will live. As usual."

"Good to hear that. We'll—"

"Take a team to San Francisco," Amanda called back. "Get to Marco. He is being targeted by a creature called Day. D-A-Y. Maybe his last name. He is a… a creature of some sort. He is after Marco."

There was a pause. "Madam Colt, I can't. There has been a ban on air travel since this happened."

"Give the tower a password. Dhampir. D-H-A-M—"

"Thank you, I know how to spell it. And you think that will get us off the ground?"

"To the moon, if you like." *I hope the code is still good. It's been twenty years.* "But you *must save Marco.* He is the target."

"I hear you. What about you?"

"I will be fine. Just save him! Before he does something stupid."

San Francisco

Merle waited for his secure uplink to the White House. The President wasn't actually at the White House, since no one wanted to give terrorists another target, but the secure link was relayed from Washington DC and all the way to Air Force One. It had been hours since the attack.

Shortly, the connection kicked in, and Merle nearly stood up in salute. He had received one of the Joint Chiefs of Staff instead of the President. Merle instead leaned back in the chair, laced his fingers together, and nodded respectfully. "General."

The old military man was used to interacting with their only Extra-Special Forces agent. There had been some problem with a creature killing military personnel over in Poland, and Merle had dealt with it. "Merle."

"What's up? I hear that the entire country has been locked down. I worry when someone locks down the Vegas Strip and closes Idaho—*again*. We have intel that some new Bin Laden wants to nuke the potato stock?"

The General smirked. "Fear. That's why they called them terrorists, Merle."

Merle nodded. "It *is* an Al-Qaeda job, isn't it?"

The General nodded. "Seems to be."

Merle's deep blue eyes twinkled with malice. "Why didn't we kill all of these people before, General? The CIA suggested it. Louie Freeh suggested it. Even *I* suggested it, and they're not my area. Yet we let these pricks live, even *after we invaded Iraq and* Afghanistan! Come on, now. Can we kill them *this time?* Please?"

The General nodded. "Do you think your special services will be required?"

Merle frowned, remembering Dalf's warning of several months ago, of something deep and dark and ugly making its move. *I have a sneaky suspicion that this was only a part of what my brother said was coming.*

"They already are." He waved it off. If there was a problem in San Francisco, he could deal with it in his own time, his own way.

*But if I left now, odds are, I'd leave in time for something to go wrong. I should at least secure home base before I try anything, in case any vampires want to play around with the confusion.* "I think there might be a bit of a local problem cropping up soon. It'll be secured in a day or two, and special situations or not, I'll be free to start going medieval on AQ ass… sir."

A raised brow. "Until we see something… peculiar… in the area, you will not be put on call. You are *not* a team player, Merle. Take care of your problems, and if we come across something we need you for, you'll be there within 24 hours."

Merle sighed. "Yes, sir. Understood. Good luck, sir."

"You too, Merle. You too."

Merle stood slowly, getting his bearings, his thoughts drifting immediately to Kristen and Arthur. *My son only just moves from New York, the new kid in San Francisco, which is already traumatic enough for a kid of his age. Now this…*

*Someone is going to pay, and I'm going to at least help cash the check.*

"Dalf," he muttered, "if you had anything to do with this, I will stake you to the ground in the middle of Death Valley and leave your stinking carcass to be eaten…and I'll see if I can get them to eat you while you're still alive, you sick son of a bitch."

"Merle," came the calm, cool voice. "You mistake me for a lower class hood. They wish to kill people. They wish to take lives… *I, take, souls!*"

Yana and Tara frowned at each other across their little corner of the dorm.

"Can you get him?" the redhead asked. Her girlfriend shook her head.

Tiffany Whitman looked over from her place in George's lap. He had one arm around her and one hand holding a *Guns & Ammo* magazine. "Who are we getting again?" she asked.

"Marco," Yana explained.

"Oh, him. Why?"

"Because his father's hospital was blown up, and we don't know how many friends and family of his were murdered."

Tiffany blinked, as though the thoughts were too much for her empty little head to contemplate, and she shrugged, turning back to George.

George glanced over his magazine. "If he's cut himself off, he probably just needs some time to himself. It's not like there's a lot of privacy around here. Compared to New York, there's not a lot of places to run."

Tara hummed with thought. "Why would he run from us? We like him. We want to support him."

George rolled his eyes and looked back to his magazine, muttering, "Touchy-feely Wiccan New Age psychobabble," under his breath.

New York

By the time Father Rodgers and his team of Vatican Ninjas had boarded the private jet to San Francisco, he was still busy trying to reach Marco. Email, IM, cell phone, nothing worked. Absolutely nothing.

"Still can't get him?" One of his men sat across from the priest, clad in the dark blue-and-green stripes of the Vatican Ninjas. He slung his sniper rifle off his shoulder and held it across his lap. Rodgers wondered if he slept with the thing. The man was more wiry and spry than anything else.

"No."

"You really think there might be a problem?" asked Ibrahim "Bram" Javaherian. He was a young Persian Catholic who had been with the Vatican Ninjas for only a few years… well, that was Rodgers' assessment. He was too young, otherwise.

Rodgers knew more about Marco than he had ever let on, but couldn't say much of it, due to the seal of the confessional. Heck, Rodgers had baptized Marco. Had taught Marco catechism. He had all but shaped Marco, or so he had thought.

When Marco had his first confession, Father Rodgers had expected very little from him. He was only seven. The first words were standard—"Bless me Father, for I have sinned, this is my first confession"—and was followed by a sincere, "Is it a sin to want to kill someone?"

Rodgers had answered just as seriously. "There are ways it is sinful. Who did you have in mind?"

"The people who knocked down the buildings."

The priest frowned. He had been worried about this from the moment that Robert had reported what Marco had seen. "We must pray for those people, Marco, so that they change their ways."

The young Marco had nodded slowly. "What if they don't change? It would be self-defense to kill them, wouldn't it? My teacher told me that self-defense was okay."

Rodgers had thought, *I should ask them what they think they're teaching in these "stranger-danger" courses.* "Yes. But it is most likely that a soldier would be the one to fight them like that."

Marco nodded and considered it. "Then when I grow up, I should do that. Thank you."

Had that been the end of it, Rodgers would not have worried. Really, he wouldn't have. Marco had been a child, and there were more than enough children who wanted to play soldier for real one day when they grew up. In and of itself, that was nothing. When Marco took Krav Maga, it had been seen as a phase, the same as with most children and karate.

Then, last year, months before the vampire plague had started, Marco came into the confessional and said, "Bless me, father for I have sinned, it has been a month since my last confession."

Rodgers had given him a big, hearty laugh. "Marco, what could you have done in a month? You're too busy to sin. I mean it, I've seen your schedule."

"Remember how we once talked about killing in self-defense?" Marco asked casually.

The priest nodded solemnly. That was a first confession he was never going to forget, even if he had tried. "Yes. What makes you bring it up?"

"You've met Lily, right?"

Rodgers rolled his eyes. He had always known that young woman would be causing trouble someday. "What have you and she done together?"

"We didn't do that much. I can't promise what would have happened next, but we had been interrupted." Marco stared at his hands absently and held them up. They were red and encrusted with blood that had already turned black. "I killed him."

The priest leaned forward. "Marco, are you all right?"

Marco squeezed his eyes shut a moment, then stared at the priest blankly. "Yes. I'm fine. Lily's fine. The gang has cleaned up most of the mess. They gave me some restaurant wet-naps to clean off my mouth." He shrugged, as though it had just been annoying. "I bit him, you see."

"Marco, wh—"

"Why did I come?" Marco finished for him, even though Rodgers had wanted to ask *What happened?* "I came here because I made him suffer. I didn't really mean to, that was just improper technique on my part. I'll do better next time. No, the problem is that I liked it. Well, that *may* be a problem, I'm not entirely certain. Isn't it a common thread from Washington to Churchill that it's so much fun to be shot at without being hit? And it's a good thing war is so terrible, otherwise we'd be doing it more often? I get that part."

Marco grinned. Some of his teeth were still stained with blood. "You see, I killed the little bastard because he was trying to kill me, and I enjoyed spilling his guts onto the sidewalk."

Rodgers nodded slowly. He had heard confessions from soldiers who had told him much worse. "Marco, if this is about the anger we've talked about before—"

Marco held up his hand. "Oh, no. My prayer life is fine. You know how I know it's fine? Because *this* doesn't happen more often."

Rodgers blinked a few times, coming back to the here and now. That was over a year ago. While he and Marco had been working on Marco's anger problems, it was something he had been worried about for some time. Marco's prayer life was…interesting. He had memorized the psalms, read a daily breviary.

Eventually, Rodgers would learn that someone had pulled a knife on Marco and Lily and tried to mug them. That man had been a one-off. Marco may have never killed anyone else ever again.

But that was before the vampires had come, and death was a daily occurrence.

Bram Javaherian nudged Rodgers with his foot. "You awake?"

Rodgers nodded and sighed. "Yes, I am. As for Marco… if Amanda believes him to be in danger, then he is in danger." He leaned into the aisle as he saw Ninja Troop Leader Hendershot in the cockpit. "Did Amanda's password get us clearance?"

Hendershot gave a thumbs up without calling back, and the jet started moving.

Bram chuckled. "Wow, that was fast. Didn't expect us to be airborne already. Especially during a terrorist lock down. It took days for even minimum air space to open up the first time this happened."

Rodgers leaned back in his seat and thought about it for the moment. "Yes. I can understand that. I believe there is much more to Madam Colt than we first expected."

San Francisco

In the beginning, Marco's job was straightforward and simple.

For example, at the very first place he visited, he had patiently listened at a crypt door for signs of life. He slowly and methodically placed four bottles on top of the crypt, two of them with rags. He calmly lit the rags, put away the lighters, then kicked open the door.

They had just torn into a new kill, already dead. "Surprise."

He ripped the Molotov cocktails from the doorway above and tossed them to the floor beyond the foot of the stairs, letting the flaming alcohol consume the floor, and block the way. He broke the next two bottles over the stairs, letting the holy water seep into the stone. Before anyone could react, he closed the doors, sliding a stake through the outside lock.

The earplugs attached to the iPod cried out the question, *"How many of them can we make die?"*

New York

Amanda Colt had had more than enough. When she got out of the rubble, she was going to make it to San Francisco and beat "Mister" Day to death.

Assuming she could beat him to death.

She even had a plan. Sure, Day would have a twelve-hour head start, but she could manage something. The country's airports would be shut down for a terrorist attack, but she had the security clearances from back in the day …

*Except that would require a plane, dummy,* she thought. *Clearances are nice, but you don't own a jet.*

It didn't matter. She was going to make it if it killed her. No matter how many different plans she came up with since she woke up, it always came down to one plan: running. Like many vampires of her age and skill, she'd been able to cross distances in the blink of an eye. But running from New York to San Francisco from sundown to sunup would be a challenge.

How fast would she have to run? Three thousand miles in about nine hours… make it twelve, since she was going west through time zones… She would have to run at about two hundred and fifty miles an hour.

*I wonder if I can move at those speeds without blasting my clothes off and shattering my bones. And can I do it without blood?*

Amanda winced, and not because she was buried under a building. She'd been buried alive… okay, buried undead… for hours already. This was after Day had beaten her to within an inch of her afterlife. Had he been thorough and not assumed the explosion would kill her, he could have easily twisted her head off. The blood she would need to heal from that alone would eat up plenty of time—a whole five minutes, which already felt like far, far too much time to waste.

But she was going to have to do it. She couldn't see any other options. She had spent every waking moment pondering the problem, and that was the only conclusion she could reach. She would have to run from Brooklyn, over the Verrazano, through

New Jersey, and… North around the Rockies? Or over them?

With that consideration laid out, she had only one thing left to do. Pray.

*Please God, let me get to Marco in time. Please. I try not to ask for too much, honestly, I don't. And I don't know how much of this is for me, and how much is for Marco, but if he needs me, I want to be there. I'm going to need speed. I'm going to need to run. I've done it for short distances in combat, but if You could help me do it over long distances? Without blood? Yes, I know I am asking for bricks without straw… or vampires without blood… but Day must be stopped. And Marco… You know how I feel about Marco. Probably better than I do, considering how confused I am on the subject.*

*I can offer You nothing, as everything I have already belongs to You, from my soul to my friendships. I just need—*

She felt the rubble shift above and around her. She started to panic. She could feel the sun still up. She could feel it directly above her.

Her heart stopped again, only in pure terror. She was going to die. She'd never see Marco again. At that moment, she wasn't entirely certain what would be worse.

Rubble disappeared right off of her, and she braced for the worst.

"Mistress Colt," came the voice of Jennifer Bosley. "Had enough of your dirt nap?"

Amanda looked up. It was pitch black—at least to the naked, human eye. The president of the New York City Vampires Association stood over her, smiling down with her great big grin.

"President—"

"I was being sarcastic, Amanda," Bosley said, and reached down. Amanda took her hand and yanked her to her feet. "I told you, call me Jen."

Amanda looked around. She knew the sun was up—every vampire did—and there wasn't even a glimmer. The entire area had been surrounded by a giant circus tent.

"How did you do this?"

"Your friend Enrico knows some people. Especially in construction."

Amanda glanced at Bosley. "Enrico? He's still talking to me?"

"He is now." Bosley smiled. "Terrorism brings out the best in people. Especially when we're all united in hurting them a little." She looked over Amanda's clothing. "You look like a building dropped on you, love. I have blood and a change of clothes put off to the side for you. Don't have any underwear." Bosley laughed. "Hope that won't be a problem."

Amanda ignored the jokes. "The man responsible is a Mister Day. He's been—"

"Around a while, I know," Bosley told her. "I know about Day. I also know he's been in town. Had I known what he'd been up to, I would have told you… and possibly the NYPD."

Amanda blinked. "You could do that?"

"You don't get to be my age without learning how to contact the proper authorities, dear. They come in handy sometimes."

Amanda nodded slowly. *I suppose I have, too.* "I have to get to Marco, warn him."

Bosley held up a hand. "I've already done the warning bit. However, if you want to get to him, we're already on it." She looked off to the side and called "Back it up!"

The tent parted a little, and a van pulled in.

"We have a coffin in the van. We'll use that to load you onto a private jet."

"You can do that? I have my own ways of doing it, but you—"

Bosley rolled her eyes. "Never underestimate the power of political donations to the right politicians. Also, I have friends with security clearance."

"We'll have to compare notes sometime."

"Right." Bosley clapped Amanda on the shoulder. "Off you go. Have fun saving your boyfriend."

"He's not—" Amanda sighed. She knew what Bosley meant. "Thank you."

"Don't mention it, love. You may not make it out alive, though, you realize that, don'cha?" she asked, her London accent slipping in.

"I know. Day is a horror."

Bosley shook her head. "Nah, love. I'm a horror. Day is a walkin' catastrophe. Haf of wha' I know about 'im scares me, and I ain't easily scared. If dere were a 'orseman of war, he'd be it. Scary as that is, I think he's not even a top man."

Amanda knew that phrasing. Last time she heard that in a discussion, it was in relation to— "He's part of Mikhail's organization."

Bosley hesitated. She cleared her throat, and her accent became as melodious as usual. "There's what I know, and what I suspect. None of it will help you kill him right this minute. Go. Save your pet. I'll be here."

Amanda nodded, turned to the van, and then paused.

Something was wrong. Yet another disturbance "in the force."

Demons Are Forever

This one was easy, though. She had felt it before, first in Poland, and then in Afghanistan—a feeling of dread as old as the dawn of time, and maybe even a little before that. It was a time when she had been known by a different name, a different alias, and where the locals had called her Sitt Alghul—Lady Vampire.

She knew very little about him, and what she did know was that him needed to be followed, hunted, and killed. Preferably before the United States of America suffered utter annihilation.

She turned toward the van and ran for it.

San Francisco

Kristen Kelly ran her fingers through her hair and wondered exactly why she had been called in today. It wasn't like anyone had expected San Francisco to have riots and blood in the street—heck, it wasn't Oakland.

Detective Kelly shook her head and pondered exactly what was going to happen next. They didn't have a large Muslim population in San Francisco, at least nothing that could even remotely rival New York or New Jersey, or even Dearborn. If she were in Brooklyn at that moment, she would have a somewhat different day ahead of her—possibly in riot gear on Atlantic Avenue.

She frowned to herself and pondered Merle's reaction to the attack in New York—his first call was to her. Ironic, since her first call was to him. Not to anyone on the NYPD, not to her relatives in New York, but to Kraft. And he had been frantic from the way he sounded. Scared out of his mind for her. It was sweet, even touching. It was…

Kristen shook her head. *But I don't* want *to be in love with him anymore, dammit.* She growled to herself in frustration. She needed something to do, anything would be preferable to just sitting there and wondering what would happen next.

A hand waved in front of her face. Her eyes snapped forward and locked on to her Lieutenant. "Yes sir?"

"Kelly. Welcome to the human race." She was handed a slip of paper. "Someone's decided to start wreaking havoc."

"Really?" Kristen asked. "Do we have a hate crime spree on our hands?"

He shook his head. "No, and that's the odd thing. Seems someone's desecrating cemeteries for some reason."

Nest number ten—the Whelan grave—developed a slight problem for Marco. Four vampires leapt over the flames and him. He locked the door, wheeled round, and tossed the knives from his sleeves, nailing both. As the knives left his hands, he reached for the stakes at the base of his neck, also cut for balance. He killed a third with a throw, but the fourth and final one leapt to one side. Unfortunately for the vampire, Marco was in the mood for hand-to-hand.

Marco grinned at him, baring his teeth. His iPod was still playing, only one earbud playing in one ear, telling him to fight until he died or dropped.

The vampire leapt for Marco. The New Yorker sidestepped and slashed down with the stake, tearing half its throat out. It rolled to its feet and smiled as it turned.

"I was in 'Nam, boy."

"And I'm from Brooklyn."

The vampire paused, wondering if this was of significance. Then he bared his teeth again and went into a decent combat stance. He had been trained for knife fighting…not for Marco.

Catalano reached for the small of his back, and drew down on him with a squirt gun, firing holy water into the vampire's eyes and chest. He fell back, blind and in pain, clutching at the burns.

Marco strolled over to him and stabbed down into his skull, driving the stake through his brain. He crumpled, paralyzed.

The vampire hunter dragged the paralyzed body over to the local Catholic Church and found they had a baptismal font for grownup full-body immersion, bigger than a hotel bathtub and five feet deep. Marco slashed the vampire's throat with a wooden blade before taking both of the vampire's hands and thrusting them underneath the water. His mouth stretched into a silent wail of pain as his hands dissolved, held there until the very bones disintegrated. Marco then lowered the vampire's feet into the pool.

It took an hour to get up to just below its heart. Marco then dissolved the arms, and then tossed in what was left of it, murmuring, "And tell them Marco says hello."

He definitely preferred violent rage to flashbacks.

# Chapter 17:

# Run For Your Life

September 12, San Francisco, 3:00 am

Marco first stabbed the vampire in the base of the spin, so it could no longer walk. He stabbed it again in the neck so it couldn't move its arm. Then he twisted so he could make it hurt some more.

At this point, Marco didn't know where he was, how many placed he had burned down, or how many vampires he had killed. What has started as an exercise in controlled rage had spun out of control.

"You seem to have been most busy, Marco Catalano of Greenpoint," a soft voice said behind him.

Marco froze, the vampire still in his grip. "Yes. What are you?"

"Someone who wants to kill you. Well, I should say you and everyone else."

"Have we met?"

"You shoved me into a tiger trap back in April."

"Thought you looked familiar."

Marco finished off the vampire before turning to look over the unremarkable person. His hair and eyes were brown, his skin tanned, his black suit something out of a mortuary supplied by Armani. His body was thin and willowy, his fingers like spider legs. He looked and sounded vaguely Slavic.

Marco held both hands behind him, reaching for a cocktail. "I take it you're not Dracula?"

He chuckled. "No, not hardly. Vlad was always too much for my taste. Too overbearing, you see. Very snobbish, flashy."

"I see. So you're not a vampire?"

He laughed, as though at a good joke from an old friend. "Hells, no. I'm something so much more than those lower-class knee breakers."

Marco arched a brow. "You're not related to a man named Mikhail, by any chance?"

The well-dressed, eloquent monster arched a brow. "The vampire? Technically, I'm a cousin of his. We in the family had been very disappointed by his actions recently, especially how he ended. Even his trainer, she spent so much time and energy on him— she has 800 years of experience, and he wasted it all."

Marco sighed. "I completely understand. I have a large family myself, I know how hard they can be on the nerves."

"Yes, aren't they so?" he cracked his knuckles. "However, he was family. And his death cannot go unanswered."

Marco nodded. "So, *what* are you?"

He smiled beneficently. "I am death."

The human looked him over, completely under-whelmed. "Wow, you just happened to pick one of the few things that I'm *not* afraid of."

"Oh, I know. You aren't scared of me, Marco. You should be, though." He gave a small shrug. "You may call me Mister Day."

Marco's eyes flattened. "Good. I hoped you'd come here."

With the Molotov cocktail firmly in hand, Marco lit the rag and tossed it at the creature. His chest ignited in flame, but he just stood there, unconcerned. "That's annoying."

He dropped, rolled, and sprang to his feet, put out.

Marco raised his brows. "Efficient."

Day nodded. "Thank you." He flexed his fingers. "Now, you get to die. Just like your vampire whore."

Marco's smile finally faded. His eyes narrowed. "Oh, really? You're the guy? You leveled a whole building just to get my attention?"

Day's smile grew a fraction. "Yes. I am 'the guy.' You seem to have forgotten that I killed your girlfriend. Does that make you angry?" He blinked. "Oh my, does it ever. You just give off waves of rage."

Marco said nothing, and simply studied Day, picturing exactly how he was going to break Day apart. There was nothing to say, really. He had expected something to come and get him, and here he was. Mister Day. Something that could track rage. *Well, he picked the right method for tracking me. Maybe he should try another hobby, like needlepoint.*

"Should I ask who else was behind it?" Marco asked. "Or should I just assume you're another lone psycho with some nifty powers?"

Day cocked his head to one side. "Oh, there are always some terrorist groups who need encouragement. I needed some help collecting the materials. ISIS or Al-Qaeda, or whatever they are this week will claim responsibility soon. All just to get you. You should feel honored."

Marco's smile became sly. "Did you think that it was going to be that easy? Just walk up, have a chat, kill me? Did you think I wouldn't fight back with every means at my disposal?" *You like rage. Well, let's try something different.*

Day grinned. "I expected it. I intend you to. I want you to. I—"

*Our Father, who art in Heaven, hallowed be thy name. Thy Kingdom come—*

Day's face lost its smile, and the glimmer of amusement shifted in a heartbeat. His teeth pulled back in a snarl, and he leapt for Marco.

Marco, however, had been dealing with things infinitely quicker than he was, and had already dropped forward, into a roll, as Day pushed off the ground. Marco was back on his feet and facing Day just as the creature rushed him again.

This time, Day stopped as he came within inches of Marco.

*Thy will be done, on Earth as it is in Heaven.* Marco's smile was back as Day looked down at the knife sticking out of his chest. "How do you find rage now, sucker?"

Merle came down the stairs to look into his shop. The college students who had been his core group of San Francisco vampire hunters were gathered in his store. Tiffany Whitman had been handling the customers as the others just sort of meandered.

George Berkeley was in the back corner, reading another magazine. His larger build discouraged some of the more obviously stoned from being a pain in the *tuchus*. Yana and Tara were the ones who were really wandering, though, like lost souls.

*Damn it, Marco, I brought you here to be a leader, not the Lone Ranger. You're supposed to be leading these people, not just leaving them hanging.* "How are all of you doing?"

"Fine," Yana and Tara moaned. George grunted, and Tiffany said, "We made $300."

Merle sighed. *Why do I expect anything different from Tiffany? Why, Lord? Why?* "That's nice. Any word from Marco?"

Yana shook her head. "He left his cell phone in his room."

"How did you know that if you haven't talked to him?"

"I broke down his door," George rumbled as he turned another page. "Don't worry. I put it back together again."

"That's good to know." Merle frowned. "Is that a lycanthrope thing? The knocking doors down bit?"

George shrugged without even looking up from the magazine. "I knocked a little too hard. It's not like I bit anyone."

One corner of Merle's mouth curled down in a frown. *If lycanthropy has more to do with the bitten, and less with the biter, I can only imagine what these people would turn into if George ever bit one of them. Gah! Though it would be nice to have George as muscle if I ever needed the backup. Hell, he's already built like a brick wall, the lycanthropy element should be a killer.* "Well, just don't bite Tiffany, no matter how much she asks," Merle muttered.

George smirked, but said nothing, and it seemed like no one else had heard him.

"Merle," Yana said, "what will happen to Marco?"

Merle shrugged. "No idea. I didn't know that you'd become that attached to him."

Yana pouted. "Well, yeah. Sorta. He's really *nice*."

*Nice? Has she been paying attention?* Merle thought.

George shrugged as well. "Yeah. He's cool. He can put a plan together." He looked at Merle. "He'd be good in a real fight, total war zone. Maybe we should consider combining more traditional tactics with fighting vampires."

Yana turned to George and said, "No. You can't possibly be thinking of…of…*guns*."

George arched a brow. "We've been handling crossbows, napalm, Molotov cocktails, and I've been building pipe bombs left and right, and those can kill more people than a whole magazine of bullets from an AK-47. And you somehow think that *guns* will be a bad thing?"

Tara blanched. "But…guns *kill people*."

George looked at her as though she was insane. "Uh huh, and what, exactly, do you think we've been doing this entire time? Did you think that vampires were just really big rodents?"

"Oh, no," Yana insisted, "rodents are part of nature."

George looked to Merle, as if to say, *What can you do?*

Merle glanced at his watch. *Shouldn't I be closing up?* He looked around the store, looking at the kids, and sighed. "You guys can all stay past closing, I just want the front door locked if you do. Okay?"

Merle sighed. *I hope that Marco is doing something productive.*

As Marco twisted the knife in Mister Day's body, Day's visage turned back from rage to amusement, as though the psychotic wrath that he had unleashed mere moments ago were a distant memory.

"I approve," Day told him.

His hand came up to Marco's shoulder and gave him a little shove that sent Marco sprawling on the ground. Marco scrambled, and Day pulled out the knife.

"Time to return to sender."

*--and forgive us our trespasses as we forgive those who trespass—*

Day turned, about to stab behind him. A broadsword suddenly ran through Day's chest and nailed him to a tree.

Rory, the vampire with the bad dye job, turned his glare on Marco, his deep green eyes flashing the yellow of his inner dark side—*So the Irish vampire isn't a perfectly virtuous monster.*

"Wha' do ya think y' doin' out here a' this time o' night?"

Marco smiled. "Hunting."

Rory turned to Day, pulled out another sword and swung it like a baseball bat through his neck. The sword bit into the neck and cut through, but Day healed so fast he might as well have been a hologram.

"Leave him," Marco growled.

Rory grimaced, but he kicked the first sword handle, driving it deeper into Day's chest.

Day reached out, grabbed Rory by the throat, and lifted him off the ground, the attack not even phasing him. "You should have stayed away, vampire. Now, I pop your head off like a zit."

Day's head snapped forward, and Rory's face was suddenly spattered with blood. The vampire pushed away as Day's grip faltered. The chatter of automatic fire broke up the night, riddling Day with bullets.

"Rory! Run!" Marco screamed.

"No need to tell me twice, laddie."

Marco ran through the graveyard, stepped up a headstone to use as a leaping point, and just kept going. He ran past three pajama-clad warriors taking cautious, slow steps backwards in retreat as they fired disciplined bursts with submachineguns. "The vampire with the neon hair is with us!" Marco called.

"Get to the van!" came a Swiss accented voice.

*If you were Austrian, you would have had a chopper. Sorry, "choppa."* Marco spotted the dark van and headed straight for it. "Rory, with me."

Rory had the back doors of the van open in time for Marco to toss himself in.

Less than a minute later, the other Vatican Ninjas piled in.

"Go!" Bram, the one with the sniper rifle, called as he ran for the van's bumper. He tossed the rifle into the van, where one of the other ninjas caught it.

Bram leapt for it. Rory and one of the other ninjas caught him by the wrists and pulled him in.

Without any warning, Day was there, grabbing the sniper-ninja's ankle before he could come all the way into the van. "I can get at least one of you!"

Marco stood, right hand held high, and cried, "The power of Christ compels you, motherfucker," as he threw what was in his hand.

Day grabbed the cord thrown at him, then screamed and leapt back as he realized Marco had thrown a rosary at him. By the time Bram was pulled in, the van was already turning a corner.

"The last thing I need is to lose one of you people, so make sure you don't get eaten by the demon!" called the driver – Father Rodgers.

Marco looked around, his perpetual smile had crept back. "Funny meeting you guys here. Just in the neighborhood and decided to stop in?"

"Amanda thought you might be in trouble."

Marco nodded slowly, as though this was something so predictable, he shouldn't have even asked the question. Though, inside, his brain was roiling with relief. All of the tension he had been unleashing on the world of vampires just flowed out of him, and he sank against the wall of the van, as though he had just now decided to take a nap.

Amanda was alive. That was all that mattered.

"Well, it's nice to see that she worries about me," Marco drawled, "but I assure you, I was doing just fine until Mister Day showed up. Does anyone know who he is?"

"Just a guess," Bram said, "but I'm going to say demon. Just a guess, mind you."

"What was your load?" Marco asked. "All of you, not just you, Bram."

"I was firing fifty-cal hollow-points filled with holy water, sealed with church wax. Forget a vampire, that should have slowed down an elephant. For Day, I don't care if he was some sort of super vampire, it should have taken his head off. Everyone else was firing our special hollow-points."

Marco cocked his head. "What's so special about them?"

Bram drew his Desert Eagle sidearm, ejected the magazine, then wracked the slide in Marco's direction, effectively tossing him the bullet. Marco caught it one-handed and held it at eye-level. The bullet was a hollow-point, nothing unusual about it. There were three types that Marco generally knew about—pin, ball, and solid. The pin or ball within the hollow-point was to felicitate expansion of the point, causing greater damage. Without the pin or ball, there was a chance that the point wouldn't flower out, defeating the purpose of using a hollow-point.

*Now, if I was to guess…*"Is the ball made of silver?" He narrowed his eyes at it. "Let me guess, you guys read Larry Correia?"

"Who?"

Marco rolled his eyes. "Never mind. Short version is that I read somewhere that silver is basically too hard to rifle. No rifling, there's no spin on the bullet. No spin on the bullet, the accuracy is basically that of an eighteenth-century musket, good for *maybe* thirty feet. By keeping the bullet made of lead, copper, whatever, you keep the accuracy, and with the ball, you still deliver the silver."

Bram cocked a brow at him. Marco smiled, tossed the bullet back, and said, "I read stuff. When my life started to look like something out of a Joss Whedon TV show, I read all the applicable treatises on it. Even if they're fiction. Trust me, Tom Clancy told me about the applicability of planes as weapons, as well as the troubles in Ukraine, long before reality ever caught up to him."

Bram chuckled. "I'm sure reality will never catch up with *you*, Marco."

"He better not. I run really fast." He looked around, closed his eyes, and sighed. He let his eyes burn with fatigue. It helped him think better. He placed his head against the back of the van and started. "So, a holy water bullet to the head and dozens of rounds will only slow this guy down. He doesn't like holy objects, but he doesn't have vampire-level allergies to holiness; otherwise, Bram's holy water bullet would have eaten away his brain. It might slow him down a little without destroying him. He also seems to react to rage. He can feel it, track it."

Bram looked across the van to another ninja with bright blue eyes that Marco recognized as belonging to Captain Hendershot. "Does that sound like a Prince of Hell to you?"

Hendershot nodded. "It does. Aamon."

Marco winced. From what he could recall, they were basically talking about fallen angels. Even worse, one of the more powerful of the fallen. "So you figure that this guy is possessed?"

"It's the only way we know of that demons enter this world," Rodgers said. "Aamon fits the bill."

Marco sighed. "Well, that's just *great*. Wonderful. Perfect. Though I've got a better suggestion for Mister Day. If we're not *too* strict and literal, how about a demon whose name was originally demon of wrath."

"Oh no, Marco," Father Rodgers said from the front. "You're not serious."

"Who else would Mister Day be, but Asmodeus," he said, pronouncing it As-mo-*day*-oose.

At which point, even Rory groaned. "Aw crap."

# Chapter 18:
# Start Of A Brand New Day

Merle had fallen asleep in his chair, though it wasn't a big surprise, considering the month he had had. Technically, it was even worse considering how the last year had been going.

The pounding on the storefront had woken him up, and he could hear someone speaking softly, in hushed, calming tones.

Merle got out of the chair, and he felt his body creak along the way. *I'm too damn young to be falling apart like this.*

By the time he had gotten out of the office and to the front, the entire task force he had assembled to fight the vampires of San Francisco were inside and waiting. There was George, the human mountain, standing behind the blonde, Barbie-like Tiffany Whitman, and on the other side were Yana and Rory.

In the middle was Marco Catalano, and he looked annoyed. "We have a problem. What do you know about a creature that can heal so fast it almost looks like he was never touched?"

Merle blinked, trying to wake up. He glanced outside the front window, and wondered if it was still dark, or if the fog had just concealed the sun. He shook his head, sighed, and sat down behind the counter. "You're not kidding, are you?" He rolled his deep blue eyes. "And I suppose you also want me to bring in my brother Dalf as well?"

Yana's eyes flared. "You're one of *those* Kraft brothers?"

Marco clamped down on the redhead's shoulder. "Down, girl, this is a good Kraft brother; he doesn't actually bite."

Merle cocked his head. "There's actually only one *bad* Kraft brother… though he seems to get all the press." He stopped and pondered Dalf a moment. "Then again, I'm not even sure that he *does* bite… sigh… I don't know a darn thing about this, so I'm not exactly the go-to person this time."

Marco's little smile increased a little. "I may know a guy."

Marco walked to the door, opened it, poked his head out, and said, "Come on in, Father."

Merle started at the sight of the newcomer. He was black, older, a little pudgy, with close-cropped hair and thick, coke-bottom classes. "Where'd you get the priest?"

"Everyone, meet my local priest, Monsignor William Rodgers," Marco said. With a look at Merle, he continued, "He deals with these things on a regular basis, much like you, Mister Kraft."

Merle merely arched a brow. "Right. So. What do we know about your bad guy?"

The priest and Marco exchanged a glance. The priest yielded the floor to Marco with a nod. The New Yorker shrugged, moved to the counter, then sat on top of it, making sure everyone could see him. "What we know thus far is that his name is simply Mister Day. That's what he calls himself. As for what he is, well, there are various and sundry theories on what he really is. He heals really, *really* fast. Holy objects *seem to* slow him down, but we weren't going to hang around for an extended period of time and test the theory. We almost lost someone just running away from him."

Merle blanched and looked around. "One of you was with him?"

Rory lit a cigarette with his Zippo. "I was there. Sort of." He flipped the lighter closed with a *clack.* "Long story."

Marco's smile didn't even twitch. He just watched Rory tell his half-truth (after all, he *was* there), and appreciated that if everyone else thought that Day had nearly killed the vampire, they would take the threat seriously.

*Come to think of it, I don't think there is a way to exaggerate this threat.*

At this point, George spoke up. He raised his *Guns & Ammo* magazine and said, "Desert Eagle? Fifty-cal?"

Rory laughed. "And didn't we try that, laddie? And a sword? The bullet to the head was what slowed him down, and not by much."

"I don't know much more than that," Marco said. "Father, would you like to explain the rest?"

Rodgers started, and it didn't get better. Rodgers had called the Vatican for everything that they had on something that even remotely *looked* like Day, and it wasn't good. Everything pointed to a creature that was older than Rory. Then again, Rory was only a 20th century vampire; Day appeared to be older than most species on the planet, including the bugs. He may have been around in Paleolithic times, but if the Neanderthals ever saw him, none of them lived long enough to draw pictograms on a cave wall.

Day's reputation was noted for killing whole cities. The Black Death took the blame for some of his kills, but they would have died if he hadn't gotten them first. According to some of the stranger conspiracy theory websites, he was also spotted in Europe throughout the first half of the 20th century, and in Northern Ireland for the 70's, and spent most of the latter half of the 1900s in the USSR. That last part made sense to Marco, since Day kept much of the accent.

The creature known as Day used to be British, apparently, working with the government during much of their later colonial period, after they had outlawed *suttee* and Thugee. Essentially, after the British had been done with any and all positive impact they could have had in the country, Day appeared. He might've been in Ireland during the 1170s, when the English first invaded Ireland, and in 1601, when they conquered the place properly, and hung around for as long as the persecutions and horrors lasted.

"You know, the British have always been such pricks," said Rory, now perched on the loft staircase like a vulture.

"Day," Father Rodgers continued, still speaking as though he was shooting for the back row of the Church, "as Marco noted, has extraordinary healing abilities, almost like he's never been hit."

"So we blow him up!" Rory said with enthusiasm. "Let's see him heal with his body parts all over the place."

Marco looked at his watch. "As of 23 hours ago, somebody decided to blow up New York City, again, so the military would shoot to kill anyone seen on a military base raiding supplies. Besides, an artillery shell would go right through this guy."

"Oh?" Tiffany said, "and how do *you* know? When was the last time *you* blew up some ... thing?"

He smiled at her. "About the last time a neuron flared between your ears."

"See!" she boasted. "I *knew* he's never done something like this."

Marco slapped his forehead and sighed. "Sarcasm just ricochets right off some people." He shook his head. "I was also on a phone call before all this hit the fan. A vampire who saw Day in World War One swears he got hit with a mortar, and a flamethrower may have even been involved."

Merle sighed, raised his hand, and said, "While the suggestions and the commentary are all very nice, can we ask a very simple question? What is he?"

Father Rodgers started, as though it was already self-evident. "A demon, of course."

Blink. That sounded strange, even to Merle. "Shouldn't demons be a little more, you know, more in appearance and power? From the way you guys have described him, he isn't... much. Aside from some strength and healing issues, there isn't a hell of a lot from him."

Marco raised a hand and a finger, as though politely interjecting. "Add one more ability. He turned to Rory before Rory made his appearance known. He can sense creatures around him. At least creatures that aren't human. I'm not sure if his range is limited, or his ability to track humans is limited to tracking rage." He looked to Rodgers. "Please continue. I'm sure you can elucidate better on the rest of it."

Rodgers sighed, slid a cigar out from his jacket, and spent a moment lighting up. "Demons can only operate within the medium they choose. Considering the power level you've mentioned, I can't imagine that he needs much more than his increased strength and healing, unless he goes up against something of equal power." The priest paused a moment. "As far as demons go, in general, if you want to be impressed, make a deal with him, or tell him your full name. Then don't be surprised if you wind up exploding from the inside out."

Merle smiled slightly. "So it would be a good idea not to get into a long conversation with him," he noted. "That should be easy enough; I work for the government, and we don't make deals with terrorists."

"That was before Obama, wasn't it?" Marco muttered.

Tara and Yana glared at him. "What? I believe in killing terrorists, not GITMO catch-and-release." Marco frowned thoughtfully. Being a Physician Assistant, he asked, "What's this guy's biology?"

There was a slight pause. Marco and Merle exchanged a glance. Merle knew where he was going but couldn't see how that could help.

"From what we can tell," Rodgers said slowly, "he's quite human except for a few changes. The healing, advanced strength. As I said, he's probably possessed someone from long, long ago."

Rory, leaning against a bookcase now, said, "How *much* strength? He tossed me around like a rag doll, but a strong vampire can do that, can't they?"

Rodgers waved the hand with the cigar, drawing a line of smoke in the air. "Oh, the usual vague terms about strength enough to level armies, that sort of thing. However, no one's ever dissected HIM, so we don't know what he looks like inside."

"I can show you your own insides, if you like."

The room turned. There was Mister Day, all bright and shiny and looking as though he hadn't been in a scuffle. With him came the scent of death, gently wafting through the store.

"How are you all doing?" Day said smoothly. "Is everyone good? I'd hate for you to be put out when I kill you all."

Everyone took a look at each other. Day hadn't been slowed down by bombs or bullets or swords or fire. So, they were running out of options.

Day stepped forward. "I think—"

Day cut himself off and looked to his right. "What the–?"

A gold streak shot up next to Day, impacting him like a wall. The demon was blasted out of sight.

Everyone looked at the newcomer, and Marco smiled like the cavalry had arrived, mainly because he had appeared in the form of a curvy, 5'6" woman with long red-gold hair that flowed down to her shoulder blades. She was also wearing a gold cheongsam that could have come from Japantown a few blocks from here.

Merle nodded towards her. "Hi, Amanda."

Merle's eyes flickered from her to Marco. *The last time I saw a look like he's giving her, it was my wedding photo, while I was looking at Kristen. This boy is so in love.*

Marco slid off of the counter, moved casually towards Amanda, and threw his arms around her as though was a life raft, and he had been holding his breath under water for four minutes.

*God, I love this woman!* Marco thought, even though he would not admit it under pain of death. "I thought I lost you," he whispered.

She hugged him back, and answered, "You almost did."

Marco didn't let go and for a long moment that was awkward for everyone else, they said nothing.

"Um, guys?" Tiffany asked. "Shouldn't we be doing something about the demon?"

They broke apart, but they didn't go too far from each other. "I think he's had enough for the night," Amanda said. "The sun will come up soon. Demons I know would rather not be in daylight if they can avoid it." She looked back to Marco. "How are you?"

Marco's hands rested on her shoulders, still not willing to break off completely. "Jennifer Bosley called, offered to adopt me as her minion if you didn't make it."

Amanda grinned. "That slut," she said in a complete deadpan. "I will have to talk with her again."

Marco's little smile lengthened microscopically. "Indeed."

Their eyes met, and for a long moment, the world ceased to exist. Literally, the entire world faded away, leaving the two of them alone in their own little world.

Or to be precise, Amanda's little world, as Marco once again slid into her mind through the prolonged eye contact of vampire to human. It was a trick he had pulled once before, to a tactical advantage. This was the first time he had ever done something like this for sociability.

Marco glanced around at the perfect blackness. "Nice digs."

Amanda noted the sudden change. "I think making eye contact did this."

Marco shrugged. "Oh well. Bram Stoker would have been the first one to have told me not to look a vampire in the eyes."

Amanda poked him in the stomach. "Hey. Last time, you used it to hack into *my* mind."

He waggled his eyebrows. "It worked, didn't it?"

She rolled her eyes while shaking her head. "And you spent that time telling me you loved me, so other vampires would think we weren't paying attention."

Marco blinked, several times, and in rapid succession. As he spoke, every time he cut himself off, his body started, as though he had been a piece of poorly edited film. "And I—knew you'd play along while I—made that—profession."

Amanda cocked her head. "Marco, what were you going to say?"

Marco's brow furrowed, and his smile remained, giving him a confused look. "Why do you ask?"

"You are skipping like scratched DVD. I didn't know anyone could hide what they were thinking when they were mind-melded."

"Oh, darling, you have no idea." Marco arched his brow and smirked. "Maybe we should talk to everyone else before they wonder if we're having a shared seizure?"

They both snapped back to reality, and Marco's hands were still on Amanda's shoulders. He squeezed her arms, then turned back to the rest of the store.

"Okay, we'll get rid of 'Mister Day' next time he comes out in the open."

Everyone looked at him strangely, proclaiming victory before a plan had even formed.

Tiffany raised a hand, and hopped up and down, disturbingly showing that she wasn't wearing a bra. Marco averted his eyes even as she asked, "And how, oh supernatural expert who's been here for only five minutes?"

Marco's eyes became hooded. "Because if we don't get it done next time, we won't get another shot, since we'll all be dead."

"Marco," Father Rodgers asked before they could wander all over the place again. "Why did you want to know about his biology?"

"Nerve points," Amanda answered for him. "There are some points on the body you hit, and parts stop working. Hands, spine, brain, et cetera. Yes, he is human. I've seen his physiology."

*This is the best part of having her for cavalry, she knows what I'm thinking ahead of time… and she feels good to hug, very soft, padded in all the right places, and even smells good… and I don't think that's a perfume to cover up the smell of death.*

Merle smiled and nodded at the two of them, looking amused. "But that only works for a few moments, and only if you can get close."

Marco peered into Amanda's eyes a moment more. They were so lovely dark and deep, he could just fall in again and… he broke off from that thought to scan the chemical shelf before Merle. What some of it had to do with magic supplies, he had no idea. He reached over for a jar of hydrochloric acid. "He can heal tissue, but let's see him heal at the molecular level."

Amanda looked at the others, then smiled lovingly at him. "Atoms of acid lack at least one electron on the uppermost level of the electron rings, an electron it *should* have. It burns because it steals electrons of atoms that hold matter together."

At Tiffany's blankest look, Yana dumbed down the explanation. "Your body is made up of sugar as the most common component. If you were to dip your hand in acid, it would caramelize."

The overly busty bleached blonde blinked. "My hand would be a caramel candy?"

"No, it would turn to a lump of coal," Marco said. *Like your brain, you stupid, bloody, idiotic, mindless blonde!*

"Oh."

Merle shook his head, rolled his eyes, then looked to the priest. "Father Rodgers? Does anyone know what attracts him? Why did Day just move here? There has to be a reason."

There was a hesitation from Rodgers.

Amanda cleared her throat. "Um, Merle… He follows patterns of rage, it attracts him."

Marco looked around at the others in the room, wondering if they knew. Merle looked at Marco. *He* knew. Yana stared straight at Marco curiously, as though wondering what he had been doing with his time since the news had reached the city. George looked up from his magazine, and then went back to reading it—he just didn't care, one way or another. *After all, the man turns into an Irish wolfhound. Who does that?*

*I must have lit up like Hiroshima at midnight of a new moon in 1945.* Marco turned to Amanda to thank her and met her eyes. "Thanks."

Rory, on the other hand, sighed, and whipped a cigarette out of his jacket, lit it casually, and said, "Do we know what the little fecker did in all these places? Or is it all just rumors?"

"They're all just rumors to start with, son," Rodgers drawled. "We just haven't the evidence, unless you know someone who survived any of those places?"

Marco smiled, and waved Rory down before the vampire could complain. "At the moment, who cares? Right now, it seems like we're going to have to hit this guy with everything we have anyway. Merle, do you want to be in on this?"

Merle said, "I'm game, but why not throw everyone at this?"

"Long story. To start with, I'm bait. From what I can gather, he wants me… I've met him once, and that's usually enough for me to piss off anybody. And for the pressure points, we need his guard down. For that, you'll need someone that isn't intimidating. Let's face it, compared to this creature, I am nowhere near threatening. Rory and Amanda are, well, vampires. You have your… reputation. But me, I'm no one."

Rory looked at the New Yorker with curiosity, as though he had admitted a deep dark secret. He glanced at his watch. "Almost dawn soon. Are we really going to place our bets on a hope that he acts like a vampire and is put on hold for a day?"

Marco nodded. "Maybe. If we're lucky. That allows us to make the time and place of our response a matter of *our* choosing, not his."

Merle: "How do you intend to do that?"
Marco smiled his most annoying smile. "Trust me."

# Chapter 19:

# Before The Storm

Merle waited for everyone to go home before he fell down onto his bed, face first.

*Dammit, who knew I could once again be sucked in by vampires and monsters and whatever else this new guy is? I should've known. Part of the reason that I had become "the Initiative" was that I not only knew how to deal with the freaky stuff, I also attracted it. I was my own walking Hell-mouth. Joss Whedon didn't need Sunnydale, I was available, and I could have used the money. Merle Kraft… freak-magnet. Oy.*

But yes, Tiffany was right. He wasn't being paid nearly enough. But with crap like the demonic highlander-as-terrorist, enough money was no longer a viable concept. He wondered if he could be paid in sleep, nerves of steel, or sanity points.

Now there was Marco's plan. Marco's plan called for Merle to stay out of the fray for as long as possible, preferably so that Merle didn't even show his face. It was psychotically brave, it was noble, it was deeply insane, and it might even work.

That didn't mean it was any less the product of a half-baked mind that relied on lots of chutzpah and just as much applied chemistry and martial arts skill. The odds of that being able to take down a who-knows-how-old demon didn't strike Merle as very good.

*What the kid's thinking, I don't know. It's borderline insane, but I at least know where he's coming from. I wanted a force that I could leave behind in San Francisco without their being a problem, and I guess it's time to test that thesis. If this goes bad tonight, not only would I probably die, I wouldn't be able to do my job outside of San Francisco for months, if at all.*

Merle sighed. *Well, then again, what were the odds that I'd be related to a brother from Hell, literally?*

Merle sighed, leaned over, tapped a cigarette against the top of his night table. He sat up and lit up. *Just when I thought it was safe on the streets of San Francisco.*

"Merlin, you're in San Francisco, it was never safe, and I should know."

Merle inhaled deeply before looking over at his brother. Dalf Kraft emerged from a shadow in the corner that Merle didn't know had been there before.

Merle exhaled in his brother's direction. "So, Dalf, this Day fellow a friend of yours?"

"Hardly. I do not deal with knee breakers."

A nod. "I would suppose you're above that… or in the ranks of hell, does that mean you're below that?"

Dalf smiled. "I told you to run and hide, little brother."

Merle turned, holding the cigarette to the side. "This have something to do with the UN again? Like last time?"

The bastard only smiled. "Did I say that?"

Merle narrowed his eyes. "You're playing both sides against the middle again." *This means one of two things: he's actually a double agent and he's on my team, or else…* "These people are onto something big, aren't they? Something big enough to kick you out of your position with whatever circle of Hell you run with."

They stared at each other a moment. Dalf smiled slightly, leaned against a glass case, tucking his wolf's-head cane under his arm. "Whatever could you be talking about?"

"Something international… someone has something up their sleeve at the UN, don't they, Dalf?"

Merle blinked, and Dalf was gone… *But maybe I should bring a camera to tonight's events… maybe I should sleep first…*

The doorbell rang in front, and Merle sighed. *Of course someone would have to do this* now! *What illiterate pothead can't read the Closed sign?*

Merle stood slowly, making it to the door, and then Merle saw a glimpse of honey-blonde hair… Kristen and Arthur were there, waiting.

Merle smiled. *Well, maybe I can stay awake for a little bit longer.*

He unlocked the door and Kristen smiled. They exchanged a few pleasantries, and when Arthur had to go to the washroom, she took the opportunity to stay behind and asked, "One thing, Merle, I may need your professional help with something."

He raised a brow. "Yes?"

"Do you know anything about several destroyed crypts lately? From the remains, they look like they were made into homes, but the way they've been destroyed, it looks like someone was having fun with napalm." Kristen shook her head and sighed. "If I didn't know any better, Merle, someone out there has personally declared war on… someone. Maybe the homeless? As far as I can tell, it could either be a strike team, or a one-man operation. You're the expert in weird—you know anyone like that?"

*Hello, Marco. Nice that you found a hobby.* "You could say that."

Marco walked into his dorm with Amanda about three minutes before the sun came up. He sat back on his bed and sighed. "Remind me to sleep before this is over."

Amanda sat on the foot of the bed. "You can do that now. I'll make sure you're not eaten by big bad demon."

He smiled. A good point. As good as when she pointed out… "Wait a sec." He shook his head to clear it. "You said you know Day's anatomy. You said you saw his insides… when did you do that?"

Amanda leaned back, stretching out along the foot of his bed. "1984… I was in Afghanistan at the time."

Marco's eyes drifted down her body. Wow, she was looking really rather good today. He could even see her legs were… very fine. The cheongsam stopped at mid-thigh, like a miniskirt, and if he didn't know any better, he would have sworn that she wasn't wearing underwear.

*Come on, Marco. Focus.*

He cocked his head at her words. "Eat any good Taliban while you were there?" She smiled and nodded. He chuckled. "Well, since Day was with the Russians, he probably followed them into the sandbox during the war. What happened, you opened him up with a scimitar?"

Amanda shook her head. "Nope. He was hit by Soviet gunship."

He started, sitting straight up. *I'm awake now.* "An attack helicopter? Crap…" *I can't imagine what else could do the job. Fine, I've a plan, and it involves circumventing Day's defenses with non-traditional attack methods… but a gunship? Sigh.*

Marco pressed his fingers into his eyes, rubbing them, slowly massaging them. He had been up too long and doing too much. The pressure behind his eyes was starting to build into nearly a headache, and it was almost enough to make him feel as though his eyes were going to pop out of his head.

Marco groaned. He started to understand why Merle Kraft looked like hell so often lately. He remembered one of the last times he and Amanda had had a conversation when he was this tired. He had fallen asleep. Not because she was boring, but because he felt relaxed enough in her presence to actually let go of the million things he thought of every moment.

Amanda touched him on the arm. "Marco?"

"I'm fine," he lied. He forced himself to grin, and then to lean back against the headboard. "So, what brings you here, darling? When you showed up, I was so thrilled that I didn't think to ask. You've already had a building drop on you, and even that has to slow you down for a little. Heck, how did you get here? Did you run the whole way? I didn't exactly see you show up at the airport. And I don't think you own anything like that, so I'm guessing you got the clothes here. Day would keep."

*Except he probably would have already killed me if you hadn't shown up. I'm getting tired of needing my backside saved every few minutes today.*

"I had some help with getting a plane ride. The clothes… are on loan." Amanda gave him a small smile. I could feel your rampage from 3,000 miles away, and I thought you would need help before you were eaten."

A grin. "Kind, sweet, gentle me?"

"Marco, you are the only one I know who even speaks sign language with attitude." She grew somber, reaching out and putting a hand on his leg.

Even that casual touch warmed his whole body. "How are you?"

He shrugged. "Armageddon arrived and didn't send a memo, how rude…" *How am I? Amanda, my dear, I'm still pissed. Not only has this bastard nuked parts of my city, now Day's come by to threaten people I love. If I could find a way to beat Day to death with my bare hands, I would. It won't make a difference, but it would make me feel better.*

Instead of all that, he simply asked, "How bad was it? Really?"

Amanda swallowed. "The hospital is gone. It's quite gone."

Marco rubbed his eyes again. The pounding was no longer just behind his eyes, it was a plain and simple headache. "Great… Just… great."

Amanda touched Marco on the shoulder, and he wanted to wallow in her touch. He wanted to turn to her, wrap himself around her, and hold on for dear life. He could feel it coming back. Everything

"Did you know," he whispered, "that I can't listen to the song 'Pompeii?'"

Amanda considered the lyrics. And winced. She knew that Marco had been very young when he had watched the entire 9/11 attack, from the very beginning until long after the towers had fallen.

"Full flashbacks?" she said.

Marco's smile flickered, more as a wince. "From start to finish." He pressed the palm of one hand into his right eye, the pressure building as though to pop it out of his head. "It's been all day. Ever since I got the news. It's usually a bad day for me, but this… Day *had* to do it on the anniversary, didn't he?"

"That was part of it." She rubbed a hand over his back. "He tracked rage. You lit up. He knows you."

Marco frowned, and it actually hurt his face. "Seriously, why come after me? I know I helped kill off Mikhail, but why come after me *first?*"

Amanda smiled. "You are troublesome mortal?" she asked in a deliberately Natasha and Boris accent.

"Maybe." He thought it over a moment longer. "Though let's face it. He didn't know where I was, and he now has you, me, and Merle in the same place. It's not stupid, I'll give him that." He took a deep breath. "Before we make our next move, you should probably tell me about the entire fight in the hospital."

Amanda nodded and did just that.

He nodded, did some math, and figured a few things into the plan he'd already been constructing. "Good. That's useful." He paused a moment and reviewed what she said again in his head. "Though the speeds you're moving at—is that new? You hit

Day so fast, I thought I clocked you going somewhere between Mach 1 and full Barry Allen."

Amanda smiled slightly. "I asked God directly for speed. He gave me speed."

Marco gave a chuckle and nodded. *Well, if her power comes from how good or evil she is, prayer would be a good way to up the power scale. I wonder what happens if she joins a nunnery? Aside from inspiring me to join the priesthood.*

*Come to think of it, why don't I do that anyway? It's not like being out in the world is doing wonders for my social life. But then, a priest with homicidal tendencies? That wouldn't go over well. Then again, the founder of the Jesuits was a soldier, so… Focus, Marco. Focus.*

"Prayer is good. Prayer hurts him. A lot. I don't know if you saw it, but I did, during my first confrontation."

"You think that would stop him?"

Marco frowned, then nodded, thinking aloud. "It would certainly slow him down. If we had *everybody* in a room, praying constantly, it would certainly act as a shield. But how long does that serve? It'll drive him off, but we don't want him driven off. We need him dead … or as dead as demons can be."

Amanda let slip a smile. "Because demons are forever?" Marco rolled his eyes. "He's got my scent now. God can protect us, but we're human. And humans slip." His eyes started to slide off to the side as he fell deeper into his own head. "We can't afford to do slip, since he'll leap from the dark and drag us into it at the first opportunity. We're going to have to kill Day, because that's the only way to stop—"

Amanda leaned forward just then and kissed him on the lips. Marco didn't even think to wrap his hands around her, just touched her on the shoulder. Her hand lay on his cheek as she pressed her lips to his.

Amanda pulled back at long last, Marco's lips following her for a split-second before he remembered himself and pulled back.

She looked deep into his eyes, her hand staying on his face. "Thank you."

*Shouldn't I be thanking her?* "For what?"

"You included me in being human."

"You *are* human. With fangs." *And a body to kill for, and a soul to die for, and I love you. And why am I not telling you this out loud?* "You're more human than some non-vampires I know."

Amanda leaned forward again, only this time, she kissed Marco on the tip of the nose. "Thank you anyway."

Marco's smile widened a little. "Though if you ever do decide to leave, I might look up Lady Bosley. She sounded cute on the phone."

Amanda laughed and slapped his arm. "You're miserable."

He laughed. "You know you love me anyway."

She grinned. "Yes. I do."

They stayed that way for a long moment. Marco could only imagine what she was thinking. Could she have pieced together what he had censored when their minds were linked before? Could she have realized that what he wanted to say was that he had meant every word said to her during that trap in the cemetery?

"I love you, too, buddy," he said casually. It was a brother saying it to a sister. A salutation between comrades. It was nothing more than that. Nothing for either of them to be worried about…

Just like her kiss.

"Listen," he said, breaking the moment like a hammer tapping on candy glass, "I'll need a favor."

She smiled. "A favor? From what you've told me, the last time you asked anyone for a favor, you crippled that high school senior."

He growled in frustration. "But I only broke his knee, blast it!"

"With a baseball bat!"

"Golf club," he corrected. "I needed it; I was only in the third grade. In any event, I need you to get me something." He told her as quickly as possible. "So?"

She raised a brow. "Do you think that will work?"

"It had better."

"I'll work on it right away."

Marco checked the time. "But it's daylight out."

She waved it away and laughed sweetly. "But it is San Francisco, the mists cover the entire city."

Marco smiled and closed his eyes. Even without seeing her, he felt Amanda's presence next to him. She smiled back, and took his hand, giving him an encouraging squeeze.

"It will work."

"I hope so."

Amanda squeezed his hand again. It was warm and comforting, and he felt her warmth spread throughout his body, despite how much time he had spent in the mists of freezing San Francisco. "The plan is to make him mad. If anyone could do it, you can."

Marco grinned and opened his eyes. "I'll take that as a compliment and run with it."

Her eyes flashed with… something. He wasn't certain what. "You should."

Marco laughed, and she departed. As usual, he prayed for the thousands who died on 9/11, and added the dead from the hospital. He also prayed that any of the other guilty bastards who were involved would swiftly be brought to justice. But he didn't cry for the attacks, the people who died.

*After all, I can't cry.*

Amanda Colt stepped outside Marco's dorm room and let out a shuddering breath.

She just kissed him!

She told him she loved him!

Then, nothing.

Well, it could have been worse. A lot worse.

"You realize that you've been up and around for over a day, don't you?"

Amanda blinked. Standing at the elevator door was Father Rodgers. "You're here?"

"Of course!" he boomed quietly—which was most people's conversational volume for down the hall. "I slept on the plane. I had my men go and pick up plenty of blood from the local bank. That can get you out and to the local church, if you want to drink from the chalice during mass."

Amanda smiled. "That would be so very nice."

Rodgers grinned. "Of course, my dear! You should also sleep. You've had a long day."

"I know."

The priest smiled at her kindly. "I also have two men at either end of the hall. Nothing will happen to Marco without a lot of noise waking him up first."

"He needs me to do something."

"Can someone else do it?"

"Depends. Do you have access to chemicals?"

At ten in the morning, Marco opened his eyes to a knocking at his door.

"Who?" he asked flatly. *Four hours of sleep, and you want to wake me up? Do you value your life and most of your sensitive body parts?*

"Me." Yana's voice.

Catalano reached over and grabbed the water pistol filled with holy water. "Come."

The redhead came in, looking well rested. The New Yorker sat up in bed and swung his legs over the side. He still hadn't had a chance to change since his rampage. "Morning."

Her smile fluctuated, unsure of herself.

Marco started. "Oh… Oh! Sorry about that, this seems a little more worrisome than something that's over—the initial attack, I mean. We still have this threat right here in River City."

"Where?" Yana asked.

*Sigh*… "I'm fine as long as Day doesn't come through my door."

"And you're not worried about the hospital?"

"Why should I?" he said, almost disinterested. "I can't do anything from three time zones away, and neither can you. We're saving the world, smoking one demonic schmuck at a time. The lives in New York can't be retaken, and remember, death doesn't bother me—mine or anyone else's. The hospital can be rebuilt, and probably will be built bigger, if only to piss off the people who destroyed it in the first place. Every other monster behind it will be hunted down and staked, probably with a 2,000-pound missile through their front door."

A shrug. "It was horrific, monstrous, evil; but I let nothing interfere with my life unless I have no choice in the matter. Besides, if I give blood today, it'll probably be without a needle and a lot more painful."

He took her shoulders gently. "Nothing to worry about, eh?"

Hope sparkled in her eyes. Yana nodded. Marco looked at her wonderful pale skin, and his thoughts drifted to his attacker. To Day.

The demon's skin had been tan, a very *deep* tan.

If he *had* spent most of the past fifty years in Russia, he wouldn't have developed a tan of any kind in the almost year-round Winter.

*However, he would've done well working in the Middle East. Especially if he stayed when the Soviets left. There would have been blood in the streets. Had he been there earlier, he could have been involved in the Iran-Iraq war, Lebanon, Palestine, an intifada or two...*

"Son of a bitch," Marco said aloud.

"What is it?" Yana asked.

"Oh. Um. Nothing important. Why?"

"You're doing it again."

Marco arched a brow. "Doing what again?"

"What you did last night. What attracted him. I can... almost feel you. What are you?"

Marco rolled his eyes. Yana was a true San Francisco native—borderline pagan. *As long as she doesn't talk to me about mystic crystal revelations and the Age of Aquarius, we'll be fine.* "Human, like most people."

Yana tossed her head from side to side. "Uh-uh, not like other people. You're different."

"So are you. Your point?" He shrugged and thought about how to explain it to her in terms she could understand, something that would sound good to a Wiccan, or a mystic, or something like that. "You've hung out with me, so you'd be more attuned to me than you are to 90% of this town, and I was possibly the only one out there last night with any emotion. The planet was numb in comparison."

Yana's eyes locked on his without any distraction. "Which is how *he* found you."

He nodded. It was hard to disagree with something that even a vampire like Rory could figure out.

She leaned forward and put her hand on his arm. "And you feel responsible for bringing him here."

He blinked at that. *A total fallacy! Slander, I say!*

She stared deep into his eyes, as though trying to read something through frosted glass. "And you're going to do something, aren't you? Something you're not telling us."

Catalano smiled weakly. "I need some rest, Yana. I'll see you tonight."

She frowned. "Okay."

"Great…" After a moment, she still wasn't leaving. "Something else?"

Yana gave a brief, thoughtful frown, then, shrugged quickly. "I dunno, you felt different last night. You feel stronger than you look, stronger than most. George feels that for Tiffany, Tara and me… But you feel that way all the time. The longer I'm near you, the more you feel that way."

*San Francisco, Pagan. She believes in getting in touch with your feelings, listening to emotions, empathy, insert your superstition here. I think I'll take a real Wiccan, even a real Druid. At least they know how to kill people.*

"I place no limits on my emotions, Yana, only on how I express them. There's nothing to be gained by reining in one's feelings; however, if I expressed mine…" He yawned and waved her off. "Ah well, I need sleep. Off with you now."

After Yana left, Marco waited two minutes before getting up again and raiding the chemistry lab. He picked the lock with needles from a dissection kit, then, quickly found glycerin, nitric acid and sulfuric acid, as well as a dozen test tubes with cork stoppers. He poured out a layer of one acid, covered it with a layer of candle wax, a layer of another acid, wax, then wax, glycerin and stopper, driving a nail through the cork and stopping halfway through the glycerin.

After doing it eleven times more, he closed his eyes and prayed. *God, hey, it's Marco... yes, that Marco... I know I'm a pain in the ass, but I've got a slight problem...*

*You see, I've got a new set of friends... heck, I've a set of friends, period. I would like to mention that this is totally selfish on my part. I like them and would feel very bored here without them. I expect You to respond despite this. After all, they are Your people. I expect You to cover their butts while I handle Day. And if I die before he does, then I'll expect You to personally smite him with enough voltage to reduce this little Buffy-like Hellmouth to ashes.*

*Oh, one more thing, about Amanda. I want you to take care of her. She's one of Your people, fine, I get that. I understand it completely. I want to make certain that You've got her back, and I don't mean in a "God on high" way, I mean in a "Thou shalt not fuck with the Lord thy God," Zeus and Olympus kinda way.*

*Her I'm sure I love. In a G-rated way, of course.*

*Anyway if I die, I'll see You soon enough... I hope.*

The first thing Marco did after waking up was hunting down Father Rodgers.

"Bless me, Father, for I have sinned, it has been about a month since my last confession."

"Have you had time to commit any sins, Marco?"

"To be honest, I can't tell you. I can't remember that far back. The only thing I can say is that I want to be able to get through today without any more sins on my conscience, and well, let's face it, I'm going to get my head kicked in one way or another. Even if I live, I may not walk away from tonight."

"So, what do you have?"

"A lot of wrath."

Father Rodgers waited a moment. "And?"

"Blind rage."

Rodgers waited another moment. "You're going to have to give me an actual sin."

"Do you count necessary brutality?"

"Against?"

"A rapist."

The priest paused, and just gave him a look. "At best, there's adrenaline. Marco, give me something."

"Impure thoughts. How's that?"

Rodgers cocked his head. "That's new. Anyone I know?"

It was Marco's turn to pause. "Maybe."

"Really? Amanda? Huh."

"How do you figure?"

"It wasn't going to be Yana, now was it?"

"Not really, no."

"Should I ask how impure these thoughts have been?"

"I want to kiss her. Make out with her. Caress her cheek. I want to date her. I'm sure I love her. I'd marry her if I didn't have the mental restraint."

Rodgers arched a brow. "I'm waiting for the impure thought. Are you pondering her nude?"

"No. Duh … Well, I am now, thanks a lot. Why would you even ask that?"

Rodgers sighed in frustration. "Marco, have you ever considered that you're bad at this?"

"I enjoy killing people. I should probably consider joining a monastery."

"I don't think the Trappists could handle you."

"Not sure they could, either. Do they have a vow of silence?"

"Ha!" Rodgers boomed. "Now that I would like to see. You with a vow of silence." The priest sighed. "Marco, are you going to tell her you love her?"

"No. That would be stupid. Not to mention jeopardize a great working relationship on fighting the army of darkness. I'm not going to screw up a war on evil just to see if I can get her to marry me."

Rodgers sighed. "Anything else?"

"Nothing that comes to mind. Then again, I've been busy, and everything's a bit of a blur."

"In which case, say three decades of the rosary, and make a good act of contrition."

"I'll see how much I can do before we have to kick ass tonight."

# Chapter 20:

# A Day of Reckoning

Marco stood in the cemetery that night and silently raged, waiting to reduce "Mister Day" to a pile of shattered glass. He scanned the tombstones around, waiting for the adversary to jump out from behind any one of them.

Catalano turned around once more and found the demon standing in plain sight. He wore a wonderful, brand-new Armani suit with a silk shirt and cheery green tie. His posture was elegant, his hair was perfect, and he smoothed his tie with a movement so suave, he must have taken dance lessons at one point.

Day smiled and cocked his head. "I'm curious, Mister Catalano," he noted, slowly slinking around to Marco's left. "What did you intend to accomplish by setting a trap for me? You know nothing can harm me."

The New Yorker grinned at him. "True. You can't be harmed. But I have no intention of harming you, I intend to kill you." Shrug. "I expected to kill the monster who's been causing havoc in the Middle

East. It took me awhile, but I noticed something. You're lazy."

Day smiled. "Oh? Pray tell, how? I assure you, I am a most industrious demon."

"Granted, but you're lazy about how far you want to move. During your history, you've moved in a definite pattern and kept going right next door: Ireland to England, to Germany, to Russia, probably sliding into Afghanistan during their war against the Soviet Union. What did you do from there? Spend a little time in the Sudan? Head back for some ISIS action?"

He grinned. "You are very wise for one who has not yet lived one lifetime."

The human smiled in turn. "And you cannot realize how nice it is to meet a demon who's at least *read* Stoker's *Dracula*. I'm only curious as to whether or not you flew one of the planes on 9/11."

Day bowed slightly. "The second plane—the one which hit the target *properly*, in the *middle* of the building." He studied Marco a moment. "I'm impressed at your mental capacity. Most people wouldn't have made such a leap. The CIA never figured out that there were 20 hijackers, not 19."

A shrug. "Might I inquire how you managed to keep the whole thing under wraps?"

Day waved it away as though it were trivial. "The President before that was no great problem to make a deal with, so long as we gave each other certain concessions. In the '90s, I even managed to get him to cut down your military to 40% capacity since the first Gulf War."

Marco arched a brow. "Always knew the Devil would be a Democrat."

"I prefer to think of myself as a Lobbyist."

"Not an Advocate?"

"Touché," he said with another small bow. "I crippled your CIA and military capacities for years. Heck, since 2009, I was able to walk back every measly effort made after 9/11, making your country vulnerable for *decades* this time."

*Doubted, but I'm not going to debate the point.* "If you live that long."

Day took a step toward Marco. "Forever." Another step. "It doesn't matter how many times you shoot or stab me, because I *am* an army of darkness." One more step and he stopped. "My *real* name is Legion, for I have the strength of many."

Marco nodded. "Actually, I was thinking it was Asmodeus."

Day's smile became sly. "Like I said, you are smart."

In five seconds, twelve metal bolts came from four separate, fully-loaded triple-action crossbows. Instead of the annoyance he had showed that morning, he screamed in agony, falling back, doubled over in pain. He glared, his eyes now pools of—literal—fire, staring as so though to burn Marco to the ground.

If eyes were windows to the soul, his was not exactly prime vacation territory. They had turned coal black.

Day cocked an eyebrow. "Why metal?"

Marco chuckled. "Think... *Godzilla.*"

Day's eyes then followed the cables streaming from each arrow, which were just then being connected to the San Francisco power grid. "Oh, nuts."

The electricity went straight into each arrow, leading directly into his body. Day pulled back his upper lips in a snarl, and turned his gaze on Yana, reloading her crossbow.

The strange and unlicensed use of the San Francisco power grid tripped a few circuits, because his body jerked one last time, then flopped to the ground.

Day was up in a second, which was three-quarters of a second longer than it would have taken him usually. He pushed up off his hands and knees in time for Rory to leap on him, driving a fist into the nerve spot behind the ear. The blow would've knocked out a human being, but only stunned Day. Rory drove a knife into his kidney before hitting the spot again. That blade was covered in the same anticoagulant that the arrows were.

Day twirled and threw Rory off with a shake that tossed the vampire over Marco's head and almost three blocks away. Day turned to Marco, eyes burning with rage. He reached up and pulled out the first arrow, and the wound healed, but not half as fast as it had during their original battle. Day dropped each bolt to the ground, extracting each with infinite patience.

Marco slowly reached for a test tube at the small of his back, a nail poking out of the top of the stopper. Marco rammed a nail through the cork and the layers in the test tube, shook the tube, and tossed it at the demon. Day caught it with graceful ease and smiled as he held it in front of him. He dropped it to the ground and stepped on it.

The resulting explosion knocked Day off his feet, severing the front half of his foot from the heel. The concussion wave sent the toes flying over Marco's shoulder before Day had a hope of healing the damage. The next tube was tossed at Day while the creature struggled to his feet. It exploded under his body and sent him sprawling, pieces of glass shining in his face. Day rolled to his damaged foot, while the other foot bled profusely.

Another chemical bomb flew at him, and Day caught it. He shook it as Marco had—but it didn't need any more mixing and exploded in his clenched fingers, blowing them off as well.

Day grabbed his hand with the healthy one, and fell back, collapsing onto one knee. "You can't do this to me!" he cried as the next explosion fell between his legs, nearly severing the other foot at the ankle.

"Wanna bet?" *I wonder how long I can keep this up before I get bored. I have eight more of these left. His Armani suit is already shredded, and it doesn't look like he can take much more… then again, he will.*

Marco smiled and brought up a large boxcutter. He smiled. "Come and get me."

Day leapt for him.

Marco burst back, just out of Day's right hook. Day swung back, and Marco met the blow just below Day's wrist, stabbing with the boxcutter. With a quick roll of the wrist, Marco broke off a blade from the boxcutter, leaving it in Day's arm, embedded so deep that he couldn't pull it out without tools.

As Day's fist passed him, Marco leapt after the arm. Marco wrapped his left arm around Day's right, holding on for dear life as he stabbed up into Day's armpit, breaking off another blade as he pulled and twisted. As Marco pulled back the boxcutter, he pushed out another blade. He drew it down Day's ribcage, opening up the demon's side like a zipper, all the way to Day's hip. Marco pulled back, stabbed Day in the femoral artery just inside the thigh, twisted the blade, and slashed across the rest of the quadriceps. He twisted it out, leaving the blade behind.

Marco dove to his left, and Day tottered. The bland little man who housed a demon blinked, confused. "Are you getting faster, or am I going slower?"

Marco simply smiled. "Oh, buddy, you have no idea."

"So, what exactly is your plan?" Rory asked. "Can I hope that it involves land mines?"

"Sort of," Marco said. He drew a boxcutter handle from his pocket. "We all know these, right? It's a non-disposable handle that gets refilled with a strip of box-cutter blades."

Bram raised a hand. "So what?"

*Marco grimaced. He wanted to spell this out so he could get the details straight. "The strip of cutters are segmented, so as one becomes blunted, they can be broken off, using a fresh one. Now, with Mister Day's regenerative properties, we know how fast he can heal. What can slow him down?"*

*"Leaving a blade in?" Rory asked.*

*"Holy artifacts?" Father Rodgers suggested.*

*"Anti-coagulants?" Merle Kraft added.*

*"All of the above," Marco said. "I've got several of these boxcutters. I've painted one side of the blade with anti-coagulants, and the other with holy water. If we don't get him with one or the other, he'll still have to heal around the blades I leave in his major muscle groups and blood vessels."*

*Amanda nodded slowly. "Assuming that he doesn't rip your head off when you blink? I went at him full speed and didn't slow him."*

*Marco nodded, appreciating that she asked the sensible question. "Yes. But you activated the protocols in the hospital for a vampire invasion. That got his attention. Slowed him down a bit, maybe?"*

*She nodded. "Yes. But he was still vampire fast."*

*His smile grew a little more. He raised his left arm, showing his wrist, where he had wrapped a rosary. "I know that they're not supposed to be used as jewelry, but I figured God isn't going to object. If holiness slows him down, I hope that it keeps him from tearing my arm off and beating me to death with it."*

*"And you'll be doing this by yourself?"* Amanda asked again.

*Marco shrugged. "On the one hand, he knew Rory was coming. So he knows it'll be a trap if you two are close by. No one ever worries about the small, unimportant human."*

* * *

Day shook his head a few more times, and looked at his right arm, as though wondering what happened.

"What's the matter?" Marco asked. "Does dying not appeal to you?"

In-between blinks, Merle Kraft popped into existence behind Day, and jammed two large syringes into Day's neck, filling him with both holy water and anti-coagulants. Day roared with the sound of a thousand voices in pain.

Marco did the math. *Right leg and arm damaged. Kicks out of the question. He turns to responds to Merle, I stab him in the back.*

*Since he can only respond with his left arm, I stand behind him on the right side. If he tries a rear left elbow, I'm out of range. If he tries a left hook or cross, I'll be out of range before he can reach me.*

As Day screamed in pain, Marco charged. Day whirled around, swinging with his left arm, and Merle wasn't there. That was perfectly timed, as Marco rammed several blades right into Day's kidney.

Marco threw himself straight back, rolling over one shoulder, springing up several feet away.

Day's eyes had gone darker. They were as deep as the dark between stars, and almost fragmented, and insectoid.

"You will regret–"

There were several metallic streaks slapping into Day's back and breaking up his dialogue.

*Amanda did not look impressed. "Do you expect Day to bleed to death?"*

*Marco shook his head. "I'm crazy. Not stupid. I'm not the trap, I'm the bait. When I have him engaged and securely in the fight, that's when the rest of you come in. You all hit him with everything we have. This includes arrows with the holy water/anti-coagulant mix and throwing Stars of David."*

*Bram smirked. "You want I should blow his head off from two klicks out?"*

*Marco shrugged. "If you can, knock yourself out. In fact, that would be great. Pardon me if I don't rely on it, though.*

*He's a demon, and if we trash his body, that's nice, but does anyone really want to rely on that alone?"*

*Rodgers leaned forward on his chair. "Marco. I need to be close enough for a full combat exorcism. The way you describe your kill box, I won't get close." He pointed at Marco with his lit cigar. "And you'll already be far* too *close."*

*"That's when things are going to get tricky. And when everyone else is going to come in and save my behind."*

The throwing stars of David came out like machine-gun fire, the really fast ones obviously coming from Amanda. One of the stars slammed into Day's spine, and the demon's legs fell out from under him.

*Bram will be so disappointed,* Marco thought. *He never even got a chance to blow Day's head off.*

Day's intact hand reached back and grabbed the star, and pulled it out. There was the sound of sizzling, but he didn't even mind.

*Makes sense, a choice between a little pain or death.*

Day took several deep, hyperventilation-speed breaths, and let out another Godzilla roar. With his left arm, he pushed off the ground to standing up straight, and spun on his "good" leg.

Marco dropped to the ground, face first. The centrifugal force hurled the Stars of David from his back, as well as several arrows and razors, sending them shooting out like bullets. There were several screams, two of them female.

Day slowed to a stop, and he staggered like a drunk, trying to maintain his balance. The demon gave a full grin, revealing suddenly sharp teeth. His body was covered in blood, but his wounds were already healing. Even his fingers were starting to grow back.

"You can't stop me," he bellowed. The voice sounded less human, and more like it had been run through a distorter or had rumbled from deep inside Day's stomach.

That was the point where the giant Irish wolfhound jumped on his arm, biting for Day's face. The demon staggered back, and delivered a quick uppercut with the partially blown-off hand, and swatted away with the other.

Marco saw the lycanthrope pass overhead, and hoped that George would heal.

Marco scrambled to his feet, charging Day head on, two fresh boxcutters in hand.

Day grinned and braced himself.

Then Marco dropped to one knee. There was the *crack* of a rifle, and Day's head snapped back. The demon took a single step back, and then doubled over, as though he was vomiting, but a .50-caliber bullet came out of his forehead.

Marco drew down and tossed two tubes on either side of Day, knocking him around in time for Marco to throw himself shoulder-first into his stomach.

They rolled on the ground before Marco showed the good sense to leap off. Day sprang to his feet and swung casually, as though Catalano was more of an annoyance than anything else, now that it was hand-to-hand. Marco dropped him with an unprofessional kick between the legs and leapt back again. Day doubled over in pain and received the gift of two more test tubes at his feet, breaking legs and feet and other parts.

But the chemicals released into Day's bloodstream had already worn off. His insectoid eyes glowed and he smiled manically. He stepped forward, ready to kill, when a bottle of acid broke against his head. He cringed, gasping as Rory followed up his attack with a broadsword through his chest.

"Die, you focker! Die!" His roar was almost as inhuman as Day's. Day pushed him away again with all his strength and sent Rory on another flying trip.

Marco smiled weakly. "Do you really want to give him so many frequent-flier miles?"

Day smiled and rushed forward, taking his time, comparatively, and brushed Marco aside, smacking him against a marble slab. Marco sunk to his knees as Day stood over him. The student looked up at him through cloudy eyes, waiting for night to finally overtake him.

Amanda had followed orders. She didn't like leaving Marco out in the cold at the cemetery, but his plan had relied solely on being underestimated.

She watched from her position in the trees as Marco and the demon danced around one another in the dark. Chemistry being used at its finest, in a combination of a close-quarters combat with chemical warfare.

Until Marco started losing.

Amanda's heart started pounding as though she were once again on her run from the airport. She pounced, growling as she leapt for Day.

The demon disappeared from the view of normal people as a streak of golden-red hair slammed him away.

Amanda's teeth drove straight into Day's neck. Her jaws clamped around his throat while her arms were clamped around his arms and upper body in a bear hug. She had already fed that day, but this was… something else. The blood flowed into her mouth, and did not taste like copper, but like honey.

Every time she ate, she became stronger and faster, and all around more alive. This was something completely different—this was to normal blood as a soft drink was to centuries-old scotch. It tasted like nothing so much as pure energy. She had never felt anything like it.

Her arms locked around him tighter as she sucked the blood from him with new vigor. At least a pint had flowed into her body, and she wanted more.

Day didn't even bother fighting her growing strength. Instead, he curled his forearms against his belly, then exploded them outward, hurling Amanda against a mausoleum so hard the stone broke. However, when Amanda went flying, her teeth held fast in his arteries, and she took parts of his throat with her.

The Armani was so bloodied, the shirt and tie were one massive red stain. Day gurgled a little as the skin formed back around his veins. He coughed and spat out a wad of blood, then straightened, studying the vampire.

Day's fire-eyes narrowed. "Amanda," he croaked. He coughed, holding his throat. "I wondered how he had become such a troublemaker. It's you again," he drawled with disdain. "You didn't die."

Amanda smiled as she rolled to her feet. "Of course, Asmodeus." Amanda licked her lips clean, leaving a slight red smudge on her upper lip.

Day smirked. The fiery gaze locked onto her. "Come, Amanda Colt, we should finish this, you and I."

A roundhouse kick to the back of Day's head slammed him face first into a tombstone.

Merle Kraft smiled. "Sounds like a plan to me."

Day snarled and whirled around with a backhand for Merle's head… and he struck thin air. Between blinks, Merle had gone from being behind Day to being perched on top of a tall stone angel. Day charged for it, crashing through the marble, and Merle vanished again.

Day looked around, wondering where Kraft had gone. Even if he had fallen into the dust and rubble, he couldn't have gotten far.

Day's legs were swept out from under him, and Merle leapt away before the demon even hit the ground—or, more precisely, before the demon fell onto two marble spikes sticking out of the ground, left after Day had charged through the stone angel.

Day rolled off, the damage healing as though it never was.

Amanda slid into place on the opposite side of Day, her amber eyes glowing. "Do you think that you can deal with the two of us?"

Day grinned, and leapt straight up, grabbing a tree branch above his head. With a quick pull, he broke it off, and held it as effortlessly as though it were a baseball bat… but carried it like a spear.

Day thrust for Amanda, and she stepped toward it, taking a long, diagonal step with her left foot, and grabbed the makeshift spear with her left palm, redirecting it. The palm of her right hand crashed into his nose, driving the cartilage into his brain. He was stunned for only a moment, then tightened his hold on the branch, and twisted, snapping it in half.

"I'm still carrying wood," Day grinned.

Amanda shook her head, tossing the piece of the branch away. "And I always thought you were classier than that."

Day charged…

And then, tripped over Merle Kraft.

A blur swooped in, driving a punch straight up, into and through where Day was. Amanda was the blur, snapping Day's head back and forth at a speed that Marco had never seen her move before.

Day twisted to one side, deflecting one of her blows, then had own flurry. A right palm to her face, a double blow to her ribs, and a grab to her throat, it was clear that Day was recovering.

Marco blinked. Still on the ground. *Can't have that. He can't recover.* "Hey, Asmodeus, can't take the lowly human?"

*Let go of Amanda. Focus on me. You came here for me. Come on.*

He rose to his feet, his smile still on his face. "Come on. Weren't you sent here as a hit man? You want me, you can come and get me, you little twit."

Day smiled. "I came to hurt you." His eyes flicked to one side, the razor-sharp grin returned, pulled back, and threw Amanda straight for a tree.

The last of Amanda that Marco Catalano had seen was her body slamming against a tree branch that had been splintered by one of the projectile Stars of David.

Amanda had disappeared so fast, Marco didn't even have a chance to even *think* "Good bye."

# Chapter 21:

# Asmodeus Ex Machina

Marco stared blankly for a long moment. Amanda was dead.

Amanda. Was dead.

That was that. Day would die.

Marco's smile was unwavering. He reached into his pocket and pulled out a chain with a bob at the end of it. He gently swung it around, casual, calm, and easy.

"I'm going to kill you now, Asmodeus." He swung the bob into his hand. "I'm going to strangle you. With this pocket watch."

Day arched a brow. "Really?" He raised his right hand, where the fingers had mostly regrown, muscles still exposed. In the blink of an eye, the bob was out of Marco's hand, and in Day's. It looked like he hadn't moved.

"I'm back to full power, Marco," Day boasted. "There is nothing that anyone can do can stop me."

Then Day pumped his hand once, crushing the bob. He stopped, becoming stiff. The blood drained from his face in terror.

Day gasped. "No."

Marco smiled. "The power of Christ compels you, bitch."

*"A pyx," Marco began, "for the non-Catholics amongst us, is a container for the consecrated host from the Eucharist. Eucharistic ministers carry these to administer the Eucharist to the sick and bedridden who can't come to church on Sundays."*

*"And what does that do?" Yana asked.*

*"The consecrated host?" Amanda asked her. "The body of Jesus in the guise of bread?"*

*Yana blinked. "I have no idea what you mean."*

*Amanda rolled her eyes. "You know, if you're going to claim you're 'multicultural,' you should learn about a few cultures."*

Day's hand crushed the pyx and stopped dead. He didn't blink, he didn't move, he even stopped breathing. His hand couldn't open, and even started turning black and necrotic. His veins turned black, racing down his arm like the most virulent infection ever.

Then, suddenly, with a full roar, Day reached with his good hand, and grabbed the rapidly-dying shoulder. The grip alone tore the material. With another Godzilla-like roar, Day ripped his own arm off and hurled it away.

Day fell to his knees and his hand. His blood gushed from his shoulder.

In the back of Marco's head, a switch was thrown. Like at the cemeteries he had raided not 24 hours ago, the tune for *March of Cambreadth* rang in his head.

Marco moved like a robot moved for Day. Marco stomped down on his skull. The ankle came down on the spot right behind the ear. He did it again, hitting the other ear.

Day tried to rise. Marco slammed his foot sideways into Day's knee, breaking it at an odd angle.

A punch to the kidney, then knuckles into the small of his back, paralyzing Day for moments. The acid burns on his head still hadn't healed, and they wouldn't—it was damage on the molecular level.

*I love being right,* Marco thought, as he bellowed, "Now!"

He drove two mixed test tubes into Day's pocket and shoved him away.

Day staggered backwards as one of the Vatican Ninjas came in on a motorcycle. The Ninja leapt off the vehicle. It slid along the ground, cutting the feet out from under Day. The test tubes exploded, ruining the pockets of the jacket and causing damage to the thing's torso. Day and the bike slid together, one dragging the other.

Marco stood to one side as the motorcycle slid by him, and whipped out a set of handcuffs from his pocket. He righted the motorcycle and quickly cuffed Day's ankles to the seat of the bike. He drove off without another word, dragging Day behind.

Marco drove straight for the docks, Day being dragged along the way.

The demon simply glanced at Marco's back, and smiled to itself. As Day bounced off the asphalt, all of his other wounds were healing. Even his arm was growing back. Slowly. Impact against concrete wasn't going to harm him any, so he let himself be dragged by the back of the motorcycle…

Because, after all, Marco had to stop sometime.

Marco didn't even think about it as he pointed the motorcycle at the docks.

He drove straight for a pier.

With the engine at full speed, he jumped off the motorcycle and into the water. The bike left the wooden planks, soaring through the air and straight down, into the water, on top of Day. With a breath, Marco dove down after him.

Day shoved the vehicle off of him easily and moved as fast as though he were above ground. Marco slammed a foot behind Day's ear, then fell onto him, driving an elbow into his solar plexus, driving the air from his lungs. Most people would be paralyzed for minutes, but that would only be seconds for Day.

Marco swam away as Day recovered.

The demon smiled as his body automatically strove for breath.

Day's eyes widened in shock as he realized he had automatically taken a lungful of seawater. Marco smiled.

Even monsters needed to breathe.

Marco moved back for Day as the demon struggled frantically with the handcuffs, momentarily forgetting his own strength. Day spared the human only a glance and punched at him, even though Marco was yards away—but the motion sent a fist of water at Marco, pushing him to the surface as Day broke the handcuffs.

The student had made it to the dock by the time Day had figured out that he needed to drop the suit and wing-tipped shoes so he could surface.

Marco glared at the water and waited for the demon to come after him. The body that hosted Asmodeus would die if he didn't get oxygen within five minutes, and not even he could resurrect himself from the dead. Unless the demon jumped bodies, he would be trapped in a brain dead shell, and Day would be the ghost.

Day surfaced and climbed onto the dock, trying to fill his lungs with air. He looked at Marco and charged, making no sounds with his open mouth. Marco smiled, bent one leg and swept Day's legs out from under him.

Marco used another test tube to blow a hole in the dock beneath Day. The demon fell through, but Marco wasn't ready to stop just yet. He turned to where the dock met the mainland. And there was Merle, as planned, with a large tank in front of him, on the ground like a missile.

Merle smiled, looking behind Marco as Day came through the wooden planks, raging, dying. Day ripped a board from the dock and rammed it through his chest, letting a hole in his lungs to release the water trapped there.

Merle looked at Marco. "I think it's time for us to leave, don't you think?"

The two of them broke out into a run.

Farther down the dock, Ibrahim the sniper aimed down his handgun at the release valve of the pressurized tank with the gun… then fired. When his bullet hit the nozzle, the tank shot off with the force of a rocket, slamming into Day…

The demon caught it, plucking it from midair like a bouquet of flowers.

Day held it in his hands, shooting Merle and Marco a look of contempt.

"Pressurized air?" he snarled with what little breath he had already regained and slammed his fist into the tank.

As he destroyed the final weapon, Marco remembered explaining this to the gang after it had arrived.

*"Where did this come from?" Rory asked, wondering why it was in the Artful Krafts.*

*"Amanda secured it for me," Marco explained.*

*"And what is it, a cruise missile?" Tara asked.*

*"An oxygen tank?" Merle inquired.*

*Tiffany: "A phallic symbol?"*

*Marco smiled and plucked a rose from the vase on the table, sliding it behind Amanda's ear. "Hold on to that for me, will you, love?"*

*Marco rolled the tank to the table and let some of the contents pour into a plastic cup. He took the flower from behind Amanda's ear and slid the open petals down her cheek, wishing it was his hand.*

*"Has anyone ever seen Terminator 2?"*

*Marco then dipped the rose into the cup, pulled it out, and then shattered it against the table as it exploded like glass.*

*"Liquid nitrogen."*

Day drove his fist into the tank of liquid nitrogen, and it exploded like the oxygen tank in *Jaws*, spraying him with the chemical over four hundred degrees below zero.

Marco stopped at the explosion and turned, facing the fog of gas. If his plan had worked, if Day had been pissed off enough, and aggravated enough, to crush the pressurized liquid nitrogen without thinking, and if the demon had been affected, there would be no reason to run.

*And if it didn't work, there'd be nowhere to run.*

Marco waited, staring at the cloud.

Marco and Merle looked at the dock once more. The water beneath it had iced over, and the dock looked like it had been dusted with a light frost.

The gas dissipated, revealing the demon known as Day.

He had been completely covered in the liquid nitrogen, freezing him like a statue.

Marco and Merle exchanged a glance, astonished smiles frozen on their faces. "It worked."

Marco carefully walked up to the dock and looked into Day's eyes. They were still alive and aware, even behind the ice. The PA student spoke to him softly and evenly, never letting his voice above a whisper.

"You, sir, attacked *my* city. You murdered my only friend. My only love. It's time for you do die. Your body is frozen to your core and your metabolism. You're dead, and you don't know it yet."

Marco looked down the pier. Rodgers had not yet been allowed near Day. There wouldn't be an exorcism just yet. He looked out a knife—a real one, not wood or a boxcutter—and he hacked away at Day's right shoulder, smashing the arm off. It shattered against the pier. He then stabbed into the open wound, making a little pocket. Marco pulled out another pyx. He slid away the knife, and carefully took out a host. He gently pressed the wafer into the wound.

"That should keep you still for a while. In case you wondered about all of those test tubes, glycerin, plus nitric and sulfuric acids equal nitroglycerin, which equals boom. Now go back to Hell." He stopped thirty feet away from him with the rest of the team, standing next to Rory and Merle, who was shooting Day with a camera. Marco didn't think to inquire.

Marco turned his back on the demon, content to let the bastard burn… or explode… or whatever movie special effect might happen when you shoved a host into a demon.

Then he heard the first *crack*. It sounded like a tree suddenly snapped in two. Marco looked over his shoulder. The frozen Day had fractured at the torso, just under the breastbone, cracking up to the left shoulder …

Meaning the lower part of Day's body that weren't connected to the parts touching the hosts.

*Oh crap.*

The upper part of Day's body was cast aside as the lower half exploded, with a giant arm shooting out and grabbing Marco. The thick fingers were like telephone poles as they wrapped around his arms and torso. The hand seemed impossibly large to have come from something as small as what was left of Day …

Except, instead of the human-looking form, this was a great black ball of mass. It began to unfurl itself, growing as it did so. First the outer layer of the ball spread out, revealing two great black wings that spread out the length of the pier. Then came the neck and the giant head, armored and shiningly black all the way down.

As it grew, the water level dropped—matter upon which a demon could build a body in the physical realm.

Marco looked up and up… and up some more, peering at the unbridled majesty and terror of a fully-unleashed demon named Asmodeus.

*Of course he'd turn into a five-story dragon. Because, you know, that's just the way my luck runs. Anything that can go wrong… damn you, Murphy, I hate you.*

Asmodeus raised Marco to eye level. It would be nice if the eyes were dead and lifeless, like if it were the end of *Sleeping Beauty*—the original animated version, not the terrible live-action re-write. But no, the eyes were very much alive, like jade that glowed.

For some reason, Marco recalled, that he had seen eyes like that once at an aquarium, in the shark tank.

Marco looked down at the hand gripping him and frowned. "If you want to crush me, what are you waiting for?"

The dragon's mouth opened a little and bore teeth in a razor-sharp grin. Asmodeus stared straight at him. "So, now what, Marco Catalano? What will you do without your love? Without your Amanda? What will you be *able* to do?" The grin became wider. "I've seen your heart, and I know what's in it. I know what darkness is in your depths. You cannot hide it from me, Marco Catalano. You can hide nothing from me. Your soul is bare for me to see. The evil. The depravity. The thirst for death and destruction. Your soul shall be mine.

"But first, I want you, little man. You want to fight evil with evil, then you get evil. You get me.

"You get to be my new host."

Marco grimaced. *Oh nuts.*

*Sorry, God, hadn't expected that twist. While I generally like to rely on the gifts You gave me, and not ask for Divine intervention, I won't object to a little here. Could You help me out a little here? Like killing me before that happens? A nice little lightning bolt to fry my synapses would be appreciated. Pretty please?*

The dragon stared at Marco long and hard. Marco heard the noises below. There was the chatter of gunfire below. If Asmodeus noticed, the dragon showed no sign.

"So?" Marco asked defiantly. "What are you waiting for?" *Seriously, God, what are you waiting for? I have no problem dying. Right now. This minute. I can hopefully join Amanda in Heaven, and not be host to a freaking demon.*

The dragon cocked its head to one side. "I cannot enter your body," it rumbled. "You cannot be possessed."

Marco wondered. *Really? I scared a freaking vampire out of my head with what's in there. Yet this guy can't possess me? Huh. Too evil for a vampire, too good for a demon? Did I miss a memo?*

Asmodeus the dragon grinned again. "No matter. If I cannot have your body, and I am forced to leave this plane," Asmodeus put his thumb against Marco's chest, "I'll merely have to kill you."

Marco looked at the finger pressing against his body, and he wondered if Asmodeus possessed retractable claws that were going to punch a hole in his torso, or if he was just going to pop Marco's head off like a zit.

*Looks like a closed-casket funeral for me. At least I'm not possessed. Thanks, God. We can talk together in a minute.*

Marco's prayer was interrupted by the sound of stone breaking.

Even Asmodeus looked off to the side. "What was—"

Something blurred between Marco and Asmodeus. It cut right in front of Marco's eyes, smashing through the dragon's wrist, and into Asmodeus' face. The dragon's head rocked back. Marco felt his stomach lurch as he began a five-story drop.

Marco's eyes were stuck open. He didn't want to miss a thing—and he wouldn't even see the concrete rushing up to meet him. He had this sudden urge to try a fall break, and instinctively spread his arms to absorb the impact.

Marco landed on his side, which is where the knuckles of the dragon's hand were. At the moment of impact, the hand around him rippled and fluxed, and absorbed the impact like it was water.

It helped that the hand turned to water, reverting back to the matter from which it came.

Marco laid on his back for a long moment, looking up at the sky, blinking. *Okay. That makes sense. A demon is like an angel, all form, no matter. It needs to co-opt matter to become physical, and if you sever the physical, it reverts to its original form. But what severed it in the first place?*

The next blur sliced through the demon's other arm, taking it off at the shoulder. It turned to water before it even landed.

Asmodeus roared in pain, his arm, wings and head thrashing about, as though he were trying to swat something. Someone touched Marco on the shoulder. "Need a hand?"

Marco looked up. The newcomer was… vague. At first glance, Marco thought that he was looking at a young Pierce Brosnan, with less-defined features. The closer he looked at his savior, though, the more it looked like the man was cut out of rock.

"Who the Hell are you?"

"Not quite Hell." The voice was light and musical and…

*Angelic?* "No," Marco said, "seriously, who are you?"

"Da'ni'el." He reached down and grabbed Marco by the arm, and hauled him up, one-handed. "Guardian angel."

Marco arched one brow. "My guardian angel is a guy named Daniel?"

The angel's eyebrow arched. "Da'ni'el."

"Right." He looked back to the dragon. "What about Asmodeus?"

"One second." The angel walked down the pier, then looked up at the dragon. "Asmodeus. You should know better than to crawl onto the natural world without a host. You should have grabbed someone more reliable than my human. It's decidedly unhealthy for you."

Asmodeus' head whipped around and snapped for Da'ni'el. The angel leapt back, swatting it on the nose. "Bad dragon, no cookie."

Marco looked at the… angel… and said, "Really? You're stealing my lines now?"

The angel looked at him and shrugged. "You're my human. Where else would I learn smack talk?" He glanced back to Asmodeus. "You, go back to Hell."

"You think you can stop me?" Asmodeus growled. "I am older than humanity. I have been on this Earth for longer than you have been—"

The angel was a blur again, this time punching through the dragon's teeth, then out the back of its head, causing the entire body to explode into a giant spray of water.

The angel popped up next to Marco again, making Marco flinch. "You made that look easy."

Da'ni'el shrugged. "Actually, you did the hard work. Fighting a demon is hard enough without supernatural backup. Let's face it, you got lucky. Well, sort of. It's complicated."

Marco's eyes narrowed. "Complicated?" He took two steps forward, coming nose-to-nose with his angel. "Amanda is *dead*, and you want to talk *complicated*? Where the Hell were you back when I could have used you? Better yet, when *she* could have used you?"

Da'ni'el looked… tolerant. "Walk with me."

# Chapter 22:

# Talk With An Angel

When Marco and Da'ni'el thought they were far enough away from the scene of the crime, the angel began, "While I've got you here for the moment, there are a few things we need to discuss."

Marco's eyes narrowed. "I can come up with a list. What did you have in mind?"

Da'ni'el looked completely unaffected by Marco's hostility. "Well, first of all, do I have to explain why Asmodeus couldn't possess you?"

"Going by *the book* of *The Exorcist*, I figured it had to do with the fact that I play with no occult toys whatsoever. I don't do Ouija boards, or anything like that." Marco shrugged. "Don't play with otherworldly crap, otherworldly crap doesn't play with you."

Da'ni'el nodded. "After a fashion. Also, you're nowhere near as bad as you think you are. Other angels tell me that their humans think they're perfect. I have the exact opposite problem with you."

Marco frowned. "I enjoy killing people. I've done it enough."

"Most of who you've killed are vampires. A lot of vampires. You enjoy thinking you're a monstrous killing machine. Have you ever considered that you're just a soldier who merely enjoys his job? Churchill and Washington were never considered sociopaths, and they had the same feelings about war than you do."

Marco rolled his eyes. "Don't start with me, buddy. I've used that line on Rodgers. You can't honestly be telling me to go forth and kill a few more bad guys?"

Da'ni'el rolled *his* eyes. "I'm telling you that you're not as bad as you think. Pride is when you give yourself too much credit. Trust me, thinking you're the worst human being to ever walk the Earth? Too much credit. *Way* too much credit."

Marco took a slow, deep breath. "I'll file that away for later. Though if you want to talk to me about something in particular, how about you tell me why you couldn't come and save my sorry ass earlier. Better yet, why you couldn't save Amanda's much nicer ass."

"Until Asmodeus slipped his human suit, he was just a possessed human being," Da'ni'el explained. "It still counted under human-on-human violence.

The best I could have done was my usual job. Some of your luck tonight was planning. Some of it was me. When Asmodeus tried to use direct action against you as a demon, that's when I could intervene."

Marco sighed. "Makes a certain amount of sense. It's why we don't see angels flying around like superheroes. Though that would be sort of cool." He nodded at his angel. "Where'd you get the material for *your* human suit?"

Da'ni'el shook his head. "It's not a human suit. Asmodeus had a real human he had possessed centuries ago. My current physical form I took from surrounding materials. Right now, there's a human-shaped chunk out of a stone wall nearby."

"Riiiight." Marco stopped and stared. He wanted to knock the angel's head off, but his better judgment made him choose against it. Not only did he have no chance against someone who was probably by design plugged into his head, the angel was *made from rock*. "It makes sense. All of it does. But Amanda is a price I wasn't willing to pay. My life is one thing, hers—"

"Is hers to do with what she wants. You both choose to stand between the darkness and everyone else on the planet. Sometimes, you die. Welcome to being a soldier."

Marco frowned. "You're really annoying, you know that?"

"All I'm doing is quoting a different part of your brain than you active use." Da'ni'el gave Marco a familiar little smile. "You can play three dimensional chess, and conversational chess. You know where this is going to go as well as I do. I don't have to work very hard. Who knows what evil lurks in the hearts of men? No idea. But I know yours. Your evils are slightly different than what you're thinking of."

"Oh really?" Marco drawled. "How exactly did I drive out Mikhail the Bear from my brain? He freaked out and nearly self-destructed, I scared him so badly."

Da'ni'el smirked. "To start with, Mikhail was essentially a Commodore 64 trying to sync with a supercomputer. Calling them incompatible is a drastic understatement. You know how Chesterton said that a mind like Martin Luther's would be lost on the map of a mind like Saint Thomas Aquinas? Same thing, only this was literal."

Marco shook his head. "Not possible. I know that slowed him down. It slowed him down a lot. But something jumped out at him and savaged him. I saw it, in my head."

"Oh. That?" The angel waved it away. "You spend half of your time either angry or in prayer. You think that doesn't make a difference? There is holiness in you. Mikhail could not have savaged your mind any more than Asmodeus could possess you. Look, I'm not going to say you're bucking for sainthood. There are better people than you. There are also much, much worse people than you. You're going to be fighting them. A lot."

"You can see the future now?"

The angel gave him a familiar cynical look. "Are you telling me that *you* can't see them coming from here?"

Marco nodded. "Point taken."

Da'ni'el looked off to one side, obviously thinking. "I'm going down the list of the various and sundry things that I want to talk with you about, and that I *can* talk with you about."

He grabbed his angel by the arm and pulled him up against a building. "You should know the state of my soul more than anybody. So I want to know about that guy I killed."

Da'ni'el rolled his eyes. "Killing someone doesn't change a lot of people. You can't really *make* a sociopath. You really can't. You can make people crazy, but most people who are monsters *choose* to be monsters, even the sociopaths. More often than not, killing someone just shows people what's inside. It tells you more about yourself, that's all. Your reaction to that knowledge, *that* changes you more than anything else. You enjoyed *killing* someone, not murdering him. You didn't seek out the engagement, and you haven't made a habit of slaughter.

"Like I said, you're a soldier in a war where evil cannot be stopped without lethal force. You were prepared early for a war that would come with or without you."

"Prepared? Does that include 9/11?"

Da'ni'el sighed. "I tried to spare you that one. You had a flat tire on your outing that day? My doing. The nail technically should have only barely touched the tire. I pushed it in. Your father was faster with the spare than I thought he would be. The full impact of 9/11 would have sunk in over time if you were watching at home on television. Live? That was a different story."

He looked off to one side, as though checking a clock. "Time's up. I don't have any good excuse to stay, and we're about to have company."

Marco looked back at Merle and Tiffany and the Ninjas who had followed him, and were busy wrapping up back at the dock. "They've already seen you."

Da'ni'el smiled. "You'd be surprised."

"Pretty mess you made," a voice stated.

Marco whirled and stared with wide eyes for a split second before lifting up Amanda Colt, crushing her to his chest as her feet dangled off the ground.

"I thought I'd lost you," he whispered without thinking.

"I'm fine," Amanda told him, once he put her down. "Of course I'm alive. I became mist before I hit. He really wasn't that smart."

They looked at each other for a long moment. Then grinned, and then grabbed each other in a firm embrace. "It worked!"

Marco buried his face in Amanda's neck, and just breathed her in as the tension flowed out of him. Everything that normal people would have felt just drained out of him, all of the terror he had kept locked away and contained, compartmentalized until it was dead. The relief flooded through him like a shower, washing him away from the top down, flushing all the terror from him in one wipe.

As subtle and as casually as possible, he kissed her neck as easily as he'd kiss her cheek.

Marco looked over Amanda's shoulder. "What happened to you?"

Yana limped alongside Ibrahim, the ninjas' sniper. She looked like she was bleeding from the arm and the leg. "Day threw the pointy things back at us," Yana said. "Amanda jumped me… I kinda hit my head." She stared at Marco. "Are you 'kay?"

He blinked away a tear. "Of course."

"You looked like you were crying."

"I can't cry," he stated obnoxiously.

They all knew better, but she wouldn't contradict him here. "Let's go home."

Tara slid up to Yana's side and slid an arm around her waist, and the two women went home together. He looked after them, thinking *Freaking San Francisco.*

George had his cell phone open, already telling Tiffany where to pick him up. Merle was, well, Merle, so he'd already vanished. Marco was left with Rory and Amanda on the dock.

"You know, you're not too bad for a WOP bastard," Rory told him. He lit a cigarette. "You know, I never did tell you the name I was born with, did I?"

Marco looked at Amanda, who only shrugged. He sighed and looked back to the Irish vampire. "No,

Rory, you didn't mention it. Why, should I know you?"

"Only if you know Irish history," he murmured. "I don't actually match any photos, I made modifications, lest I scare the bejesus out of anyone after I died."

The New Yorker raised a brow. "Your death by vampirism was a public event?"

Rory inhaled, then, shook his head. "No. I was machine-gunned the night after I died—and it was a full audience, and someone else was taken out with me."

Marco blinked. Rory said he was an early 20th-century vampire. Add an Irish brogue, that made him one of the original Irish Republican Army. "Which one of the hard men were ya, laddie?"

"Ever hear of Shawn Treacy?"

Marco concentrated. "I have."

Shawn Treacy was the Irish rebel equivalent of John Dillinger, quick on the trigger and heavy on the bullets. He was the first one to shed blood after the Irish Republic declared independence in 1919. He and his friend Dan Breen had cut a bloody path through the Irish countryside. Until, one night, Treacy had been engaged by a British Army contingent, and he went hand-to-hand. He was winning until the others stepped back and machine-gunned Treacy and the British soldier he—

The face and the body didn't match what photos Marco had seen of Treacy, more like photos of Barry Fitzgerald. But considering all the things that vampires could do with their bodies, that shouldn't have surprised him.

"So you really are a cold-blooded butcher of the first caliber—thirty-eight caliber, to be more precise. Well, I know why you don't react well to crosses—you're not exactly a saint, are you?"

Rory—Shawn Treacy—narrowed his eyes and took a step toward him. Before he could take a second step, Amanda took another step closer to Marco's side. He glanced at the two of them, waved, turned around and left.

Marco smiled. "Thanks. I wasn't in the mood tonight for tussling with him."

"Understood." She patted him on the back, then, slid her hand up to his shoulder. "You're wet."

He chuckled and put his hand on top of hers, making sure she didn't move it. He had to look up whether or not death contributed to the smoothness and softness of someone's skin. He doubted it. "Better than the alternative." He looked to her. "Will you be staying long?"

Amanda looked at him… strangely, was the only word he had for it, as though she were searching for something in his eyes. "I can stay longer, if you want me to."

He smiled. "I'd like that… and if I time it right, our sleep patterns will match up." He slid his other arm around her back, hugging her to him by the waist. They started walking towards his dorm. "So, what are you going to do when you go back to New York?"

Amanda paused for a long moment. Too long. "Research Day." She looked at him. "You get into such trouble, Marco. I want to know how."

"You mean my sparkling personality isn't enough of an explanation?"

"Not this time. You have somehow managed to attract a demon on par with armies."

He shrugged. "And we still wiped the floor with him. Color me impressed when we get our asses handed to us, or if we lose people… which would pretty much be the same thing."

She wrapped an arm around his waist and pulled him against her side. He didn't try pulling away. "I just hope you are not the death of me."

Marco snorted. "Funny, I didn't know I looked like a giant piece of wood."

She laughed, then reached up and kissed him on the cheek. "I would not even take that opening."

He gave her a wicked smile. "Aw, pity."

# Chapter 23:

# Coming Home

Amanda walked Marco back to his dorm, and she was starting to regret the idea. They talked congenially, nothing more than friends…

And she was starting to think she was an awful actor.

Certainly, almost one of her kind could pick up exactly what she was sensing. They could hear Marco's heartbeat pulsing mellowly along. They could catch the faint hint of sweat, a light musk mixed with Ivory soap and Pert Plus shampoo, and especially the tinge of blood from the cuts where Day had struck him.

But any vampire older than a week undead would have been able to ignore every last bit of sensory input, otherwise they would all have to smoke like a Bristol chimney just to block out all the data in an urban environment. Hundreds of years ago, that kind of mental control was necessary, but the progress of years had made it even more so. There were millions of intrusive sounds and scents—cars, trucks, food, garbage, EM-waves from electronics, thousands of people crammed into high-density areas like Bombay… or New Jersey… with natural and chemical scents. Without an ability to cut off that data and focus on others, a vampire would be driven mad.

Amanda was a hundred years old, and a vampire for over eighty years, and perfectly sane, and could cut off anything from overwhelming her…

Except Marco.

Amanda had not noticed until he had left New York. She knew where he was every second of every day… but that could be explained by cell phone communication…

She knew what mood he was in by his scent… but that could be explained because they were very well tuned to each other…

And, now, after only a few weeks of being apart from him, she was being driven crazy by the amount of data he was throwing off… and she couldn't block him out.

As they walked down the hall to Marco's dorm room, she became very, very aware that she only wore the cheongsam that she had acquired from Jennifer Bosley. The skirt was short; she had no bra, and no underwear.

And she was going to Marco's private dorm room, just the two of them.

"By the way, how'd you get the clearance?"

Amanda started, looking at Marco as though he had suddenly appeared. "What do you mean?"

He gave a casual shrug. "Standard government protocols after a terrorist attack is to ground all flights and make the entire country a no-fly zone. But you wrangled clearance for two planes today. The commandos and the jet Bosley sent you. How'd you pull off that trick?"

It was just that simple. He was just curious. It wasn't a big deal, just a cute trick she'd managed. He didn't accuse her of keeping a secret or of being anything other than she was. It was odd.

"You don't sound upset," she stated.

Marco furrowed his brow and bunched up one side of his mouth in a frown. He stared off to one side with the intensity and focus of a supercomputer geared to one problem. "Why would I be? You're easily four times my age, and I presume that you have a long bio. You haven't exactly written it down, so what should I have a problem with?"

Amanda gave him a little smile. "I keep forgetting you're different from other people."

His smile turned into a grin. He stepped in front of her, dramatically wrapped her arm around her waist, put his lips next to her ear, and said, in a voice four octaves lower than usual, "Oh darling, you have *no* idea."

Amanda's breath caught. Her knees went weak, and parts of her lurched in ways that were completely unfamiliar to her. She caught herself on his chest. He gripped her arms.

"Are you okay?" he asked, worried.

She trembled in his grasp. "I - I should go back to New York. I've been giving the gang members personal treatment."

"How so?"

"I've been biting them… lightly, of course. I haven't been drinking, but—"

Marco nodded. "I get it. From what you described to me, they were lucky to stay alive. If you're the only thing really keeping them in one piece, then, by all means…"

Marco's face hadn't changed, but his scent had. Maybe she was imagining it, but it was possible that he was as lonely here as she was in New York …

The idea that he was in love with her, though, didn't even enter Amanda's mind. After all, she was a vampire. He was a human. And that was that.

Marco nodded slowly, unlocked his door. "Maybe you could at least stay around for a quick bi—?" He glanced over his shoulder again… and discovered her gone.

He stepped into the dorm room and closed the door behind him.

Marco Catalano slumped against the door, closed his eyes, and sighed.

He never did find out if she was wearing underwear.

Merlin Kraft went home to his little shop in San Francisco and sent the photo of Day to his employers of unknown name, and had them run facial recognition software.

The first stop was something simple and basic… on AOL news.

There was a photo of the explosion from the second World Trade Center building, where a giant face formed in the flames.

And it looked a little like Day.

The next hit came from the security videos of the United Nations building.

Day was a regular, almost weekly, visitor to the Secretary General of the UN. Merle swore he heard Dalf's malevolent chuckle echo in his mind.

Merlin narrowed his eyes and scowled. He reached over to his secure phone, when it rang. He paused. Clairvoyance had never been his strong suit, but now… "Hello?"

The general he had spoken to the day before didn't even bother introducing himself. "Merle, we've something that's right up your alley, and we need you on point in Afghanistan. Satellite imagery shows us two improbable scans. On thermal, we see nothing, but in optical, we have moving human beings."

*Hardly human… I can at least tell Kristen that I really am going to be hunting these bastards.* Merle was about to reply when a firm pounding on the front door reached him.

It had to be George Berkeley; no one else matched that knock. "One moment, General."

Merle moved to the door. George immediately said, "I want to kill them."

This was new. "Anyone in particular?"

George's hulking frame heaved with his enraged breathing. "The terrorists."

Merle looked George over. He was big, strong, experienced and motivated. And Merle was about to head in-country against vampires. It was a perfect match.

Merle raised the phone to his mouth and said, "General, I'll need to bring someone with me."

By September 14th, things had gotten back to something resembling normal. There were even some flights here and there throughout the country. Her son could finally be allowed back in school, now that San Francisco had come to the conclusion that no, Arab terrorists did *not* want to nuke San Francisco.

Kristen sighed and thought back to the news she had seen that morning. People known as International ANSWER had already decided to rally in response to the attacks—rallying *against* the United States. "ANSWER" stood for "Act Now to Stop War and End Racism." For some reason, before the US even had an enemy, discussed war plans, or even knew for certain who was behind the hospital attack, these people had come to the conclusion that "they" were being treating unfairly… whoever *they* were.

*A cute trick since we haven't* done *anything yet… in response to this, or anything at all as far as this administration is concerned… then again, it is San Francisco.*

*Hell, even the definition of "normal" doesn't work here,* Kristen Kelly thought as she looked around the police bullpen. It wasn't really the type of thing she was used to. Back in New York, the Detectives were lined up two-by-two, desks nose-to-nose with their partners. They didn't even have the decency of a large cubicle.

Now, in San Francisco, she was trying to figure out whose bright idea it was to put the police department in a building with genuine wood-paneling, hard-wood floors—even the desks were made of solid wood. Okay, the entire building was older than she was, and apparently in fairly good shape… but there was just something *wrong* about a police station that was this *clean.*

Kristen looked at the reports scattered out along her desk, and she instantly decided that she was on the "new guy" shift. She didn't even have a partner with her yet, possibly because of the "new guy" factor.

It wasn't bad enough that the SFPD had given her every strange case to hit town since she did. But every unsolved case from the last five years had landed on her desk with a solid "thud." Murder cases, an ever-increasing body count… she had even taken to organizing them by month. They were in neat little piles on her desk, because that was the only thing she could do with them—play her own personal game of solitaire.

Kristen stared down at it and shook her head. She just hoped she could get back to something like a real workload soon.

She sat down, still staring at the piles before her…

And blinked.

The piles, organized by month, had been getting smaller.

Kelly had never been much of a numbers person. She always preferred people. She knew each and every one of these people dead in the files, because they were her dead, now. She was responsible for them. They were hers, and she would take care of them to the best of her ability.

And her ability was limited. People kill strangers these days. Most murders were easy—the average murder victim was most likely to drop dead in their own bedroom between one and four in the morning, killed by someone they loved. These files, of course, had none of those instances. The murders were savage, the victims unconnected, and probably not even connected to the killers. She could remember what most of the dead died from, and the only way to link them would be to try using ESP to divine one… which had already been tried. Twice.

She also knew that a cut throat wasn't much of a signature. Especially when it was being done by different weapons, tools, and in dozens of different fashions. Gang rituals had been discussed, strange initiation ceremonies for Wiccans or Goths, or vampire wanna-bes. In fact, it was so strange, the strangest thing about it was that she was surprised no one had gone to Merle Kraft—expert in anything remotely resembling "strange."

The thought of Merle made her think of something. She wasn't sure what, but she was certain that Something. Was. Up.

Kristen leaned forward and very carefully grabbed the telephone, staring at the piles of folders as though they may run away from her if she took her eyes off of them. She dialed the file room. "Hey, Freddy, how's life in the darkness? Yes, that is rhetorical. Could you tell me how I can get the numbers on murder rates in the city? Online? Freddy, you're in records, and you remember everything, just give me a quick breakdown. Have things been up lately? What do I mean by 'lately'?" She eyed the piles. She already knew that the murder rate was down since she arrived… "How about the last five years?"

She waited a moment. She didn't even bother grabbing a pen. This would be burned into her brain for a while. "Up for the last three years, declining for five months… up in August… down for the past two weeks… Okay, Freddy, thanks."

She hung up and thought a moment. Six months ago was April … when Merle had asked her about Marco Catalano, and Amanda Colt of dubious origin. After that, the murders by throat-trauma dropped… until August…

Kristen looked at her pile for August. In July, there was a definite gap, only one murder of the strange variety. On the top of the next pile was the first corpse of August.

She grabbed it. The young woman had been named Sarah Bell, student of martial arts, and death by …

Kristen tried not to gag at the crime scene photos. It looked like she had been killed in a war, ripped apart by artillery. She had been literally torn apart and partially eaten, with bite marks of odd origin—not quite human, but too much of an arch to be animal. In fact, the entire alley looked like an actual war zone.

But there was only one body by the time it was found at daybreak.

All of the people questioned were found, tracked down, and interviewed at Merle's store…

Kelly shook her head. No, Merle couldn't have been involved. He had been in New York that day, with her, helping her and Arthur pack for the move to San Francisco. There was nothing he could have done to be even remotely…

She stared at one of the witnesses, one of Sarah's friends. Tiffany Whitman *worked* for Merle, in his shop. Another was her boyfriend, George Berkeley, a friend named Yana Rosenburg, and her girlfriend Tara… and supposedly there was someone with a bad dye job hanging out there by the name of Rory—no last name.

She flipped back to the date. The day after—or that morning, depending on how you looked at it—Merle had received a phone call that sent his mood through the basement and him half out the door.

*So, Merle's involved in keeping the murder rate down. He put together a team of Buffy-lites, puts them in place in San Fran, and something goes wrong. One of them gets butchered. He hears about it, doesn't feel like talking about it. But he only put it together in April…because he only learned about it in April. Did he* learn *anything from Catalano and Colt?*

*Well, you have the phone number for him around somewhere, use it.*

Kristen quickly tapped out the New York area code she knew so well and slowed down a bit for the actual number.

"Doctor Catalano."

"Hello, sir, my name is Kristen Kelly of the San Francisco Police Department, I would like to talk with your son, Marco. Is he there?"

There was a long moment of silence, and then he released his breath. "Oh, sorry. I heard SFPD and worried for a moment. I assume that you don't know that Marco's *in* San Francisco."

*Uh huh.* "That would be correct, sir. My apologies. When did he move here?"

"September, with the start of the semester."

*When our mystery murder rate started to drop again.* "Ah, thank you sir, I'll get a hold of him here. Thank you."

*Young Mister Catalano comes to San Francisco, and suddenly, the murder rate plummets, and that kind of killing motif almost disappears once again. On Tuesday, there's a small rampage through cemeteries, with no bodies, even though there looks like they had been taken over by the homeless, or someone else...*

Kristen's phone rang, and she arched a brow at it before she picked it up. "Detective Kelly."

On the other end was a man who sounded a little confused. "Oh, hello, Detective. My name is Peter Sharpe, with the FBI. I wanted to talk with you about some samples that had been collected from a few cases you'd been working on."

She blinked at the folders on her desk. "Oh? Which samples?"

"Well, you can probably find them in the murder books under 'strange biologicals'. Your coroner sent them to us, and we've decided to take over your cases."

She looked at her piles once more and considered getting a copy machine ready. "Oh?"

"Yes. They are a part of another investigation already in progress. I'm sure you'll be glad to get these off your desk, Detective."

She leaned back in her chair. "Oh… you'd be surprised, Agent Sharpe. You'd be surprised."

*Hello, Merle… what are you up to this time?*

# Epilogue

New York

Amanda Colt walked into the chambers of Jennifer Bosley. The President of the NYC Vampire's Association leaned back in her desk chair, bare feet up on the blotter. The glass in her hand looked like red wine.

Bosley gave Amanda a big grin. "Care for a glass?"

Amanda shook her head. "I do not drink… wine."

Bosley laughed. "Quoting *Dracula*? How long have you been holding on to that one?"

"A while."

Bosley waved at the bar off to the side. "Well, this isn't wine, but we have more than just booze here."

"Thank you, but no."

"Suit yourself, love." Bosley took another sip and looked at Amanda a bit more intently. "Something the matter?"

"I love Marco."

Bosley grinned and laughed aloud. "Wonderful. How'd he take it?"

"Fine. He told me he loved me, too."

"Great! Cheers!" Bosley saluted her with her glass and was about to take a sip when she paused. "Not great?"

"Not great." Amanda took a slow, deep breath. "I told him I loved him as a friend. He said it as the same."

Bosley's smile froze on her face. She automatically took a long, healthy sip from her glass. She put it off to one side, still staring. "May I ask why?"

"I might hurt him. He might even let me."

Bosley tossed her hands up, not even bothering to shrug. "I think that's called love. Period. Welcome to everyone else's problem. Get over it."

"I am a blood-sucking monster, Jen. That's worse than some headache."

"I dunno, I think I'd have preferred my heart literally ripped out a few times," Bosley muttered as she reached for her wine glass. "What if he felt the same way about you? Ever think of that?"

Amanda cocked her head, confused. "What makes you say that?"

"I talked with your boy when you were still a pussy in a box, mate."

"What?"

"Schrodinger? Cat in a box? Maybe dead, maybe inn'it?" Bosley prompted, her urban accent thickening. "Dunno 'til you open and look inside. You were the pussy in the box when the hospital dropped on ya. He was not happy about it. He's not exactly detached. If he's not in love with you, I'll eat Kalsey's heart out myself. I mean it, too."

Amanda smiled at the idea of the vile bar owner with his heart ripped out and being used as snack food. "Tempting."

Bosley pointed at her like a stern schoolmarm. "Trust me, young lady. If your human knew what we were talking about this minute, he would personally jump you himself. Were I you, I'd let him. He's not bad looking."

Amanda sighed. "I suppose I will have to take it under advisement."

"Don't give me that. I think I *invented* the term as a replacement for 'Get stuffed.' When are you going to see him next?"

"Around Christmas."

Bosley smiled broadly. "I can't think of a better present to unwrap."

Amanda sat back in the chair, wondering what Marco really would think.

San Francisco

Marco Catalano sat down at his laptop and started to compose an email. For a man who had just gone toe-to-toe with a demon with as much worry as the average citizen might have against a mugger, the email terrified him out of all proportion.

*Dearest Amanda,*

*I have a secret to tell you. Not too surprising, is it? My very smile must appear to be a mask at times.*

*In fact, I have two secrets to tell you. Neither may surprise you. Or both will. Though which would surprise you, or surprise you more, I couldn't begin to say, or guess. After all, if there's anyone who knows me better than my father or my confessor, it would be you.*

*I've told you before about the night I lost Lily for the first time. Yes, it was before I met you, but I think I told that story vividly enough. It was a mugging. The man held me at knifepoint, and I killed him. I told you the truth in that I did have to kill him. I made a mess of it. What could have been a quick disable or kill turned into a bloody mess in more ways than one. I hurt him. And I kept on hurting him until he stopped moving.*

*What I didn't tell you is that I liked hurting him. I liked making him suffer. I enjoyed making him bleed and die.*

*In short, Amanda, I am a bit of a monster. You need blood to live, and you have only killed when you needed to, but I'm the one who enjoys it. I enjoy the stab, the slice, the twist of the knife.*

*However, I've been made aware that I might not be quite so insidious and monstrous a human being as I thought. Apparently, my time in prayer and church and confession may not be 100% for naught.*

*My second secret is at the same time both much more innocent, yet much creepier at the same time, given secret #1.*

*I love you, Amanda. That is my big secret.*

*It sounds stupid to say it, but I love everything about you. I love your accent. Your hair. Your smile. I love how smart you are. I love how you think. I love your eyes, and the way they sparkle. I like just being around you. I even like who I am when I'm around you.*

*Do you remember what I told you in the graveyard as we "pretended" to make out and profess our love to each other, so we could bait Mikhail's vampires? I wasn't pretending.*

*Everything I said to you was true. Everything I did, I meant.*

*No matter what, Amanda, I will always love you.*
*Marco*

Marco reached to click "send."

# About The Author

Declan Finn lives in a part of New York City unreachable by bus or subway. Who's Who has no record of him, his family, or his education. He has been trained in hand to hand combat and weapons at the most elite schools in Long Island, and figured out nine ways to kill with a pen when he was only fifteen. He escaped a free man from Fordham University's PhD program and has been on the run ever since. There was a brief incident where he was branded a terrorist, but only a court order can unseal those records, and really, why would you want to know?

He can be contacted at DeclanFinnInc@aol.com

Follow him on Facebook and Twitter @APiusManNovel

Read his personal blog: declanfinn.com

Listen to his podcast, The Catholic Geek, on Blog Talk Radio, Sunday evenings at 7:00 pm EST

# More From Declan Finn

## Love At First Bite

Honor at Stake
Demons are Forever
Live and Let Bite
Good to the Last Drop

## The Pius Trilogy

A Pius Man
A Pius Legacy
A Pius Stand
Pius Tales
Pius History

## The Convention Killings

It Was Only On Stun
Set To Kill

STEPHEN OLIVER
PARANORMAL CITY

J.F. POSTHUMUS
THE FAE'S AMULET
A LADY OF DEATH NOVEL

Or take a look at some of our other award winning series at https://threeravenspublishing.com/series-universes/

Visit us at
Https://www.threeravenspublishing.com and sign up for our newsletter for the latest and greatest news on upcoming titles and events.